Darlene

"Darlene"

Bob Holt

For information contact; bobLholtco@yahoo.com

Book and Cover design by Bob Holt

ISBN -13: 978-1544619200

ISBN-10: 1544619200

In Memory

Kenneth Waters

I met Kenneth in 1962 when my career in Restaurant Equipment sales began. Over the years, we became close friends and worked on several projects together. He was a building contractor and no one cared more about his clients than he.

Divorced, he never remarried choosing to remain single turning all his attention to his work. During my single years, we were together often enjoying dining out and just "talking." Though very hard of hearing, he was an excellent conversationalist.

Kenneth lost his battle with cigarettes in 2004. I think of him often remembering the good times.

Darlene

"Not me, I don't remember."

Darlene awakened with a start, her feet were wet. She raised up on her elbow looking down at her feet. Small wavelets washed onshore and were almost touching her knees. She backed away from the hardpan and pulled her knees up under her chin.

Looking at her watch, she realized it was a little after three in the morning. The fog in her mind began to lift. She and Arlene came down Friday for the beach music festival. They were staying at the Islander Motel. It was scheduled to start at 11 a.m. on Saturday and she remembered walking over to the travel park with their wheeled cooler, packed with beer and sandwiches, trailing behind.

Inside the roped off area, the crowd was already swinging and swaying with the live band; It seemed that everyone was drinking beer. She counted seventy Porta John's lined up on the right side. The bands were on the left and picnic tables, butted end to end, formed a barrier between the festival area and the rest of the park. Huge muscular security guards, that looked like football players, walked constantly back and forth along the tops of the tables.

She had no clue why all that was necessary but as the afternoon wore on, she would.

By two p.m., lines formed at all the Porta John's, twenty or thirty deep, and by three, the revelers were just peeing on the grass. Some of the females, of all ages, scrambled across the picnic tables disappearing between the campers that lined the outer edge of the park hoping to relieve themselves in some degree of privacy but by then, it didn't matter. The gusher would come, with or without privacy. Some of the campers tried, without success, to ward them off. It didn't matter, their bladders were overflowing, they had to pee.

Darlene and Arlene were on their 4th beers when General Johnson and the Chairman of the Board began singing, ***Carolina Girl.*** The crowd went wild, and grew crazier, and louder, with each song.

When the festival was over, she vaguely remembered not knowing where Arlene, or the cooler, was? The cooler didn't matter. Beer was the last thing she needed.

She dimly remembered sitting on the beach in front of the Gazebo and it was already dark. She was stoned and wasn't going anywhere. Now, she'd lost ten hours and didn't have a clue where she'd been or what she'd done.

Looking around, she realized she was on the beach in front of Queens's Court and didn't have a clue how she'd gotten there. She still had her shorts, panties, top and bra. Apparently she hadn't been raped although it could have been consensual. In her state of drunkenness, in court, it still would have been rape. If it was, it would have been her first time. She and Arlene were brought up knowing right from wrong. They'd come to down to experience the festival, not get drunk out of their minds.

The pounding in her head made her eyes hurt, she needed relief. Reaching in her pocket, she found the key to her room. At least she could get some relief there. Arlene had a bottle of aspirin.

She opened the door finding the room empty. The beds had not been slept in. Now she began to panic. What could have happened to

Arlene? She was a big girl. Maybe she found Mr. Right and was…No, not Arlene. She wouldn't call 911, not yet.

~ D ~

She awakened a little after nine a.m. Her head wasn't pounding nearly as much but it still hurt.

Looking around, she realized that Arlene was lying across the bed and appeared to be fully clothed.

Darlene slipped into the bathroom washing her face again. She'd showered earlier and just wanted to get the sleep out of her eyes.

Dressing, she slipped quietly out of the room getting 2 coffees from the restaurant.

Arlene stirred when she walked back in the room saying,

"Holy God, I'm dying. My head's killing me. What time is it?"

Darlene replied,

"It's almost ten, you must have had a good time last night."

"Me? You're the one that disappeared. Me, all I done was party, I think."

Darlene didn't remember any of it and right then, didn't want to know. It was checkout time and they had to get moving.

~ D ~

On their way back to Washington, they talked little. It was easy to see, looking into her eyes, that Arlene was having a rough time but she still smiled and chuckled to herself. She remembered her night, most of it anyway.

"Are you going to tell me what I really did?"

Arlene tried to laugh but couldn't. The pain shooting through her head wouldn't let her.

"How much to you remember?"

"Probably 2:30 or 3 p.m. I'd just tried to use the Porta Johns and the lines were too long. I couldn't wait so I climbed over the picnic tables and was running towards the campers but I kept falling."

Arlene, trying to stifle a laugh, replied.

"I know; I was right behind you. You ran into the arms of a guy that was trying to keep you off his lot. You just plopped at his feet and peed on his feet. You were a mess."

"What did you do?"

"About what? It was all I could do to pee without wearing it. Besides, he picked you up and got you into the hammock behind his camper. After that, I don't have a clue. He said you could sleep it off in the hammock."

I crawled across the sand dunes and lay on the beach. That's when Gary came along. Remember him? He works in palliative care. Anyway, he was about as wasted as I was.

"We got to laughing about how everybody was peeing all over everything and I guess I sobered up a little. He was staying at Queen's

Court with two other guys. We went to the condo and set around talking.

"He invited me to have dinner with him so I came back over here, changed clothes and we went somewhere in Swansboro. The shrimp were good and it helped me sober up some but then we went back to his room, the other two guys and I guess, their girlfriends, were boozing it up on rum.

"They all left about nine saying there was a dance down near the Food Lion. We went there too and I woke in the condo No, don't ask, I don't remember. I slipped out and came back here."

"Were the others still there?"

"Yes, they were scattered all over the room."

Darlene had more questions but she wasn't her mother. Besides, she had no clue what she'd done. All she knew was, okay, they'd been to the beach music festival but no more; not for her anyway.

She'd probably never live it down if anyone recognized her. She was too ashamed to even want to know what she'd done. She couldn't believe she'd peed on a man's feet but with any luck, she looked awful and nobody would have recognized her.

~ *D* ~

They arrived back at their townhouse a little after four p.m. First things first, their clothes had to be washed; they reeked of stale beer.

What's this? Inside the pocket of the top she'd worn, was a Ziploc sandwich bag with a piece of paper inside. *Miss, I put you in the hammock behind our camper. You were too drunk to stand up. My wife checked on you later and found you covered in vomit. She said you had wet yourself again. I hosed you off as best as I could. Sorry about your wet clothes. Later, when I checked, you were gone. I found you on the beach asleep. It's not my place to judge you. I hope you are feeling better when you read this. John 3:16*

She was sure he was her guardian angel. He had to be. Apparently she'd done nothing wrong…Nothing wrong! If their parents, even their brother, Dale, had seen them, even though they were twenty-one; they would probably have gotten the worst whipping of their lives and they would have deserved it.

~ D ~

They'd talked about moving to Greenville but still had five months left on the lease. Pamlico Village was nice and being located on the river's edge just down from Mimosa Shores made it convenient to Food Lion and the country club if they'd ever get an invitation. So far, that hadn't happened. The closest that ever came to happening was last year when they bought tickets to the fund-raiser golf tournament.

There were men galore but every one of them seemed to be chained to a wife. They knew Mac Cox wasn't but he was too wrapped up to even notice them.

If Darlene could have gotten close to him, she could have gotten his attention. She was 5'6" slender, nice shape, long blonde hair, not even remotely platinum, more medium blonde, hazel eyes, and full lips. Dressed right, she could command any man's attention but she was too shy.

Arlene's hair was lighter but beyond that, they looked almost like identical twins but she didn't possess that sexy way Darlene had of smiling.

Growing up between Swan Quarter and Engelhard didn't offer many opportunities to put together a "Come to me" package. They lived east of Swan Quarter on Great Dutch Road near Last Chance. Their daddy, Owen, had a huge produce farm. Most of his crops were trucked up north, mostly to Maryland, Delaware, and New Jersey.

Darlene and Arlene, born on April 4th, 1994, spent almost all their time working on the farm when they won't in school or church on Sundays. Their brothers, Dale, he was 2 years older, Evan, 2 years younger, and Billy, he was the baby, did the same. Besides, there wasn't anything else to do. It wasn't like there a dance hall or something in Nebraska, North Carolina. It wasn't anything but a bump in the road anyway.

Sometimes, they'd go to the outer banks and spend a day but that was about it. Dale played basketball at Mattamuskeet High School and daddy let them go to the games. Sometimes him and their mama, Martha, would go too.

He did take them to Martelle's Feed House near Engelhard, once a week, for the best fried seafood they'd ever eaten. That's how Darlene got the waitress job her senior year. She'd been hit on so many times, it rolled off her like water off a duck's back.

Jimmy Balance wouldn't leave her alone but he smoked and his teeth were yellow. No way would he ever get past go with her.

Daddy's brother, Russell Snell, owned a fleet of fishing and shrimp trawlers in Engelhard and he sent most of his seafood up the Delmarva Peninsula too.

~ D ~

When they graduated from high school, they moved in with their aunt, Bessie, she was mama's sister, an old maid that lived on 2nd street in Washington. They'd gone to Beaufort Community College getting an associate's degree in radiology.

They applied first at Vidant Beaufort to work in the radiology department but found nothing. Following a suggestion, they applied at Vidant Health in Greenville finding positions there.

That's when they leased the townhouse thinking they wanted no part of Greenville. There were too many people and they drove like they were crazy. It was bad enough commuting but at least, at night, and when they were off, it was much quieter in Washington.

It didn't take long to realize that quiet had a downside too, no eligible bachelors. It wasn't as if they were panicking. Not yet, but it was getting close.

Darla, she was in the radiology department too, had told them before to get to work 30 minutes early.

"That's when all the guys are in the dining room. That's the best way for them to see you. After that, it's up to you."

Monday morning, fresh from their wild weekend, at seven a.m., they were in the cafeteria, sitting near the Starbucks counter, in the back corner, watching hundreds of guys come in, get coffee, look their way, smile, some twice, and leave to punch in.

The second morning, Doug Trip, came over introducing himself.

"Good morning, ladies. May I join you?"

He was nice enough but beyond that, no ring, dark wavy hair, cut business-like- slim, six-feet tall, wearing a black polo and comfortable looking slacks. He shoes, black too, appeared to be very comfortable with thick soles. Darlene was surprised she noticed, his eyes had blown her away. They were greyish blue and so soft, she could easily have fallen asleep, just looking into them.

She jumped ahead of Arlene replying,

"Please do, we'll only be here a few minutes more, we have to punch in."

He took a seat facing them.

"Thank you, I'm Doug Trip. I work down the corridor in rehab. I haven't seen either of you before. How long have you been working here?"

Darlene was out front again,

"About seven months, we're in radiology."

"Oh, you live in Greenville?"

Arlene wasn't fast enough. Darlene was already answering,

"No, we live in Washington. We'll probably relocate when our lease is up in a few months.

"How about you?"

He replied saying,

"Actually, I live between here and Washington in Pactolus. I grew up on a farm about 4 miles from there on Hwy 30. I thought I didn't want to live in Greenville but I was wrong. I prefer eating out to cooking and I end up driving back here almost every night. I'll probably move over here in the next few months"

Darlene was out of the gate first again.

"Where are you looking? We don't know anything about Greenville, just how to get here."

"Mostly over on Allen Road, there are tons of condos and townhouses scattered from Stantonsburg to Dickerson Avenue. If you'd like, one day after work, I'll show them to you. Which parking area are you in?"

Arlene had given up; Darlene was driving the conversation.

"Thank you, Doug. We're in the one by the Wellness Center."

"I am too; would you like to look around one afternoon this week?"

Darlene glanced at Arlene replying.

"Yes, we would. Will tomorrow be good for you?"

It was set. They'd park in section C and ride with him.

~ *D* ~

All during the morning, Arlene was all over her about driving the conversation.

"You wouldn't let me get a word in edgewise."

"Arlie, he was looking at me, not you. What was I supposed to do? Let him get away. Don't you remember daddy saying that you when you get a nibble, you have to set the hook. I did."

~*D* ~

That afternoon when they got back to Washington, they changed clothes and drove to the waterfront. It was their favorite place when they lived with Aunt Bessie. They'd sit for hours dreaming of boarding their yacht and sailing down the Pamlico waving goodbye to Oriental and the Crystal coast on their way to the Caribbean and beyond. Now, there was no yacht but a girl could dream couldn't she?

In the Estuarium, they picked up a few pamphlets and walked back to the other end near the bridge. The supper bell was ringing and it was ringing for Bill's Hot Dogs. the girls walked along Washington Parkway crossing West Main Street onto Gladden Street finding Bill's Hot Dog Stand on the right All orders were to go and there was no seating in or outside. The girls ordered two each, picking up Pepsi's from the vending machine before walking back to the waterfront.

"I'm going to miss these when we move to Greenville but I'm sure we'll find something over there we'll enjoy just as much."

Arlene giggled replying,

"You're right, men! Looks like you've already set your hooks into Doug. That's okay, there's plenty more where he came from."

Darlene replied,

"I set the hook but he's not in the boat yet. For all I know, he's just pretty on the outside. If I get him in the boat, I'll see what's under the scales."

That brought laughter from both of them.

~ D ~

Next morning, they had coffee with Doug confirming their rendezvous in the parking lot after work.

"Ladies, join me for dinner after we look around, my treat."

That was a no-brainer, of course they would.

Doug took them to Willow Spring, Waterford Place, and Crystal Apartments at Medford Point. There was an open house and they toured the property really liking what they saw. There was no river but getting to and from work would be a breeze. "Restaurant Row" and the mall on Greenville Boulevard was just minutes away too.

Even the price seemed reasonable. It was higher than what they were paying but they'd save that much on gas plus shave 40 minutes off their travel time. It was a no-brainer but they couldn't do anything for five months.

Doug sealed the deal saying he was impressed too. He was going to put his move together soon.

"All right, ladies, join me for a 'Cubbie's' burger. They're the best in Greenville. This is on me."

They were more than ready. He took then back to their car and they followed him down Arlington Blvd to Cubbie's in Arlington Village. Inside they found seats along the outside wall. All the seats around the counter were full.

Doug suggested they try the double cheeseburger and cheese fries.

"That's some good eating."

There was so many entrees that begged to be tried but since he was buying, they went with his suggestion ordering a frosty beer knowing they would only have one. Their food, as advertised, was delicious. It was easy to tell by the taste and texture, that the hamburger patties were hand formed from fresh ground hamburger.

"Are you ladies joined at the hip or can you be separated?"

Darlene jumped right on his query saying,

"We're joined but it's with Velcro. We can be pulled apart."

"That's good news, I'd like to ask you out. May I?"

Darlene threw her special smile at him, replied.

"Yes, I am available and would love to go out with you."

Arlene kept quiet while the matchmaking was in progress. Darlene would probably be trying to set the hook soon. It was time for her to bait her hook.

That evening, after getting home, they walked along the waterfront enjoying the ambiance of the setting. The quieting solitude was only intruded by sounds of traffic crossing the bridge.

Up in the star-lit sky, the cresting moon bathed the water's surface with a silvery shimmer. There was little movement of the water against the docks and the sway of the boats was barely noticeable.

They sat on one of the benches enjoying the peacefulness of the early evening.

"You know we're going to miss this,"

Darlene stared out across the water replying,

"Yes, we will but it's time to get on with our lives and it's not happening here. We're already 21. We've to get something going."

Arlene slumped a little, replying.

"I know you're right. Still, we're going to miss it. I'm looking forward to living in Greenville. The pickings sure look good."

~ *D* ~

Next morning, Doug joined them for coffee.

"Did you ladies have a nice evening? For me, it was Facebook."

Darlene replied that they'd spent a couple of hours on the waterfront. It was nice.

Doug, looking at Darlene, asked?

"Are you busy Saturday? If not, would you like to ride down to Oriental and have lunch?"

Darlene's mind was racing, *At least he's not trying to get into my panties on the first date. That's a plus.*

She replied saying,

"That sounds like fun. What time do we leave and where do we meet?"

"9 o'clock, I'll pick you up. That will give us time to walk along the waterfront before lunch. Oriental is the sailing capitol of North Carolina. Afterwards, if you'd like, we could drive to Minnesott Beach near Arapahoe, and enjoy the scenery there.

Darlene was ready, it sounded like a fun date, not a battle.

"That sounds like fun, I'd love to."

They exchanged addresses, email addresses, FB pages, and cell phone numbers.

~ D ~

Saturday morning, the weather was gorgeous and Darlene was ready. Doug arrived at 9 and they drove down Hwy 17 to Chocowinity, turning left on Hwy 33, following it to Hwy 306. At the intersection with Hwy 55 in Grantsboro, they turned left and passed through Alliance, Bayboro and Stonewall before entering Oriental about an hour later.

The waterfront was beautiful. It faced the wide Neuse River as it flowed towards it's confluence with the Pamlico Sound. It appeared to be the perfect place to launch sailboats and there were dozens of them anchored out in the protected harbor or tied to the docks. Darlene thought the catamarans looked like fun. The sailboats appeared to be a bit crowded to her but then, she'd never been on one. Her only experience with boats were aboard her uncle's fishing and shrimp trawlers. They were far from being fun.

After spending an hour on the waterfront, they walked along the streets, seeing shops, churches, and a bed & breakfast.

A little before noon they walked over to the marina to have lunch at the Oriental Marina Restaurant. Inside, they were seated by a window that offered a perfect view of the marina. Watching what could only be described as "old salts" mending nets and doing other chores created a wistful longing to live that kind of life. Reality quickly replaced that dream with a bucketful of reality. Their wrinkled facial features that looked leatherier than skin. It didn't get that way by itself. Mother Nature extracted the tribute with sun, wind, salt water and air.

"Darlene, what are you thinking about? You seem to have drifted off?"

"No Doug, back when I was growing up, I thought I wanted a life on the water but after Arlene and I spent a couple of weeks on Uncle Russell's shrimp trawler, we changed our minds. It looked like a lot of fun but it wasn't. I'm back now."

They ordered the three-seafood special. Darlene chose the shrimp, flounder, and sea scallops. Doug wanted the deviled crab, shrimp, and flounder. Both wanted the usual fries and slaw with sweetened iced tea. They munched on hushpuppies slathered with butter while they waited for their seafood platters.

"Doug, are you doing what you want to do or is being a physical therapy assistant just a step? If I'm prying, tell me."

"No Darlene, you're not prying. I guess, to me, it's just a first step. I go to classes at Pitt Community College two nights a week, and online, getting some of the required subjects completed that are required for my four-year degree.

"I may take a leave of absence next year and enroll at ECU. With my online and college courses, I would get my bachelor's in two semesters. After that, I'd go back to my job and start on the next phase. Becoming an associate is my dream. We'll see."

Darlene was sure that whatever he set his sights on, he'd accomplish. He appeared to have the drive and determination.

"Enough of me, what are Darlene's dreams?"

"Doug, I think I'm already there although I still wonder what it would be like to own and operate a restaurant. It takes a lot of money and I don't have any. Maybe opening a little café after I retire from Vidant would suffice. Right now, other than moving to Greenville, I'm good."

"What, no marriage, no children, no grandchildren?"

Darlene was laughing now.

"One step at the time, I have to find Mr. Right first."

~ D ~

After finishing lunch, they crossed the bridge following Oriental Road that became Janiero Road. They stopped and spent a few minutes in Janiero, standing on the bridge that crossed Dawson's Creek.

Afterwards they encountered the next road name change. Now they were on Buckland crossing Camp Don Lee Road. They'd heard of the camp and now knew where it was located. At the Hwy. 306 intersection, they turned left following it to Minnesott Beach.

Parking, they walked down and watched the vehicles unload off the Cherry Branch-Minnesott Beach ferry then the waiting vehicles loaded and they watched the ferry begin another crossing to 2300 Ferry Road just outside Havelock, NC.

Afterwards, they strolled in a westward direction down the beach until they reached the country club entrance, then they retraced their steps stopping along the way to enjoy watching families alongside and in the water.

It was late afternoon and time for their return trip. Hwy 306 took them back to Hwy 33, then Hwy 17 N, Main Street and River Road.

Arriving, he opened the car door and walked her to the door.

"Darlene, I hope you enjoyed today. I have very much. May I ask you out again?"

"Doug, I had a very nice time, yes, I hope you will."

She could sense that he wasn't going to try to kiss her. She leaned forward and kissed him lightly on the lips.

Smiling, his eyes were sparkling when he said

"Until Monday…"and turned and walked away.

~ *D* ~

"Well, did you have a good time? What did you do? Talk to me!"

Arlene was all over her.

Darlene plopped onto the couch with a smile on her face that refused to leave, replied.

"I had a wonderful time and I'm ready to do it again!"

She had Arlene going now.

"Was he nice, did he have a thousand hands. Is he a good kisser?"

"Arlie, it was a day date. No, he didn't try anything. I had to kiss him goodbye."

~ D ~

Sunday morning, they went to church at Woolard's Pond Church of Christ. They'd been a few times but probably not nearly as often as they should have. If Aunt Bessie was there; they'd sit with her.

That guy was there; the one that couldn't keep his eyes off Arlene. He'd already asked her out twice and she couldn't really say why she wouldn't go. He just wasn't…she didn't know, but this time; he clicked and Arlene was ready to meet him.

It was fifth Sunday and that meant 'dinner-on-the-grounds.' They hadn't planned on staying and didn't bring anything but after seeing Ken... Was that his name? Arlene insisted on staying and she didn't want to sit with Aunt Bessie either.

"Let's sit close to him. I'll figure something out."

She did, he hadn't finished his drumstick before Arlene had moved in. They were chatting up a storm right through Kay Finch's double chocolate cake.

She had a date next Saturday night with Ken Brooks. He was divorced, 29, and lived on Market Street extension near its intersection with Hwy 171. He grew up near Pinetown just off Hwy 32. He was a job superintendent for a building contractor in Raleigh and had a mobile home in Clayton just outside Raleigh. He went up on Monday mornings and came back on Fridays.

"He's taking me to dinner at Blackbeard's Saturday night."

Darlene was tickled for Arlene; now they both had new boyfriends.

~ D ~

June turned into July and Doug took Darlene to Belhaven for the 4th of July festivities. It was fun being with him and their relationship seemed to be ripening. No rush, just one date at the time. He was picking her up Sunday mornings taking her to Eastern Pines Church of Christ on Portertown Road, just east of Greenville saying when they moved, it would be a lot closer.

They attended the traditional service at 9 a.m. Darlene wasn't used to all the instruments or songs used in the contemporary second service although it was the one folks their age attended and was, by far, the largest.

After church, he would take her to dinner at any restaurant she chose. Most times, it was either, Moore's Barbecue or Parkers. The afternoon would be spent enjoying a movie or they'd go to the Washington waterfront. She loved their relationship but it was moving too slowly for her. There hadn't been a passionate kiss yet but! It would be soon She'd see to that.

"Two months? That long?"

"That's bull!"

On Wednesday, they met for their usual early morning coffee and she could tell immediately that something was wrong.

"Good morning, I guess it is. My supervisor emailed earlier this morning. I'll be training for the next two months at the University of Tennessee outside Nashville. I don't have an option, neither does Janice or Skip. They're married but it doesn't matter. There are new techniques and we have to be trained or it counts against accreditation. I have to leave Friday. I'll be back in November. Will you miss me?"

"Darlene was frowning,

"A little, I guess…You know I'll miss you… A lot!"

That afternoon, she sent Arlene on without her. They were going to eat at Logan's

Her steak was good and Doug's company was caring but she was deep down in the dumps. Two months! That was bull!

~ *D* ~

They messaged on Facebook mornings and evenings and talked on their cells two or three times during the week and several times each weekend but time, her time, seemed to in flux refusing to move forward.

She didn't have Arlene to pal around with anymore; she and Ken were gone somewhere every weekend. Weekdays, they'd go to the waterfront or go up on 15th Street for fast-food or pizza.

With Arlene gone, she went to church every Sunday finding friendship in several of the older members. Oftentimes, they'd invite her to join them for lunch.

~ *D* ~

The week before Doug was to return, her mother fell in the kitchen and fractured her hip. Her left arm was broken in two places and her left ankle was broken too. She'd be incapacitated for six months or longer. Somebody had to go back home and help. None of her siblings or her daddy could cook, wash clothes, and probably couldn't clean the house either.

Arlene said she'd go but Darlene refused. She asked her supervisor for a leave of absence, bought a used car, and moved back home.

It was a call she didn't want to make but had to.

"Doug, you're not going to believe this but here goes, mama fell in the kitchen and broke herself all up. I have to move back home to take care of my siblings and daddy. I'll probably be gone six or seven months. There aren't any options. None that I know of. Daddy can't afford a full-time housekeeper. That leaves me… I know but I don't see any other way… I'll miss you too. I hope we can get back together when this is over… I sure hope so; either Thanksgiving or Christmas, maybe both… Okay, I'll see you on FB in the morning, bye."

That night, she cried herself to sleep. Arlene tried to comfort her but to no avail.

Next afternoon after work, she bought a 3-year old Toyota Corolla with 40,000 miles on it. It was transportation and that's all she needed.

~ D ~

November turned into December and they'd gotten a chance to date once. Doug drove down the day after Christmas and they rode over to Mattamuskeet Lake spending several hours watching the geese and just being together. The setting wasn't what she wanted but there was finally the passionate kiss she'd dreamed about.

There was nothing to do now but to mark time and take care of her mother and family.

Taking her to the doctor proved to be interesting. There was no way to get her into Darlene's car so her daddy had to take her in his Super-Cab F-150 half-lying, half sitting, in the back seat. Because of how it was used on the farm, the 4-wheel drive had been jacked up 8" and that added to the drama of trying to get her mama into, and out of it. The over-sized tires roared like lions at any speed over 40 MPH.

~ D ~

That March, she got a call from the administrator at Pungo District Hospital in Belhaven asking her to come in for an interview.

She couldn't believe he wanted her to join the staff as the assistant radiologist. She wouldn't have given it a second thought but he'd sweetened the pot saying how difficult it was go get anyone to come to Belhaven. They also needed and assistant dietary director. The position was essentially administrative. Nellie Wiggins, the director, oversaw the complete operation.

"You could easily fill both positions giving you an annual income double what you're now receiving. Think about it, Miss Snell, and let me hear from you."

It really didn't require a whole lot of thought. Double her income, the mileage was about the same but the traffic would be dramatically reduced and working in dietary would give her the opportunity to learn something about commercial foodservice. She still harbored dreams of opening her own restaurant.

Her mother's casts had all been removed 3-weeks previously and she'd resumed most of her family duties. Darlene had planned to call Vidant on the following Monday about resuming her position but now an opportunity was staring her in the face. One she didn't think she could reasonable walk away from.

That Friday, she packed up and returned to her home in Washington. When Arlene came in from work, she was bubbling with,

"You're not going to believe this, Ken proposed and we're getting married!"

Darlene couldn't believe what she'd just heard.

"What? Tell me again! You're going to do what?"

Arlene was giggling now as she grabbed Darlene.

"You heard right; we're going to get married! Ken proposed last night. After we're married, he wants us to move to Elizabeth City. He'll open a general contractor's office and focus mostly on new construction along the outer banks. I'm so exciting! Can you tell?"

She had her solitary right in Darlene's face.

"See?"

Darlene was happy for Arlene but totally caught off-guard. She knew they were dating heavily but marriage; she was floored.

"When's all this happening?"

We're getting married on Valentine's Day. It's only a month away. It's going to be a very small wedding, nothing formal, just his mother and our family. He's a member at Woolard's Pond Church of Christ and that's where the ceremony will be held."

Darlene was stunned, she was happy for Arlene but she was caught totally off-guard. For the first time in her life, except for the past few months, she would not have Arlene as her constant companion. All their life, they'd been glued together. Yes, she knew the day would come and now it was here. That put the glue on her life too. Yes, she would accept the positions at Pungo District Hospital.

~ *D* ~

Monday morning, she first called the administrator accepting his offer.

"When do I start, sir?... Yes, sir, I'll be there at 7:30 Wednesday morning… Yes, sir, thank you."

Next, she called Vidant Health saying she would not return at this time but may apply again later. She knew not to burn bridges.

Afterwards, she messaged Doug sharing what was taking place in her life. Although they hadn't seen each other since the kiss; she felt she should keep him in the loop although she didn't think they had a future. She thought a lot of him but love; She was pretty sure it didn't exist in either of them. It was probably time for them to move on.

"Pungo District Hospital"

Belhaven, NC

Darlene arrived Wednesday morning, a few minutes after seven, finding the dining room. She purchased a cup of coffee and took a seat in the rear of the seating area. There were probably 10 other people seated and a few others came in getting beverages and mostly pastries before exiting the room.

At 7:25, she approached Mr. Fulcher's receptionist asking to see him.

He welcomed her saying,

"Let's get you introduced."

In the radiology department, he introduced her to Dr. Pulver.

"Miss Snell, this is Dr. Paul Pulver. He heads up our radiology department. Dr. Pulver, this is Darlene Snell, your new assistant."

Dr. Pulver welcomed her saying he looked forward to working with her.

Saying he had other introductions, she followed Mr. Fulcher to the dietary director's office.

"Mrs. Wiggins, this is Darlene Snell, she is your new assistant. Miss Snell, this is Nellie Wiggins, our dietary director. You two can get together later in the day. Miss Snell, I'll take you back to Radiology."

Darlene thanked him saying,

"I can find my way Mr. Fulcher. Thank you, sir."

When she entered the department, Dr. Pulver said they only had one procedure scheduled for 2 p.m.

"There's nothing else scheduled for today. Other than that, I'll page you if something comes up."

She walked back to Mrs. Wiggins' office knowing it was going to be difficult to adjust but she'd do it. The money was too good not to."

"Call me, Nellie, may I address you as, Darlene?"

"Please do, Nellie."

She didn't appear to be more than 30 at the most and she had a pleasant personality. Nellie led her into the kitchen introducing each of the workers to her. There were two cooks, one assistant, a dishwasher, and Mr. Cahoon was responsible for setting up and taking down the serving line. The cooks, and him, loaded the patient carts at 6:30 for breakfast, 10:30 for lunch and 5:30 for dinner. "We rarely have more than 15 or 16 patients." Jim Bridgers was in charge of the stockroom. Rena Dawson was the cashier.

Back in the office, Nellie showed Darlene her desk saying the bookkeeper, Janice Tew, would get her online and acquainted with their software.

"It's 10:30, let's go to the kitchen and I'll show you how we set up for a meal. A lot of what you'll be doing is ordering food, equipment, and supplies.

"We deal mostly with PYA and Sysco Foods. We have contract prices and for the most part, don't have to deal with their salespeople. If we do, I usually call Frances Pierce with PYA. She's pushy but knows her stuff, you'll see.

"Equipment repairs are done by Hobart. They're located in Kinston, NC. Your contact is Brad West, he's the owner. There's a place in Greenville that's closer but I refuse to use them. They ripped me off once, that's quite adequate, thank you.

"With food and disposables, we place the PO's. Smallwares and equipment, we have to do a requisition through Clyde Hicks. He's the purchasing agent. He's nice, you'll like him. All these contacts are in your computer. Janice, will acquaint you with the file.

At 10:30, they watched the patient trays being loaded for lunch. The items were placed in insulated plates and bowls and assembled on 14" x 18" trays before being placed in fiberglass carts, each held up to 8 trays. The insulated coffee/tea dispensers were on top of the carts.

Next, the cooks placed the lunch entrees in stainless steel pans and covered each before placing them on a stainless steel cart ready for Jim Cuthrell to roll them to the serving line. When the line opens for lunch, one of the cooks becomes the server while the other begins preparation for dinner.

Darlene stood behind the serving line watching as the customers, mostly hospital staff and employees, went through, selecting from the offered entrees for their lunch. The server addressed most of them by name. She knew, if she stayed long enough, she would too.

4:30 finally arrived and she was ready to go home. It had been an interesting, but boring day and she knew adjustments had to be made. Right then, all she wanted was a pizza and a pitcher of beer. Arlene said she'd be with Ken until late leaving her with a 12" pepperoni and sausage pizza. It had been cooked just right and the frosty pitcher was just what the doctor ordered.

~ D ~

As she began to acclimate to the amazingly docile schedule, she felt more comfortable, with each passing day, doing almost nothing or that's how it seemed to her.

Procedures in radiology were never more than two in a day and many days, there were none. She really wasn't needed but the rules dictated that there had to be an assistant. If she didn't have the position in dietary, she couldn't have stayed but then, if it hadn't been offered, she wouldn't' have been there in the first place.

At lunch, Mr. Hicks, the purchasing agent, asked if he could join her? Darlene welcomed the opportunity to have someone to talk to. He was retired military and was just looking for something to supplement his retirement income. He, and his wife, Mary, lived at Pamilco Beach near Bath, NC.

"It's boring most of the time but the people here are nice if they accept you, if not, it's time to leave. Where are you from?"

"I'm from Swan Quarter in Hyde County. It's about 30 minutes from here down Hwy. 264. I grew up on produce farm about 5 miles on the other side of Swan Quarter. I live in Washington now with my twin sister. She's getting married on Valentine's Day. I guess I'll be alone then.

"I worked at Vidant Health for a year until my mother fell and was in a cast for six months. I went back home to take care of the family."

"Young Lady, you're too pretty to be alone. I can't believe you haven't been cornered yet."

Darlene, smiled replying,

"Not yet but my day will come."

~ D ~

That afternoon, one of the doctors came in asking about sources for stainless steel pans. He was young and good-looking too. Where had he been hiding?

She brought up PYA's online equipment catalog saying that was where theirs came from. He pulled up a chair beside her. She'd already sized him up. Tall, probably 6 feet, blonde hair, business cut, NO RING! His blue eyes were kind and his smile, inviting. What in the world was he doing in Belhaven?

"Darlene," he'd read her nametag, "How do I order these?"

"Dr. Hardy," She'd read his too, "We fill out a requisition form and take it to Mr. Hicks in purchasing. May I help you fill out a form?"

She noticed Nellie peeping from inside her office. She had a grin and knowing look on her face.

"Would you please, Darlene."

They spent about 20 minutes filling out a request that normally would have taken five but he kept asking questions and she kept answering them.

When he finally left, she was on cloud nine but knew it was a fluke. Doctors didn't associate with the staff.

Nellie stuck her head out of door,

"He likes you."

The next day, she spent the entire 3-hour lunch period in the dining room pretending to be observing the interaction between the server and the customers. He didn't show. Where in the world was he? Surely he ate lunch and there were not that many places in Belhaven to eat. Doctor's didn't eat fast-food or did they?

~ *D* ~

That evening, Arlene wanted to talk about the wedding.

"I'm not spending money on a wedding gown, I think I found what I want in Arlington Village. Will you go with me Saturday to look at it?"

Darlene hugged her twin saying,

"You know I will, Arlie. Let's have breakfast at the Egg Yolk first."

"That place is so busy on the weekend, let's do Denny's instead."

"Where are you going on your honeymoon?"

"We're going on a cruise. Ken says we'll drive to Fort Lauderdale, spending one night on Hilton Head Island on the way. We'll sail the next day on the Carnival Glory.

"He says we'll be on it six days going to places like Key West, Grand Cayman Island and Cozumel. We'll be on deck eight with a balcony. He has a pamphlet showing all the decks. The pool is on the 5th level, the casino is too.

"He says we can eat 24 hours and day. Sleep in when we want to and order room service. Darlene, they have soft-ice cream machines and they operate 24-hours a day. We'll be gone eight whole days.

"I told you that we're going to live in Elizabeth City, Ken bought a house near the hospital just up beyond the country club. He showed it to me last weekend. I love it. It's on Parkwood Drive. Darlie, it's brick and has a huge master suite, 2 other bedrooms, a full hall bath, great room with a fireplace, dining room, laundry room, a nice kitchen, and double garage with a mud room.

"His office will be across the bridge, going to towards Camden, just beyond Barnhill Contracting. From there it's only an hour to the outer banks. I'm so excited.

"When we get back from our honeymoon, I'm going to the hospital and fill out an application. Dr. Kozale says I shouldn't have any problem getting on there."

~ *D* ~

It was Friday and still no Dr. Hardy. He was a ghost; he must have been. She couldn't find him.

"Mr. Hicks, I helped Dr. Hardy fill out a requisition earlier this week. What department is he in? I found some additional information he might be interested in."

"Let see, Dr. Raymond Hardy…Here he is. Darlene, he's attached to Duke Marine Lab. He has an office… let's see, okay, it's down the corridor, beyond the dining room. The last one on the left. He's rarely in. He spends most of his time out in the sound or over at ECU. Here's his extension and email. Will that help?"

She smiled, replying,

"Yes, it will, Mr. Hicks. Thank you very much."

He probably read right through her but so what, he wasn't married and neither was she. One thing for sure, if he was there, he was hiding. Maybe next week he'd come out of hiding and she'd be waiting.

~ D ~

Saturday morning, Darlene and Arlene had breakfast at Denny's first. They chose the double berry banana pancake breakfast. Arlene wanted her eggs scrambled and chose sausage. Darlene wanted her over-easy with bacon. Afterwards, they drove to Arlington Village and Sara's. Arlene walked straight to her dress and pulled it off the rack.

"What do you think?"

The light-blue dress was A-line, all-over lace, lined, crew-neck, short sleeve, and knee-length.

"I'll wear a single string of pearls with matching earrings."

"I love it; you'll be beautiful in it. All you need are matching heels."

"And… it's my size"

After picking up a few pieces of lingerie and a peek-a-boo nightie, they went to Belk's and picked up two pieces of luggage. Arlene was ready to become Mrs. Ken Brooks.

"I can't believe it's happening this fast but I'm so ready."

~ D ~

Next week, just when Darlene had given up all hope of ever seeing Dr. Hardy again. There he was, coming down the corridor towards her. Should she speak, she didn't have to guess. He spoke first.

"Darlene, remember me and my pans?"

Yes, Dr. Hardy, did they arrive yet."

"No, but it doesn't matter, I've been this long without them."

And then, right out of the blue.

"Would you join me for lunch?"

Would she!

"Yes, that would be nice; what time?"

"Will 11:30 work for you?"

Anytime, anywhere would work for her.

"That's fine, I'll see you then."

Her heart was pounded. Was he just being nice? Doctor's didn't fraternize with the help and she was just help.

He was waiting when she walked into the dining room and he followed her through the serving line telling the cashier they were together. She was too shaken to eat choosing only a salad. He ordered the salmon, broccoli, and steamed carrots.

Seated, he began by saying.

"Thank you for joining me. I'm here so little, I hardy know anyone. You were so helpful last week. Thank you."

"Thank you Dr. Hardy: I … He interrupted saying,

"Please call me Ray, I know protocol demands that I be addressed as doctor but not while we're eating."

She continued,

"Thank you, Ray; I was happy to help you. I'm new here and haven't had a chance to meet many of the others yet. I know how you feel."

"Tell me about Darlene."

"There isn't much to tell. I grew up in Hyde County down east from here. I have a twin sister, Arlene. We attended Beaufort Community College getting our associate degree in radiology. We found positions at Vidant Health and moved to Washington.

"My mother fell about seven months ago and was in a cast on her left side for six months. I took a leave of absence and went back home to help out.

"Mr. Fulcher called wanting to see if I'd be interested in a positon here as assistant radiologist. I wasn't until he sweetened the offer adding assistant director in dietary to the package. At that point, I couldn't refuse. The compensation was too great to turn down and so, here I am."

He looked at her with a big smile asking,

"You appear to be single, how is that possible. You're much too pretty. No, I'm not prying, just interested."

"Not married, not engaged, not going steady. I'm still waiting for Mr. Right."

"Bravo, there are still a few of you left. Darlene, I'm from Cary. I went to UNC-Chapel Hill, first getting my BS. I entered medical school and did my residency at Rex in Raleigh.

"When I finished, I enrolled at Duke in their marine biology program and here I am.

"I've been here 3 months and spend most of my time out in the Pamlico River or aboard their research vessel docked at Beaufort. Any other time I have left is spent at ECU. I rented a cottage on the outskirts of Bath in Teach's Cove. It's not much but considering how little time I spend there, it' fine."

"What are you doing for Valentines? Would you have dinner with me?"

Now she was floored.

"Ray, I would love to but my twin sister is getting married and I have to be there. We've been there for each other all our lives."

"Valentines is on Saturday. What time's the wedding?"

"4 o'clock. It's in a church just east of Washington."

"Could I possibly go to the wedding and then take you out?"

"Ray, we're country folks. You may not be comfortable there."

I'll do just fine. "Is it formal, informal?"

"Informal, I doubt if any of my family will be wearing coats or ties. The groom and pastor might be. It's private and only for the family. There is no reception, or anything after the wedding. They'll leave immediately for their cruise out of Ft. Lauderdale spending their first night in Hilton Head. Are you sure you want to do this?"

"Yes, very. We'll drop your car off and go out to dinner. I'll go to the wedding, open collar, if that's what you prefer, but I'll put on a coat and tie for our dinner date."

She'd tried to warn him but he refused to be dissuaded. She so much wanted to go out with him but attend the wedding, she wasn't sure. It didn't matter, he was going.

Coat and tie? She was going to have to buy a cocktail dress. It would have to be that afternoon or tomorrow.

When they looked around, they realized they were the only ones left in the dining room.

They exchanged cell numbers and email addresses before parting.

"Darlene, I've enjoyed our lunch and I'm really looking forward to Saturday. I won't be here tomorrow. I have to attend a conference in Greenville. I'll call Saturday before the wedding."

Sitting at her desk in dietary, she tried to calm down. She couldn't believe what had just transpired. He was definitely her idea of "Mr. Right" but she felt too far out of his league. She smiled knowing she'd enjoy one date with him anyway. The wedding, there were a lot of misgivings about that.

~ D ~

She punched out at 4:30 and rushed to Greenville to the same shop Arlene had found her dress. There were dozens of cocktail dresses, which one?

She liked the emerald green long-bell-sleeve lace one with the jewel neck. It came to just above the knees. She had cleavage but he wasn't going to see it on what she hoped would only be their first date. It was the one. 4" heels, her gold chain necklace and matching earrings would complete her ensemble. She was ready.

~ D ~

Back home, she found Arlene in a tizzy trying to pack for her honeymoon.

Seeing Darlene come in with a clothes bag, she stopped for a moment asking,

"Darlie, where have you been? Did you buy a dress for my wedding? I told you no to."

Darlene flashed a huge smile at her, replying.

"It's a dress for my date tomorrow night."

"Date, what date, who…what's going on?"

"Ray asked me to join him for dinner after the wedding."

"Ray? What Ray? All right, what's going on? Why don't I know Ray?"

They were sitting on the couch now.

"Because I just met him a week ago. He's a doctor at the hospital."

"A doctor? How in the world…Wait just a minute, I'm lost? Tell me about Ray!"

Dr. Ray Hardy is from Cary. He has an office in the hospital. He's doing research in the Duke Marine Lab program spending most of his time on a skiff on Pamlico River or aboard the Duke Marine Lab vessel that's docked in Beaufort. He's… she was grinning now… He's about 6 feet tall, blonde hair, gorgeous blue eyes, nice smile, tanned, I'm sure it's not a farmer's tan. Arlie, to me, he's Mr. Right."

He came into my office asking about pans for one of his projects, we had lunch a few days later and he asked me out for Valentines. He's coming to your wedding too."

Arlene was tickled for Darlene but a doctor.

"How's this doctor thing going to work? It's like he's up there and you're down here."

"I don't know, Arlie. If it's only one date, that's fine, but at least I'm going out with Mr. Right one time. Let me show you my dress."

Arlene loved it.

"Darlie, it's you! That emerald green is perfect with your eyes. Try it on, I've got to see you in it."

Darlene was in it in minutes.

"Well, what do you think?"

She twirled around and gave Arlene her sexy smile.

"You'll knock him off his feet. He won't stand a chance. Where is he taking you?"

"I don't have a clue. It doesn't matter. Anywhere will be fine. When he said he'd be wearing coat and tie, I knew I needed a dress."

"You better get packing, girl. You've got a wedding to go to."

Watching Arlene pack and unpack was better than any TV show. She'd looked at the suggested list of clothing and other items Carnival Glory had supplied but still, she wasn't sure.

"I may need this, maybe not, but then, there's always a chance. I better pack it…No, I won't need that but I'd rather be safe than sorry."

Darlene shook her head, all of that was over a sleeveless top. It would only take all evening if she was lucky.

"Arlie, are you hungry, you must be. You've got to eat something. How about pizza? Domino's can deliver or we can go out."

"I don't have time to go out, order one from Domino's.

"Garbage?"

"Why not, go for it."

Twenty minutes later, they were munching on a 12," thin crust, with everything, sans the anchovies, pizza, washing the slices down with Bud Lights."

"Does Ray know that you get drunk and pee on people?"

"Darlene laughed replying,

"Does Ken know that beer runs though you like a river?"

That remark required more beer but only one more. Neither needed, or wanted, a hangover on Arlene's wedding day or Darlene's date with Mr. Right.

~ D ~

"Mr. and Mrs. Ken Brooks"

We do!

Next morning, Arlene's wedding day, they had biscuits at Hardee's before spending an hour on the waterfront. They walked, hand-hand, to the Estaurium and back. They knew that after today, they'd no longer be "attached at the hip." Ken had ripped the Velcro asunder and was running off with Arlene. They knew it would happen sooner or later and now it had. At 4 p.m. Arlene was going to run off with her knight in shining armor. Darlene's day would come, sometime.

Getting close to lunch, they walked to Main Street and enjoyed Philly Cheese Steaks at "Down on Main."

Back at their apartment, Arlene's nerves began to unravel.

"Lord, I'm beginning to get the shakes. Is that normal?"

Darlene laughed, saying,

"How would I know? You're the one getting married but I am taking notes."

Her cell phone alerted her. It was him.

"Hello… Yes, I'm ready. Are you still going?... Yes, sir, Dr. Hardy, I'll see you at four."

Now her nerves were shot. *It was him, her Mr. Right.*

By three, Arlene's marbles were running all over the place. With Darlene's help, she was dressed. All she needed to do was apply makeup and she'd be ready.

"Where's the ring?"

"Right here, in my purse, I think. Yes, it's here."

It was time.

"Arlie, we have to go. Let's load your luggage. Daddy is giving you away, isn't he?"

"Yes, I guess, I forgot to ask him."

They arrived at the church seeing daddy's and Dale's truck, a Nissan, probably the preacher's, Ken's Malibu, and a white QX80 Infiniti? Darlene guessed it must be Ray's. Nobody she knew could afford to drive an Infiniti. She'd never seen one that she remembered.

They walked into the vestibule seeing everyone up front. She peeped in seeing Ray seated on the back pew.

"Are ya'll ready? Daddy, you're supposed to give Arlene away. Come with me."

She led him to the vestibule saying,

"When the music starts; walk down the aisle."

She stepped inside the sanctuary and looked at Ray, He was wearing an open collar, white, long sleeve shirt, He stood and escorted her to the third pew behind her brothers.

The pianist was waiting for her cue.

"Ladies and gentlemen, please stand."

It was time. The pianist, she lived beside the church, began playing as Arlene and her daddy walked slowly down the aisle. Ken was waiting.

Darlene whispered,

"Daddy, give her hand to Ken and step back. Stand there, don't sit down yet."

So far, so good. Now Darlene was standing behind her daddy whispering,

"He's going to asked who's giving Arlene away. Just say 'Her mother and I' then sit down."

"Who gives this woman in marriage?"

Her daddy turned and look at her.

"She shook her head whispering,

"Now."

He looked at the preacher saying,

"Reckon me and her mama do."

He was looking at Darlene again.

She whispered,

"Sit beside mama."

The vows and rings went without a hitch. Somewhere in the middle, she realized that Ray had reached over taking her hand.

"Therefore, what God hath joined together, let no man put asunder? Forasmuch as Ken and Arlene have consented together in holy matrimony, and have witnessed the same before God and this company and have pledged their love and loyalty to each other, and have declared the same by the joining and the giving of rings, I, therefore, by the authority of God and of the state of North Carolina, I pronounce that they are husband and wife, in the name of the Lord Jesus Christ. Ken, you may kiss your bride. Everybody, please stand.

The music began and the bride and groom walked back to the vestibule waiting for their well-wishers.

"Mr. and Mrs. Brooks, this is my friend, Dr. Ray Hardy. Dr. Hardy, this is my twin sister, Arlene and her husband, Ken Brooks."

He extended his hand,

"Arlene, you and Darlene are beautiful ladies. May I kiss the bride?"

Arlene's eyes were glowing,

"Dr. Hardy, you certainly may."

He leaned forward and kissed her on the cheek.

"Ken, you're a lucky man. Congratulations!"

"Dr. Hardy, this is my mama and daddy, Owen and Martha Snell. Mama and Daddy, this is my friend, Dr. Ray Hardy."

He extended his hand saying,

"Mrs. Snell, now I know where Darlene and Arlene get their looks. You are a lovely lady. Mr. Snell, it is a pleasure to meet you, sir."

"Ray, these are my brothers. Dale here is the oldest, then Evan and Billy's the youngest. Dale, Evan, Billy, this is my friend, Dr. Ray Hardy.

He shook each of their hands saying it was a pleasure meeting them.

There was one more.

"Ray, this is my aunt, Bessie. She's mama's sister. Aunt Bessie, this is my friend, Dr. Ray Hardy. "

He took her hand and warmly greeted her.

Fifteen minutes later, the bride and groom were on their way to Hilton Head and her family had left for Last Chance.

~ *D* ~

Ray followed her to the apartment and went inside, carrying his coat and tie. Their reservations were for seven. There was no rush.

"Ray, make yourself comfortable, there's Pepsi and Bud Light in the refrigerator and the bathroom's across from the dining area. I'll be upstairs changing."

He put his tie on and opened a Bud Light before sitting on the couch. The picture of Darlene and Arlene on the coffee table occupied his time until he heard her coming down the steps. He turned just as she reached the bottom step.

"Darlene, you're absolutely beautiful. The dress, your hair, your eyes, yes, you are beautiful. I'm honored to have you dine with me tonight. Let's get going."

"Be My Valentine"

The QX80's leather interior was luxurious. She'd been in a car with a leather interior but nothing like this. She was out of her place and knew it but it was her one night with Mr. Right and not only was she was going to enjoy, she was going to remember every minute of it.

They followed Hwy 264 to Greenville taking the bypass exiting on Hwy 43 west. Just past Rock Springs, they turned left on VOA-Site C Road. Their destination was just ahead. The sign simply stated, **Bobby's**. She'd never heard of it but she hadn't heard of a lot of places. Parking, he took her arm and led her to the entrance. Inside, the hostess greeted them.

"Good evening. What name is the reservation in?"

"Dr. Ray Hardy."

"Very good, sir, please follow me."

Darlene looked at the richly appointed décor. No wonder she'd never heard of it. Her pocketbook wouldn't have let her in the door.

"This is your table, sir. I hope it meets with your approval."

"This is fine, thank you."

She stood by while Ray seated Darlene and then himself.

"Your waiter will be right with you. We hope you will have a memorable evening. The music will begin at nine."

The waiter arrived asking about beverages.

"Darlene, would you like a glass of wine or something else, a cocktail, beer?"

She knew absolutely nothing about wine. Her daddy made Scuppernong wine but she was sure it wouldn't be served here.

"A glass of wine would be nice. I'll let you choose."

He looked at the wine menu ordering a California white Zinfandel.

Darlene was curious,

"Do you eat here often?"

"No, only once or twice at lunch. I haven't been here for dinner. Until you, there was no one I wanted to bring."

He'd warmed her heart but just seeing him did that.

"Good evening folks. I'm Bobby Carraway. Welcome to my restaurant."

He handed Darlene a long-stemmed rose.

"I hope your evening with us is a very special one. Happy Valentine's."

He walked to the next table and Ray commented,

"I'm told he has the best steaks this side of the Angus Barn in Raleigh. We'll soon know."

The waiter was back with their wine. After tasting it, Ray nodded his approval and the wine was poured.

He raised his glass to Darlene,

"To my Valentine."

"Thank you!"

For starters, the waiter suggested the crab-stuffed mushrooms or coconut shrimp.

"Darlene?"

She looked at him replying,

"The crab-stuffed mushrooms sound good."

"I agree, waiter, we'll start with them.

"When the music starts at nine. Will you dance with me until midnight or does your carriage turn into a pumpkin? Actually, I think they close at eleven."

He reached over touching her hand.

She looked into his eyes, replying.

"Yes, I'd love to. My carriage may turn into a pumpkin but I'll still be me."

Their starters arrived and were delicious. She'd eaten a lot of crabmeat but never like this.

The waiter was monitoring them and when they appeared to be finishing their starters, he was back asking about soup or salad.

"Salad or soup?"

Ray looked at Darlene and she replied,

"Maybe a salad."

"Waiter, bring us a wedge salad. Do you have a house dressing?"

"Yes, sir, Mr. Carraway offers an Italian dressing with a twist."

Ray looked at Darlene.

"Would you like to try that or something else?"

"Let's try that."

She was sure he realized that she was totally out of her environment. He should have known when he brought her there.

The salad was delicious with the special dressing. It was time to order their main entrées.

Looking over the menu, he suggested the filet mignon.

Darlene concurred choosing the 6 oz. one cooked medium rare. For sides she chose the baked potato and grilled asparagus.

He chose the 8 oz. filet, medium rare, with a baked sweet potato and broccoli.

He was so attentive; it was as if he was there just to accommodate her. She wanted to hope it wasn't all just a dream but how could it be anything else? He lived in his world, not hers.

No, she didn't aspire to live this lifestyle but just to be with him, she'd try anything. What was she thinking? She hardly knew him and he knew little more about her. Yes, he'd met her family and didn't turn and run. She wasn't embarrassed about them. She was one of them but it was as if he lived on the moon while she and her family lived down here below.

"No, it's delicious and the grilled asparagus are perfect."

She'd almost missed his question. It was time to enjoy her one date with him. After tonight, Mr. Right would turn into a pumpkin and she'd be back cleaning the floors for the others.

Ray reached over taking her hand.

"Darlene, I'll be attending a seminar for the next two weeks in Durham. I hope we'll remain in touch."

She squeezed his hand, replying,

"I hope so, Ray, please text or message me."

Was this his out? Did he think she'd forget him in two weeks? *No way Mr. Right. I will not forget you.*

The music began while they were finishing a double chocolate dessert they'd shared.

"May I have this dance?"

"Yes you may."

She could have hugged Arlene for suggesting they take dancing lessons at Beaufort Community College.

The band was playing **Unchained Melody**. A tune made popular by the **Righteous Brothers**. He held her close and she lay her head on his shoulder. He was such a smooth dancer and she followed him perfectly.

They danced two more songs before going back to their table. Now, they were sharing tapers of champagne. Everything she'd ever dreamed of, hoped for, wished for, was happening right then.

They were back on the dance floor. It was as if they were alone, the whole dance floor was for only her, holding him, Mr. Right, but their evening was slipping away. The band was playing the last song. It was one of her favorites, **Olivia Newton-John's**, **I honestly love you**.

She melted into his arms and closed the rest of the world out. For now, this moment, he belonged to her but then it was over, and too soon, they were standing at her door.

"Darlene, thank you for being my special Valentine tonight. I do not remember ever enjoying a Valentine like this one. You are a very special lady. I will miss you over the next two weeks."

They were holding hands and he leaned forward kissing her tenderly on her lips. It wasn't a peck; it was a tender kiss with feeling. She wanted to throw her arms around his neck but he stepped back.

"I'll text or message you often. Goodnight."

Inside, she knew he was gone but she was still in the stratosphere and wouldn't come down anytime soon.

She was in the apartment alone now. Arlene was gone but right then, her heart was too full to notice. Cupid had shot an arrow and struck her in her heart. Sleep came easily as they waltzed together in each other's arms until dawn.

"Was it a dream?"

No, she'd pinched herself twice.

She awakened Sunday morning hugging one of her pillows. A smile radiated from her face. Yes, it had been a dream but before that, she'd been in the arms of her Mr. Right.

There was no hurry to get up. Church didn't start until eleven a.m. and it was only eight but excitement surged through her body. She couldn't lie there. Moments later, she was dancing around the bedroom with her pillow still in her arms. Last night was to die for. If it was never to be repeated throughout her life, she'd always have her evening with Mr. Right to remember.

She walked downstairs and cranked up Mr. Coffee. The light on her cell was blinking. Who'd texted her last night?

Hi, it's me on the way to Cary. Miss me, I'll miss you. R

She couldn't believe he even remembered her this morning.

I already do. Be safe. D

It was going to be a wonderful Sunday. She could already tell. What? Another text?

It's me, we're on our way to F. Lauderdale! Happy, Happy! Love U. A.

Have fun, Mr. and Mrs. Love U 2. D

Arlene and Ken were on their honeymoon. One day she'd have one, maybe?

For breakfast, she had a bowl of cereal, then showered and dressed for church.

~ D ~

After the service, she lunched at Wendy's. A single combo was all she wanted. The February weather was too chilly for a walk along the waterfront so she contented herself watching an old movie on the tube.

She was missing Arlene now but knew she had to adjust. A new chapter in Arlene's life was just beginning, her's too, but unlike Arlene's, she was alone.

She received another text from Ray a little after seven.

Hi, Having dinner with my bro, Steve. Showed pic I took of U. Say's U R beautiful. I agree. G-nite, R

Tnx, say hi 4 me. Sweet dreams, D

She couldn't believe he still remembered her. She was so sure that by now, he would have slipped away.

Maybe he really does like me? The old movie she was watching was just a blur. Her mind and heart were too full of memories from her date with Ray. There was no room for anything else. Not then, maybe tomorrow when reality kicked back in.

"Monday again"

It began with cereal and a shower. She was ready for another week.

Arriving at Pungo, she picked up a cup of coffee, and took a seat near the exit waiting for 7:30.

"Darlene, is that you?"

She looked up. It was Gail Gibbs from her class in high school. She stood saying.

"Yes, it's me. What are you doing here?"

Gail, dressed in scrubs, excitedly replied.

"I work here. This is my forth day. What in the world are you doing here?"

Darlene couldn't believe it.

"Me too, I've been here about a month. Join me, please."

"Darlene, I'm so glad to see you. I don't know a soul here. I thought you and Arlene worked in Greenville."

“We did, you heard about mama falling? I went back home and stayed six months until the casts were removed and I was offered the radiologist’s position and the assistant director’s position in dietary. As they say, it was an offer I couldn’t refuse and here I am. Are you living here or commuting?”

“I rented a room on the other side of River Forest Manor. It’s okay and the landlady is nice. Where do you live?”

“Washington. If I didn’t have a lease, I’d probably move here. We have to get together soon, here’s my cell, what’s yours? Oh, I almost forgot, Arlene got married last Saturday. She and Ken are on their honeymoon now, down in the Caribbean. What time’s your lunch break? We can catch up a little more then. It’s time to punch in.”

She knew she’d gotten a text but wouldn’t look until she was at her desk.

Happy Monday, R

U 2, D

At least, he hadn’t forgotten her yet but it was only Monday. By Friday, she’d probably know.

The morning passed quickly. There was a procedure in radiology and the steamer broke down in the kitchen.

When she got back from radiology, the bookkeeper said Mrs. Wiggins wanted to see her.

She tapped on the threshold,

“Did you want to see me?”

"Yes, have a seat. The steamer went down and I want you to see the procedure we follow to get it, hopefully repaired. If not, replaced and we don't want to go there unless we absolutely have to.

Remember me telling you about Hobart in Kinston? She picked up the phone and dialed.

"Hello, this is Nellie Wiggins in dietary at Pungo District Hospital. Is Mr. West in?... I need a repairman, who should I talk to?... It took a few minutes… Gary, this is Nellie Wiggins… Good, when can you come?... That's the earliest?... We'll expect you in the morning, thank you."

He'll be here about ten in the morning. Meanwhile, let's go to the kitchen. We'll have to plan our menu without the steamer." She laughed before continuing,

"We've been here before many times."

The cooks were preparing the entrée's that didn't require the steamer. They knew the ones they'd use but Mrs. Wiggins had to give her approval.

It seemed cut and dry to Darlene but procedure was procedure. She was glad Nellie wanted her to learn. One day, she hoped to have her own restaurant but didn't look forward to breakdowns.

Gail joined her for lunch and they decided to meet at Pizza Inn that evening. She'd been in touch with most of their classmates that were still close by and a few that had moved away.

~ *D* ~

That evening, they did the buffet with a pitcher of beer.

"So tell me, Gail. How many of the old gang are still around?"

Gail took a bite of pizza and replied,

"Probably fifteen or sixteen, some of them commuted to Washington getting their two year degrees. I think twelve went off to college and seven went into the service. You knew that Kay Elks died?"

"No! When?"

"Last summer, she drowned near Buxton. She was out there with her family and the rip-tide got her. It's so sad. She was supposed to have gotten married back in December. Things just happen, I guess."

"Tell me about you. Arlene's married. You must be close."

Darlene laughed, replying,

"No, not even close. I dated a physical therapy assistant, from Vidant, a few times, nothing serious though. I guess I'm just too hard to please. He's out there somewhere. All I have to do is find him. Are you still dating, Roland Mackey?"

"Yes, we've been dating since tenth grade. He's so, I don't' know, Darlene… old fashioned, country…I don't know what I'm trying to say. It's like he's living back in the old days. He's still helping his daddy with the oysters but they've been gone so long out of Rose Bay, it's takes them two or three hours to get to the beds They did start crabbing last year. I think they've got about 200 crab pots now and that's a big help. He said they were building a molting shed. They'll be doing peelers when the season opens in March or April, depending on the weather.

"Thing is, Darlene, I'm pretty sure I don't want to spend my life down there. Life up here's got to be so much better. I want to get on at

Vidant in Greenville but I want to get a little experience at Pungo first. Is that crazy? Am I?"

Darlene laughed, replying,

"Look at me, I left. There's no way that I'm going to spend my life in Last Chance, no way. We were going to move to Greenville in January when our lease ran out but then mama fell and now, Arlene's married and I'm working at Pungo. That's about as far east as I plan to go. Now, when I win the lottery, I might want to live near Duck, but that's not going to happen, I don't even buy tickets. I guess I'll just have to marry a rich man."

Gail laughed.

"Me too…fat chance of that happening. I don't think that I even know one."

"What are you doing Saturday, Gail? Let's go to Greenville and have breakfast."

"Sounds good to me, meet at your place, nine o'clock?"

"Perfect, follow me and I'll show you where it's at."

When they arrived, Darlene pointed down River Road saying,

"Just follow River Road to where it forks off to the left. It's called Broad Creek Road. It will take you to Hwy 264 at the community college. See you in the morning."

Darlene knew she'd gotten a text earlier but wouldn't look until she got home.

Hi, ck FB R

She brought her laptop online seeing his message on Facebook.

Hi, I had such a long day but now I'm finally in my room. I hope your day was nice. May I have this dance? Ray

Smiling, she tapped in her reply.

Yes, I'd love to dance with you. I had dinner with one of my classmates that started to work at Pungo. We've doing breakfast Saturday morning in Greenville. I'm glad Gail is here. It's already lonesome without Arlene. Sweet dreams. Darlene.

~ *D* ~

Her morning began the usual way. Put the coffee on, shower, dress, Special K and she was out of the gate.

At the hospital, Gail was having a cup of coffee when she walked into the dining room. She looked up saying,

"Get a cup of coffee and join me."

Darlene walked through the line picking up coffee. The donuts looked inviting but she managed to turn her head.

She joined Gail observing,

"It's cold out there. I wore my winter coat this morning. No snow yet but there's still time. Are you a snow person?"

Gail laughed, replying,

"Snow? Really? How many times do you remember snow in Hyde County?"

"A flake here and there except that one time. Remember, we got three-inches and school closed 2 days. Up here, I've seen as much as six-inches. It doesn't last long but it's pretty coming down."

Her pager was vibrating. She looked at it saying,

"Got to go, see you at lunch?"

Gail was up too; it was time to punch in.

"I'll be here."

Darlene walked down to Radiology putting her lab coat on.

"Good morning, Dr. Pulver. Is there an early procedure?"

"Yes, Miss Snell, eight forty-five."

He wasn't much of a conversationalist but she didn't expect anything less from a doctor. She was used to that.

At nine forty-five, she was back at her desk in dietary. There was a note to meet Mrs. Wiggins in the kitchen.

The Hobart Tech was already there when she walked in.

"Gary, this is Darlene Snell, she'd my new assistant. Darlene, this a Gary Alphin with Hobart. He does all our repairs."

Darlene offered her hand,

"Gary, it's nice to meet you although we hope we don't see you very often."

Gary laughed, replying.

"I guess I understand that. As I was explaining to Nellie, the solenoid is sticking. I have one on the truck and I'll have you up and running in about 30 minutes. I keep telling Nellie that if you don't put a good filter on the steamer, You're really going to have a big, expensive problem. This coarse filter can't do the job. Let me get to work. Nice to meet you…ah…May I call you, Darlene?"

"Yes, please do, Gary."

By eleven, the steamer was back online. It was just another day at Pungo District Hospital.

She ran into Gail just as she was entering the dining room. They walked through the line together. The chef salad beckoned to them. It, along with ice tea, constituted their meal. Ranch dressing and captain's wafers completed it.

Just as Darlene sat down her phone announced a text. She wasn't going to wait an hour to look.

Hi. Cell died, I'm back. Later FB R

Catch U then, D

"What would we do without our cells? I don't know how our parents ever made it. No cells, no computer, no tablet, no internet."

Darlene laughed, totally agreeing with her.

"I'd be so lost. They must have led a very boring life. I still can't figure out how they managed to date. I guess it was through school. In the summer months, it must have been hard."

She was on cloud nine. He hadn't forgotten her and it was Tuesday.

The afternoon would have been a complete waste if the PYA rep hadn't stopped by.

Nellie introduced her to Darlene.

"Frances Pierce, this is Darlene Snell. Darlene, this is Frances Pierce."

"May I call you, Darlene?"

"Yes, please do, Frances."

She asked if she could share a few specials with them. Opening her laptop, she listed several items, mostly meats and seafood but had a very special price on green beans. They're only available in case lots of 20 and it will take a while to use them but look at the savings. It was substantial and Nellie gave her an order and also included 2 cases of tilapia.

Thanking them, she was gone.

Nellie observed that Frances made about thirty calls a day and couldn't linger. She had to enter all her orders online by two p.m. for delivery the next day.

"She also juggles food around if one of her customers gets shorted or back ordered. I wouldn't want that kind of regimen. I'm only twenty-nine but it would wear me out."

Darlene agreed that it would probably do the same to her.

~ D ~

That evening, she stopped by the Chinese takeout, near Food Lion, picking up sweet and sour pork, an egg roll, and a container of egg drop soup.

At home, she first changed into sweats. Now she could leisurely enjoy her meal. A Bud Light was the perfect beverage.

Online, she checked the message from Ray.

Hi, my cell died last night and it was after nine this morning before US Cellular retrieved my data and gave me a new phone. I hope your day was better than mine. Ray.

Hi back, that had to be a hassle. I had a better day. Darlene

Arlene was online. She'd just messaged her.

Hi Darlie, we'll dock in Cozumel tomorrow afternoon. Key West was fun but those people are crazy. I've never seen so many chickens running around loose in my life. Cats are everywhere. We took the trolley tour but ate all our meals onboard. Ken can't stand the smokers. They're everywhere.

I sure miss NC's rule against smoking in restaurants. It's time for dinner, we dine at eight p.m. The other couples at our table are fun. One couple is from Oregon. Jim and Mary Sweeney are from Virginia Beach, they're nice. Dan and Virginia Scott are from Arizona; they have a horse ranch. Gotta go, Ken's calling. Love you!

She grinned knowing how much fun they must be having.

Looks like you're having a ball. You'll never guess who's working at the hospital? Gail Gibbs, I know you remember her. She was in our class. She's a nurse in surgery. We caught up on the class last night. It's nice to have someone from back home to eat with. We're going to Greenville Saturday for breakfast.

Oh! I've got to tell you about my date Saturday night. We went to a place called Bobby's on the other side of Greenville. It was a swanky place. It was all fixed up for Valentines and they had a live band. Arlie, he's a divine dancer. It was like being swept along in a dream and when he kissed me goodnight. Oh! I was in heaven.

Stay in touch. Love you.

~ D ~

Thursday morning, Darlene was awakened by a text alert.

G-morning- will call tonight R

B waiting D

He was going to call. She couldn't wait. While Mr. Coffee perked, she showered and dressed. Wishing the day away wouldn't make it happen. She would just have to wait it out.

She was having coffee when Gail walked in.

"Good morning."

"Good morning, Darlene, coffee first."

She returned taking a seat.

"No surgery today or tomorrow. It's going to be a long two days."

Darlene smiled, saying.

"I know what you mean. We don't average two procedures a week If it wasn't for my dietary job, I'd go crazy."

The morning turned into noon and lunch with Gail. The afternoon was sluggish at best but as it wore begrudgingly forward, it slowed to a snail's pace.

By four-thirty when she punched out; her nerves were shot. When she walked into the apartment, she made a B-line to the refrigerator grabbing a Bud Light. It never stood a chance. The second one waited until she changed clothes. Now the waiting game began. He didn't say what time he'd call. It didn't matter, she'd wait.

After fixing a chicken salad sandwich, she watched the local news at six and then the national news at six-thirty. If he didn't call soo…Her cell was ringing.

This is Darlene…Ray, I've been waiting for your call *Darlene, what are you doing? You never tell a man you're waiting for his call* No, not long… It doesn't matter, we're talking now. How's your seminar going?... I'm sorry, you have another whole week…Of course I'd love to… No, my schedule is very flexible... Saturday week is fine… I hope that we'll text or Facebook before then… I will, you have a nice evening too. Thank you for calling, bye."

He called, he said he would and he did. Now she could relax. It was only eight days before she'd see her Mr. Right. She was almost hyper-ventilating. He wanted to see her again!

~ *D* ~

Friday morning finally arrived. It had been a struggle. Sleeping almost didn't happen. She was too excited. When it finally came, sometime in the wee hours, she held her pillow closely, dreaming that it was him, her Mr. Right.

After coffee and cereal, she drove to work knowing at the end of the day. There would only be seven more to go.

"What gives, you look like you won the lottery."

Gail sat down wondering about Darlene's demeanor, Employees working in hospitals were usually less than happy and she appeared to be bubbling over.

Darlene smiled radiantly replying,

"Oh, nothing, okay something. I'll tell you about it tomorrow. If I try now, we won't punch in on time."

She knew there was a text. She'd heard the alert. It really sounded like two, not one. Sitting at her desk, she realized there were two. She opened the first one.

Hi, it's TGIF. B happy, I am. R

I am 2! D

The second one was from Arlene.

It's Ken, Arlene sick. Will call tonight.

Arlene sick? That let all the air out of her balloon.

The rest of the day was a blur. She shared the text with Gail saying,

"I may have to cancel tomorrow. I'll text you tonight or in the morning.

She'd skipped lunch and by the time she checked out, she felt weak. Knowing she had to eat something, she picked up a Big Mac combo on the way home.

Changing clothes, she sat at the table nibbling mostly on the fries. After a couple bites of the burger, she tossed it all out. Nothing had any taste. There was nothing to do but wait for the call.

She answered it on the second ring.

"This is Darlene…Ken, what's wrong?... Throwing up, vomiting, temperature, sounds like the flu… Well, what do they say?... Really, what did she eat?... That probably wasn't a good idea… He related that they'd left the tourist sector in Cozumel and she'd insisted on trying some of the local fare. An hour later, whatever it was, jumped on her and by the time they got back to the ship, she was deathly sick. They kept her in the infirmary two hours before EVAC transported her to Miami-Dade. They were there now and she was in isolation. "Isolation, Ken!... When will they know?... Ken, you call as soon as you know something. I don't care what time it is. You call me… Okay tell Arlene that I love her… Okay, when they'll let you see her, bye."

Arlene sick, in isolation, in Miami? All the air in her happy bubble was gone. Now what? Cancel on Gail? No, she was probably better off with company. Call the family? No, not yet. Not until she could tell them what was wrong.

She texted *Gail Come by here at 9*

Okay C U 2-morrow

She went on Facebook wondering if she should share her dilemma with Ray? No, she'd only dated him once. Her problems were not his. She tossed and turned most of the night. There were no happy dreams of being in Ray's arms, only nightmares about Arlene.

~ *D* ~

At five, she gave up and turned to Facebook. It was too early. Most normal people were still asleep. All but one. He had just signed on. She messaged him.

Good morning. Can't sleep either?

Top of the morning to you too. No, I'm meeting my brother at seven. We're going to Charlotte. There's a car he wants to look at. Why are you awake?

Should she tell him, she wanted to?

Too much on my mind, my sister's sick.

Arlene?

Yes, Ken called yesterday. They were in Cozumel and somewhere tourists don't go. He thinks she ate something. She's in isolation in Miami.

Isolation! Has CDC been notified?

I don't know. Ken's supposed to call when he knows something. I'm sorry, I guess I'm just afraid. I don't want anything to happen to her.

Now there were tears in her eyes.

Pack your bag, we're going to Miami. I'll pick you up in two hours.

Ray, you can't leave your seminar.

It will be scheduled again. Let's worry about Arlene right now. Bye.

She rushed to pack the only piece of luggage she had.

Gail, she had to text her.

Gail. Arlene sick. talk 2 U when I get back.

"Mount Sinai Medical Center"

Miami, Florida

Ray arrived at ten after seven. When she opened the door, he took her into his arms.

"Are you ready?"

"Yes, I'll get my bag."

They drove to Pitt -Greenville airport and boarded a Gulfsteam G650 private jet.

"It belongs to our company."

In moments they were on the way to Miami. She couldn't believe that she was on a private jet. They were the only passengers.

"Have you heard anything else?"

She nodded no,

"No, Ray, I'm so scared."

"Everything will be all right, you'll see. We'll be there in about five hours. Recline the seat and try to get some sleep."

It only took moments, seated beside her Mr. Right, for restful, peaceful sleep to overtake her.

"Darlene, wake up, we'll be landing in forty-five minutes. Eat this, you'll feel better."

He raised her seat up and sat the tray in place. They enjoyed a linguini salad with Ranch dressing and chicken tenders.

"It's delicious, Ray. I'll never be able to pay you back."

He grinned at her,

"Pay me back? You already have...well maybe you owe me a few more dances."

Knowing she must still be in a dream world, she pinched herself again. She wasn't dreaming.

When they landed, a car was waiting to take them to the hospital.

"I'm Arlene Brooks' sister. Can I see her?"

The greeter looked down the list.

"I'm sorry, you can't, she's in isolation."

"I'm the family doctor. I'd like to talk to the doctor in charge of her case."

"Yes, sir, Doctor. Take the elevator to the tenth floor and go to the nurse's station."

He took Darlene's arm and led her to the elevator.

"I'm Doctor Hardy, I'm Arlene Brooks' family doctor. I'd like to see the doctor in charge."

"Dr. Marchez is in a conference sir, you may wait in his office. It's down hall C on the right. His name is on the door."

"Thank you. This is her twin sister; she'll be with me."

In the office, they found seats on the leather sofa.

"Will I get to see Arlene?"

"Darlene, if she's in isolation, no. I'm sure CDC is here or on the way There are stringent protocols that have to be followed until they know what they are dealing with. Let's wait and see what Dr. Marchez says."

Twenty minutes later, Dr. Marchez walked in. Ray stood introducing himself.

"Dr. Marchez, I'm Dr. Hardy, I am Arlene Brooks' family physician. What can you tell me about the case?

"Dr. Hardy, please sit down, at the present, not very much. Mrs. Brooks slipped into a coma before she arrived. Because of where she was flown in from and the charts that accompanied her, we had no choice but to place her in isolation and notify CDC. We expect someone from Atlanta within the hour. As I'm sure you are aware, cases like this must follow strict protocol. Not ours, but CDC's. Until they arrive, this is all we have."

He handed the chart to Dr. Hardy.

Ray studied it for a few moments before handing it back.

"Thank you, Doctor Marchez. Here is my card. I would appreciate hearing from you when CDC shares their finding or if there are any other changes. We'll find our way out."

The car and driver was still waiting when they emerged outside. Driver, where have accommodations been made?"

The Breakers, sir. Two blocks away."

"Please take us there.

Arriving, the bellhop took their luggage while Ray checked in. It was a formality; the paperwork had been completed before they arrived. They followed him to the penthouse floor.

Inside, Darlene realized it wasn't a room, it was a suite of rooms including two bedrooms, kitchen with a fully stocked bar, dinette, and spacious living room that led out to a balcony affording an amazing panoramic view of Miami Beach.

Ray tipped the bellhop and he excused himself.

She looked at Ray, with tears in her eyes saying in an unsteady voice.

"Ray, I don't belong here. I'm so out of my comfort zone. Please don't get me wrong. I cannot express how grateful I am but I don't belong here."

He pulled her into his arms.

"You are with me. You belong anywhere I am."

He kissed her on the tip of her nose.

"Now, come sit down with me. He led her out on the balcony. The air was so warm and inviting She couldn't believe people lived like this.

There was a knock at the door. He answered it and a tray was rolled out on the balcony. It contained cold cuts, cheeses, breads, pastries, French bread, condiments and a bottle of Chardonnay.

"Let's enjoy a snack while we're waiting for a call."

The wine was different, tart, woody, but seemed to go well with the cheeses, especially the Brie.

"Ray, is this the way you live? How can you be happy in Beaufort County? How can you work at Pungo? Most of all, sir, how can you be interested in someone like me? I'm a country hick, Ray. I'm so out of place."

"Darlene,"

He reached for her hand pulling her up. He took her face in his hands and kissed her tenderly, like before.

"First of all, I'm in Pungo because I like the area. I have an office there because I like the relaxed atmosphere. I enjoy what I'm doing with Duke Marine Lab because it gives me the opportunity to be away from all this. Most of all, I'm with you because you fill my dream. You are the epitome of my dream. I wa…his cell broke the spell.

"Dr. Hardy… Thank you. Will they begin tests today?... That's fine. I check back in tomorrow morning.

They won't begin tests until in the morning. We will not be able to see her until after the tests are completed. Hopefully, we will be able to then. Do you have Ken's cell number?"

"Yes, it's in my cell."

"Good, let's call him."

"Ken, Darlene, we're here in Miami… No we flew down. Ray wants to speak with you."

"Ken, are you still at the hospital. Oh okay…Can you have dinner with us. I told the doctor in charge that I'm Arlene's family doctor and I've seen the charts. I may be able to share some thoughts with you if you'd like… I don't' know, Ken. Probably several days. It depends on what CDC says… Center for Disease Control…They don't know yet…Okay, we'll pick you up at six. Bye."

He looked at Darlene saying,

"The cruise line put him a hotel near the airport. That's close to the restaurant. We'll pick him up at six. Oh, we'll finish our conversation later. It's 3 o'clock. Let's walk on the beach."

"Ray, I didn't bring anything to wear. I'm sorry, I didn't know."

"Come with me, young lady."

They exited the elevator on the mezzanine level. It was lined with shops and boutiques. They walked onto one finding shorts, tops, bathing suits, bikinis, sandals, flip-flops, and sunglasses.

"Look at this Darlene, this will be perfect on you."

He held up s string bikini that could have hidden nothing. The look on her face was amazing. He laughed, trying to appear embarrassed before leading her to the shorts and tops. Pick up something you like. Get a couple of outfits and sandals. You'll need sunglasses too."

"Ray, you can't keep doing this. You hardly know me."

"I know all I need to know, Darlene; this a tax write-off. It's all being placed on the company account."

"How can you do that?"

"Easy, I'm on the board of directors. It's complicated Darlene. I'll explain it all to you later. Come on, let's walk on the beach."

Back in the suite, she changed quickly and they strolled along the beach, hand in hand, for thirty minutes before returning to the hotel taking seats at one of the tables by the pool.

"Sir, would you care to order a beverage?"

"Yes please, two Pina Coladas and a bowl of cashews."

When their drinks arrived, he signed the tab.

"Have you tried these?"

"It looks delicious, no, I haven't. Ray, it's so good. What's in it?"

"Pineapple juice, coconut cream, white rum, dark rum, and of course a parasol and wedge of pineapple.

They relaxed for about an hour before returning to the penthouse. It was time to dress for dinner.

"Darlene, we'll dress casual, almost everybody down here does."

She hadn't compensated for the climate difference. She could wear the slacks she brought, one of her new tops and her flats.

"Will this be okay; I didn't expect to be eating out. Ray, I guess I wasn't thinking. All I knew was that Arlene was sick."

"You are fine, Darlene, we're going to a Cuban place. La Casa is very casual.

"Cuban?"

He smiled, replying,

"You'll enjoy their cuisine; just wait."

Out front, the car and driver were waiting.

"Ramos, we're picking a guest up at the Best Western near the airport on 107th avenue."

He looked at Darlene saying,

"Call Ken, ask him to meet us at the front entrance. Are you hungry?"

"Yes, thank you. Are you?"

He smiled, replying,

"Starving for some Cuban; you'll love it."

She wasn't sure about that but she trusted him.

Ken was waiting when they arrived. Ray stepped out extending his hand.

"Ken, it's good to see you again. I'm sorry about the circumstances. Sit up front with Ramos. It will be more comfortable there.

The La Casa on Seventy-Third, Ramos."

It was only minutes away in Little Havana. Inside, they were seated at a table for four. The waiter asked about beverages.

Ray looked at Darlene and Ken.

"Would you like a Cuban beer or something else?

They both replied,

"Yes, thank you."

He looked at the waiter saying,

"Tres Bucaneros por favor."

Ray looked at Ken saying,

"It will probably be a couple of days before CDC completes their tests. Hopefully, by then, we'll have some answers.

"Arlene being in a coma isn't uncommon. Our brains use a coma to protect us when it doesn't know what's happening. When the anxiety subsides, Arlene will awaken.

"There's no need to explain to us what happened. I'm sure you've already been asked a dozen times. I know it will be difficult but please try to relax. I can give you a prescription if you think that will help. Just know that we're here for you."

Darlene couldn't believe what he said. He was there for them. She'd only known him a couple of weeks and he acted as if they'd been together forever. Her Mr. Right was becoming her hero too.

The waiter arrived with their beers asking about appetizers. The Americanized menu was easy to read.

Ray looked at Darlene saying,

"The Tostones Rellenos De Camarones are delicious. The shrimp and Creole sauce is a perfect combination. Would you like to try it?

"Yes, please. It does sound good."

"Ken?"

This…I can't pronounce it; the fried pork chunks look good."

"Waiter, bring my lady and I, the Tostones Rellenos De Camarones and Mr. Brooks will have the Masitas De Purercos."

They were on their second beers when their appetizers arrived and Ken was beginning to loosen up.

Dr. Hardy, I can't thank you enough for bringing Darlene down here. I've got more on my shoulders than I've ever had and Darlene, you, being here… I really appreciate it."

Ray looked over at Darlene, then Ken,

"We're here for you, Ken. Try your pork, I think you'll like it. It's not eastern North Carolina barbecue but it's good. What did you think of the Caribbean food? Most of what you experienced was probably 'Jerk,' and spicy best describes it."

"It was spicy; we were on Tums the whole time. I've got some in my pocket now."

Ray laughed, replying,

"If I'm going to the islands, especially Jamaica, I take my Prilosec with me."

"Darlene, how's your shrimp dish?"

"It's good, the sauce is really good. Thank you for suggesting it."

The waiter was back asking about their main entrée's?

He looked at Darlene asking, "May I order for you?"

"Please."

"My lady and I will have the Bistec Empanizado A La Milanesa. For sides, we'll have the Moros and Maduros.

Darlene was trying to follow his order looking at the menu. Breaded beef steak topped with tomato sauce, Mozzarella and Parmesan cheese au gratin with white rice cooked in black beans and fried sweet plantains. It sounded delicious.

"Ken?"

He pointed to the Chicharrones De Pollo saying he'd have the same sides as them.

Darlene found it too, crispy fried chicken chunks topped with Cuban Mojo and onions. He was going to need those Tums.

Looking at them, Ray asked about another round?

Ken concurred but Darlene asked if she could have iced tea.

"Waiter, bring my Lady a glass of Te Frio and another round of cervezas for us."

Their food was delicious. Darlene really enjoyed the breaded beef steak and Ken, after taking a couple of Tums, enjoyed his chicken chunks.

"Ken, Darlene tells me that you're a building contractor and you're opening an office in Elizabeth City. Oceanfront Property, is that correct?"

Ken replied,

"Yes, mostly new construction in the private sector. I've been in commercial for the past seven years.

"Oh, where?"

"In the Raleigh area. I was job-super on the Six-Forks North job."

"That's beside Northside Mall, that's one of our properties. My brother and I are the principals in Prime Properties. Our office is in Cary."

Ken smiled replying,

"We did some work for you two years ago. It's a small world."

"What made you want to get out of commercial?"

Ken smiled,

"Working for the other man."

"I sure understand that. That's why I'm in marine biology. For the most part, I'm my own boss; especially when I'm on the Pamlico River and sound."

"Dessert anyone? You've got to try their Key Lime Pie."

They were in agreement.

"Waiter, Tarta De Lima for each of us along with cups of your Cuban coffee.

"Ken, my brother says our advisory board is interested to doing a property in Duck adjacent to the Sandpiper's Traceg Resort. Would you have any interest in that?"

"Yes, very much but my pockets aren't nearly that deep."

"Where there's a will, there is always a way. We'll talk about it later.

~ D ~

Back in their suite, they stood on the balcony enjoying the beautiful Miami evening. Looking out over the Atlantic Ocean, the cresting moon painted as shimmering glow across the, almost becalmed, ocean surface.

Ray moved up behind Darlene, placing his hands on her shoulders.

"You've had a long day. A good night's sleep will do you good."

She replied,

"Maybe a little longer, I don't want my dream to end."

"Doctor's orders, your dream will be here in the morning."

He turned her, gently around, kissing her tenderly before leading her back inside.

Sleep came quickly as she and her, Mr. Right, danced the night away in the shimmering sands of Miami Beach.

~ *D* ~

He was having coffee on the balcony when she came out of her bedroom.

"Good morning. Was your doctor right? Is your dream still here?"

Her eyes sparkled as she replied,

"I can't believe it. Yes, he is."

"Coffee?"

"Yes please."

By now he knew, one dollop of cream, no sugar.

"Try these Danish, they're delicious. We'll have brunch before going to the hospital. There's no need to get there before eleven. They'll be running tests until then."

The Danish was fresh and delicious and the coffee, it wasn't anything like the hospitals's or even hers.

"Ray, you speak fluent Spanish, your brother and you own a huge corporation that retains suites like this plus own corporate jets and there you are, a doctor in Pungo District Hospital with ties to Duke Marine Lab. Who are you? Please help me to understand. I'm totally lost."

"Darlene, I'm just me. Dan, my older brother and I, bought into a strip mall project at the intersection of US 1 and Wake Forest Road about nine years ago. Roy Poole gobbled us up quadrupling our investment.

"A year later it happened twice; one in Cary and the other near Garner. The property our father left us adjacent to RTP was purchased for 30 million dollars and we invested it in our corporation, Prime Properties.

"Today we have assets in excess of 1.1billion dollars. Dan is the brains of the operation. He loves it and I hate it. We talked about him buying me out but right now, we prefer to leave well enough alone.

"Tax-wise, it would be foolish. We're looking at properties in Europe and Australia now. We're scheduled to visit Australia in June. I may be gone a month but our number crunchers are dying for us to get over there. Me, I don't really want to go but I'd love to tour the outback and Great Barrier Reef.

"That's my story and I'm sticking to it."

Darlene was blown completely away. She mind was spinning. There was no way for her to begin to comprehend what was taking place but here she was. She could only enjoy his company until the bubble burst and she knew it must.

"Australia? What will happen to your project?"

"I'll table it unless they approve my request. If that happens, I'll be in Australia for a year and I can do our company's study at the same time. The study here is on-going and my input is only a small part of the entire project. I think it's important but my endeavors will only be merged with the others. The main thing is to preserve our marine environment."

"Come with me."

They took the elevator back to the shops picking out three casual outfits plus an evening one. Her repeated protests fell on deaf ears."

After she changed, they had brunch at one of the restaurants in the resort complex before leaving for the hospital. She'd never had, or heard of, Baklava pancakes. Now she had and with maple syrup and fresh fruit; she loved them.

"They're delicious aren't they?"

She could only smile and mirror his remark.

"Yes, they are."

"Tomorrow, we'll try their Greek omelets. I think you'll like them too."

~ D ~

The driver dropped them off at the hospital few minutes before eleven. Inside, they took the elevator to the tenth floor and Isolation. He walked up to the nurse's station asking if Dr. Marchez was available.

"I'm Arlene Brooks' doctor."

The nurse pulled her chart finding his name.

"No doctor, He's with the CDC team. They should be wrapping up their tests any time now."

"Thank you, may I see the chart?"

It looked no different from yesterday other than fluctuations in her temperature that continued to be erratic. A brain scan had not been scheduled.

"Sir, you may wait in his office if you'd like."

"Thank you, nurse. We'll be in the dining room. Please notify me when he comes in."

They checked the waiting room not finding Ken. He was probably in the dining room. They were sure they'd find him there.

He was sitting in the coffee court reading a paper.

"Go join him. Do you want coffee?"

"Yes, please."

"One milk?"

She smiled, he remembered everything. She'd only just met him but was already wondering what she was going to do when he was gone.

She walked over taking a seat with Ken.

"Good morning. Did you sleep well?"

"Not really, I guess my nerves are about shot. How about you?"

"Yes, Ray fixed hot chocolate. I think he put something in mine."

She knew what was in hers. He was. They'd danced all night. Her dream seemed so real and she wished so much that it could be, would be, but reality's ugly face indicated otherwise.

"Good morning, Ken, catching up on the news?"

"Dr. Hardy, this paper must weigh five-pounds. Is it printed every day?"

Ray laughed,

"Yes Ken, you ought to see the Sunday edition.

I checked Arlene's chart. There's no change. CDC should have completed their tests by now. We'll kno…

"Dr. Ray Hardy, please call extension 9011"

Seeing a phone on one of the many columns, he dialed the extension.

"This is Dr. Hardy… Thank you, I'll be right up."

"Darlene, do you want to wait here with Ken?"

She wanted to hear firsthand but reasoned that it would be better coming from Ray.

"I'll wait here with Ken."

Dr. Marchez was waiting,

"Dr Hardy, please have a seat. The initial tests have been run and the preliminaries indicate trauma from swelling of the tissue surrounding the brain. We think it's Arbovirus Encephalitis but won't know until further tests are run this afternoon and tomorrow. If our suspicions are correct, she will be moved out of isolation and treatment will begin. As I am sure you are aware. No one can guess how long the patient will remain in a comatose state."

"Dr. Marchez, does CDC suspect it's possibly Tuberculous Meningitis? I only ask because of isolation."

"Dr. Hardy, she was out of the county when she exhibited possible systems. CDC dictates isolation and I fully concur."

He stood, thanking Dr. Marchez saying he'd be in contact tomorrow.

Handing him his card, Ray said,

"If there is an emergency, please contact me"

He found Darlene and Ken, still seated by the coffee court.

"There's really hasn't been any change. Tests have been run for Arbovirus Encephalitis and they've ruled out Spinal Meningitis but suspect Tuberculous Meningitis. The location of where she became sick is the reason she's still in isolation. In either case, the fluid surrounding her brain will have to be reduced significantly before the trauma on her brain is relieved. In layman's' terms, the swelling will have to come down before Arlene will awaken.

Darlene was hanging on his every word.

"How long?"

He reached over taking her hand.

"Darlene, nobody really knows. It may take weeks before the pressure is released. They may install a stent. I don't know. In any case, it will most likely be week's, even months, I'm sorry."

He looked at Ken.

"What are your plans, I'm sure you have to go back to North Carolina to save your business and home."

"Dr. Hardy, I don't want to leave Arlene but I have to do something. You are right, we will lose everything if I don't."

He looked at Darlene then back to Ken.

"Come over to the Breakers about seven. We're on the penthouse floor, suite three. We'll work this out."

~ D ~

Back in their suite, they spent a few minutes on the balcony while Ray tried to explain what the doctors were doing. She'd been in hospitals about eighteen months and basically knew what was happening. Diagnosing the problem came first, family concerns came second. The CDC was totally new to her. She, of course, was familiar with them but had no experience or understood the authority they had.

"Darlene, Arlene and Ken were in Mexico and out of the tourist sector. They should never have been there but they were. Whatever bit, stung or otherwise got into her system had a very traumatic effect. It's the mandate of the CDC not to allow viruses or infections into our country. It's quite a responsibility and they take it very seriously. They overrule any local or state statute welding a federal mandate. Dr.

Marchez does not think it requires isolation but it's not his call until CDC releases the case. Hopefully, that will come in a couple of days.

"I'm going to suggest to Ken that he go home and take care of their home and his business. When they release Arlene, I will fly her to Vidant Heath. They are qualified to handle her case once she's out of isolation. Are you comfortable with my suggestion?"

She looked at him with tears in her eyes. He was talking to her not down to her. It was as if he considered her as his equal.

"Ray, I don't know what to say. I haven't from the moment we met. I cannot comprehend how I'm here. I'm so out of my comfort zone and only remain because I want, so much, to be with you. Why you are willing to go to so much trouble for me, us, when you've only met Arlene and Ken once and me just a few short days ago. I can only thank my guardian angel for bringing you into my life. I am so blessed."

He stood pulling her gently into his arms. He spoke softly,

"Darlene, I want you in my life. Please know that I do. He kissed her a little longer this time and she melted into his embrace. Her life was in such a turmoil but his strength had overcome every obstacle.

"I don't know why you are doing this but I'm ready to place our lives in your hands. I can never repay you."

The phone rang.

"Yes… Please give him the code. He is expected."

Moments later, Ken was welcomed in the suite. He'd never seen anything like it.

"Ken, join us on balcony, I'll get you a beer."

"We've been talking about your situation."

He went on to share what they'd discussed.

"What do you think?"

Ken, like Darlene, did not know what to say. That has to be expensive, Dr. Hardy. I cannot afford it. I guess we could reach some kind of financial arrangement.

"Ken, you leave tomorrow. Meet us here for breakfast and pick up your car in Fort Lauderdale. I'll arrange transportation.

When Arlene can be moved, She'll fly back with us. The G650 is designed to remove seats to accommodate ambulatory patients. We fly mercy flights several times a year. It's a tax write-off for us. We'll either use a medical flight crew from here or one from Vidant Health. I'll set it up with Dr. Marchez tomorrow."

Ken, still in disbelief, asked,

"Could I have another beer. I haven't quite caught up with the plan yet."

~ D ~

That evening, there was a slight bit of joviality in the air and Ray suggested they walk down to Surfer Rays for a few drinks and enjoy Mahi with baskets with fried onion and calamari.

They began with Margaritas. Darlene was admonished that two would be her limit. They had to walk back. Laughing, Ray remarked.

"I'll carry you back if I have to."

Darlene didn't know if it was the Margaritas or the way the fish fingers were prepared but they were delicious and the calamari, she'd never tried it, was delicious.

After her second Margarita, she knew she'd reached her limit and Ken hadn't finished his second one.

Back at the hotel, they put Ken in a cab saying they'd see him off in the morning.

In the suite, she wanted to sit on the loveseat, snuggled in his arms.

"Ray, I'm so afraid I'll wake up soon and you'll be gone. I'm trying desperately not to fall in love with you but it's hopeless. Please, I beg of you. Let me down gently."

Neither was responsible for what happened next. It just did. In the heat of their kisses and embraces. His caresses, her caresses, it happened. They were one. Their embrace was unbreakable. Neither would let go, neither wanted it to ever end. The moment was theirs and would forever be etched in the annals of their hearts and minds.

Their becoming one was inevitable from the beginning. From the first moment they saw each other. Now they were one. She awakened in his arms and lay still just looking at him, her Mr. Right. He wasn't hers but right then, at that moment in time, he belonged to her.

They both knew it was her first time. It was so apparent. Whatever she'd done at the beach music festival, getting laid wasn't part of it.

It wasn't his first time; his frat brothers made sure of that. He didn't date. As far as they were concerned he must have been a virgin. Jeremy had gotten him drunk on beer and the others were waiting in a motel room with their favorite hooker. Roxanne worked him over good or so they said. He didn't remember any of it.

He awakened and pulled her close.

"Good morning pretty lady. May I have a kiss."

He could have all of her. She wanted him to and in moments, they belonged to each other again.

Thirty minutes later, he glanced at the clock.

"We have to go. We said we'd meet Ken for breakfast.

~ *D* ~

After breakfast they waved goodbye to Ken before checking on Arlene.

Dr. Marchez said that Meningitis had been ruled out. All the tests pointed to the Arbovirus Encephalitis. They planned on moving the patient out of isolation that afternoon.

"She'll remain in ICU until the swelling begins to subside. However, I think we'll install a stent just above each ear. That will facilitate drainage tremendously."

"Doctor, I want to move the patient to Vidant Health in Greenville, North Carolina as soon as possible. She'll receive the greatest possible care and I'll be there to carry her through each stage."

Doctor Marchez agreed with the transfer saying the procedure to install the stents would be scheduled tomorrow morning. She should be ambulatory by the weekend.

"Have you made arrangements for the transfer?"

"Yes, I'll schedule a mercy flight as soon as you're ready to release her. I'll have a team from Vidant Health to accompany her."

Dr. Marchez observed that sometimes mercy flights were difficult to schedule.

"Not this time, Doctor, it will be aboard my company jet."

Doctor Menchez had no further questions.

~ D ~

That afternoon, Darlene napped in one of the lounge chairs on the balcony. Ray had fixed Mai Tai's for them and the second one sent Darlene into dreamland.

While she slept, he called his brother asking about the project at Duck.

"Dan, I have a contractor we've dealt with before and he's gone out on his own. I'd like for you to take a look at his work. I'd like him in on the project if our advisors approve it… No, he was the job super on the Six-Forks Mall job… Yes, that's the one… Okay, check on it for me… Oh, you didn't tell me. 4500 sq. ft.? Sounds nice. Is that something my contractor can look at too?... Thanks… No, it may be an another week… Yes, it's Darlene's sister…Later."

A little after six, he sat on the edge of the lounge chair kissing her gently on the forehead.

"Sleeping beauty, it's time to awaken."

She opened her eyes and seeing him, a smile spread across her face. He stood and pulled her into his arms.

"We're going out tonight. Would you like to go for a swim first?"

"That sounds like fun but…"

"Yes you do, try one of these on."

"Where did these come from?"

"I had them sent up. See if there's one you like."

He'd done it again. She couldn't believe it. The red bikini was perfect.

"Do you like this."

"I love it. Here put this on."

It was a flutter sleeve cover up.

He'd already changed. She had been right. There was no farmer's tan. His slender, muscular body was perfect.

On the beach, they strolled along the hardpan enjoying the wavelets as they splashed across their feet. It was heaven but she knew it had to come to an end and probably soon. She was getting too used to his lifestyle. They got into the water and tried splashing water in the other's faces but when they locked in each other's arms, the horsing around turned to making love.

~ *D* ~

That evening, they dined at The Stone Crab. It was upscale and Darlene wore the dress Ray picked out earlier.

He slipped something to the Maître D' and he seated them in a secluded nook with a view of the beach.

He ordered cocktails first and when asked about starters, suggested the coconut shrimp. She agreed knowing that whatever he ordered would be fine. Being with him was all that mattered to her.

They finished the shrimp and were enjoying their calamari salads when their waiter returned asking about their main entrée's?

Ray looked at Darlene saying,

"I know you grew up on blue crabs. Down here, stone crabs rule. They taste entirely different. I hope you'll try them."

"You order for us, please."

"My Lady and I will have the stone crabs. For sides… Darlene?"

She chose the pineapple Cole slaw and steak fries and he chose the twice-baked potato and pineapple Cole slaw.

"Ray, you're a doctor and I've tried not to bother you asking a lot of questions about Arlene. Is she going to be all right? Please tell me the truth."

He took her hand, replying.

"I cannot be one hundred percent sure, Darlene, but it appears to be something that only time can cure. With the stents in place, the healing can begin. It may take days, weeks, even months, before Arlene awakens. We just don't know but, Darlene, she will get better."

They were going to do a brain scan in the morning. He chose not to mention that.

"Ray, these are delicious. Our blue crabs are good but these are sweeter. Thank you for letting me try them."

Smiling, he replied,

"A few years ago when I first tried them, I couldn't believe it either. You can't get them in North Carolina unless they're special order and then, they cost a fortune and a lot of times, they're fake. You realize it as soon as you taste them but by then, it's too late. Do you like the pineapple in the slaw? That's a little different too."

"It is different, but I like it too."

There was no way they could end their dining experience without sharing a slice of key lime pie. When in Florida, you almost had to.

Back in the suite, he ordered coffee and they enjoyed it out on the balcony.

She reached over taking his hand.

"You are going to sleep with me tonight, aren't you?"

He squeezed her hand.

"I am if you want me to."

There was no way to put into words their evening of love. They kissed, caressed, explored, and came together time after time until exhaustion and sleep finally overcame them.

The next morning, they were still in each other's embrace.

~ D ~

The procedure to install the stents was scheduled for six a.m. and would only last an hour. Nothing invasive except a small hole drilled into her skull just behind her ears. The brain scan would be performed when the anesthesia wore off. Dr. Marchez said that the results should be available by noon.

There was no need to go over until then. While they were having brunch, Ray surprised her again.

"Transferring Arlene can't take place until Sunday. After we meet with Dr. Marchez this morning, we're flying to St. Croix for a couple of days. There's a property we're interested in and Dan wants me to take a look. I think you'll enjoy seeing the island."

"But I don't have a passport."

"It's in the US Virgin Islands, no passport required but I want you to get one as soon as when get back home. We'll leave Miami about two this afternoon and arrive there around four-thirty. We'll fly back here Saturday and transfer Arlene to Greenville, Sunday morning."

He'd blown her mind again and she was beginning to wonder if she could ever keep up with his schedule if given the opportunity. Her feet still hadn't touched the ground.

~ D ~

The procedure was successful and the brain scan was nominal. That was a relief to Ray but he hadn't shared his concern with Darlene before and wasn't about to now.

They arrived at the Henry E. Rohlsen Airport on St. Croix and picked up a rental car driving across the island to the Buccaneer Resort.

They checked into their room and enjoyed wine spritzers on the private patio.

Later, they dined at The Terrace. There was a magnificent view of Christiansted and the bay.

"We'll drive down tomorrow and take a look."

The waiter had given them the menu and taken their beverage orders.

"What would you like for starters?"

"Ray, I'll let you order, I'm not familiar with any of this."

"Let's do the baked brie. I think you'll enjoy it."

She did enjoy the taste, especially the salted pistachios and honey. The berries were delicious too but she didn't know what they were.

"What would you like for dinner?"

"Ray, order for me. This doesn't look like Logan's menu."

"All in good time, let's try the Chef's signature fish piccata. I'm sure you'll enjoy the jasmine rice and vegetables."

"I'd really like a Big Mac and fries. No, not really, I just don't know what any of the entrées are but I'm confident that whatever you choose will be delicious."

"You'll have to watch me. Sometimes I get crazy."

"I'm sure of that, sir, but I enjoy watching you. I'm going to miss this when we get back to Beaufort County."

"I'll be around, not every day but you won't be able to get rid of me."

"You know that I don't want to, ever."

The piccato was delicious, but she knew it would be, he suggested it.

After dinner, they walked around the property while he shared some of its history. The buccaneer opened in 1947.

"It's the first hotel on St. Croix. The family that opened it arrived in 1922. It began with 11 rooms and as you can see it's grown quite a bit. Now it includes a spa, golf, 8 tennis courts, 3 beaches, a fitness center, banquet and meeting spaces, a shopping arcade and boutiques, history and nature walks and of course, there's no way we could leave without seeing the crabs race. He continued to amaze her.

"You've certainly done your homework."

Back in their room, Ray made notations about his findings and then the rest of the evening was theirs. First on the patio and then in each other's arms. Their tropical paradise was filled with romance and they enjoyed every moment on the enchanted island.

~ *D* ~

Next morning, they enjoyed the sumptuous buffet on the Terrace. The offerings seemed endless. It included: the daily egg specialty, breakfast meats, pancakes, waffles, French toast, hot and cold cereals, freshly baked breads, muffins and pastries, fresh cut fruit selections yogurt, juices, coffee, and fine teas. The open-air dining was so refreshing and the food was so delicious or was it the ambiance of the setting.

"You have a ten o'clock appointment at the spa. I'm sure you will enjoy your massage."

"Massage? Ray, I've never had a massage!"

"Get ready, My Lady, you'll love the experience and while you are, I'll finish reconnoitering the Buccaneer for Dan."

They met at the Mermaid for lunch taking a table under a palm tree.

"Tell me about your spa experience. Did you enjoy it?"

"How could I not have? It was wonderful, delightful, enchanting, oh so relaxing. Apparently, I've missed so much in my life but since I never experienced it. I never missed it. Have you ever had a massage?"

"Yes, several times but the first one was back when I was in college. A group of us went to Banner Elk to ski. On a dare, I had the works and loved every minute of it once I was sure I wasn't going to be raped. My college roommate told everyone that I had been. You cannot imagine the ribbing I took after his remark. Since then, I've probably had three."

"Now that you're all relaxed, how about lunch. See anything you like?"

"Yes, but you're not on the menu."

He smiled,

"Yes I am. Look under desserts but I know your mother told you that desserts never came first. What would you like before dessert?"

"The tropical chicken salad including crisp mixed greens with bell pepper, carrots, cucumber, red cabbage, sprouts and tomato served with almonds, mandarin orange and toasted coconut topped with grilled or crispy chicken beckoned to her. I'll have that. What are you having?"

"I'm going to have the barbeque pulled pork sandwich with the lightly smoked pulled pork and caramelized onions with a zesty BBQ sauce, Applewood smoked bacon and Swiss cheese on a toasted ciabatta roll. They both came with fries, slaw and fruit. That's a lot for lunch. Let's begin with a rum punch."

After lunch, they found their rented power boat at the east end of the boardwalk on King's Wharf in Christiansted and cruised to Buck Island Reef National Monument only 30 minutes away spending the afternoon snorkeling, shell hunting and enjoying each other.

Making love in the water was the high point. A point visited several times during their four-hour get away. She was falling deeper in love with him. There was no use trying not to. She kept telling herself to live for and enjoy each minute as if it would be the last with her, Mr. Right. Coming down would be devastating but it would have been worth it. Her time with him would be enough to last her a lifetime… she hoped; it would have to be.

Back at the Buccaneer, they spent the late afternoon sipping Pina Coladas on the beach. Their stay on St. Croix was coming to a close. Tomorrow they would fly back to Miami and Sunday; they would take Arlene back to North Carolina. They made a pact to make love when the approaching sunrise flooded their room with a myriad of tropical colors. It would be another experience to add to her growing list of memories with her, Mr. Right.

That evening, dining in the Terrace, Ray suggested they try the mussels with Portuguese chorizo sausage, garlic, tomato, and fresh herb broth for starters.

Their frozen rum runners had already arrived and Darlene thought they were delicious.

She'd tried mussels back in Hyde country and didn't really like the texture but for him, she'd try anything.

"Ray, these are delicious. I wonder why folks back in Hyde country don't prepare theirs this way."

"Darlene, everywhere you go, food and drinks are prepared differently. Most times, what we grow up on will always be our favorite way. I'm glad you like them. I want you to try something very different for our meal. The shrimp saltimbocca is served with artichokes, prosciutto, sun-dried tomatoes, capers, fresh lemon, sage, jasmine rice, and vegetable du jour. I know it's so different from what you're used to but try it for me. Shrimp prepared this way are delicious."

"I believe in you, Ray. Let's try it."

She couldn't believe how succulent and delicious they were.

"Ray, I knew the shrimp would be perfect. What am I going to do when I get back home?"

He laughed replying,

"Do just like me, wherever you are, enjoy the way food is prepared locally."

They ended their evening sharing a slice of Key Lime pie and coffee. Their real dessert would follow when they returned to their room.

~ D ~

After dinner, they strolled, hand in hand, around the resort. It encompassed thirty-four acres and there was such a variety of activities available to their guests. Out on one of the beaches, a wedding banquet was in progress. The wedding apparently had taken place earlier. The arch, covered with mandevillas and other tropical flowers, still appeared vibrant and fresh.

Seeing it, Darlene dreamed of a moment when she might wed her, Mr. Right. She knew she was dreaming but since she was living her dream at that moment in time, why not dream for the prize. A life filled with her, Mr. Right.

He was saying something but her mind, her heart, had floated up into the clouds.

"Darlene, where did you go? Come back to me."

She knew she would never left him, only fast forwarded into a dream world that could never happen.

"I'm still here. Seeing weddings always stirs a woman's heart. I'm back now. I'm sorry, what did you say?"

"It doesn't matter, this does." He took her in his arms and caressed her, running his fingers through her hair as his lips crept along her cheek to hers.

"You do know you make me very happy, don't you?"

"You have no idea how happy you make me. I'm so far above my world but right now, in this moment, I'm here and I'm with you. There can be no greater happiness for me."

They stood looking into each other's eyes knowing they were where they wanted to be. Soon, he would return to his world and her to hers but she would not feel empty. She had memories that would last a lifetime.

Back in the main complex, he insisted they go into one of the dress shops after seeing a beautiful cocktail dress in the window. The emerald green asymmetrical neck dress with long sleeves, drop waist, and ruching at both side seams caught his eye. Inside, he insisted she try it on.

"Darlene, it's you. You'll need shoes."

She couldn't believe he was doing this but hesitantly picked out a pair of 4" high heel strappy sandals.

When they returned to their room, dessert was served. They came together as one. Holding, caressing, whispering words of love, as the excitement, intensity, and exhilaration of being in each other's embrace climbed higher and higher.

"Dr. Hardy, your diagnosis on my condition was perfect and your prescription is working perfectly. May I have another dose please."

"I was just getting ready to apply it, Miss Snell. Are you ready?"

"You know I am, sir!"

~ D ~

Rays from the rising sun flooded into their room through the open patio doors filling it with hues of red, yellow, and magenta. She lay in his arms feeling the soft rhythmic beat of his heart as his breathed so easily and softly, it was almost imperceptible.

She knew that in a few hours, they would depart this paradise and end yet, another romantic chapter in her journal with her, Mr. Right. Her heart couldn't contain the joy, exhilaration, and happiness she felt throughout her whole being. There was no way in her country girl's wildest dreams could she have ever dreamed what had and was happening now. Never, how could she? She never knew that lifestyles like this even existing and... Dr. Ray Hardy. No way could she have conjured up a Mr. Right even remotely like him.

"What are you thinking?"

"About you, about here" Could she say it? Probably not but… "About us. I'm living in a dream world and I know that any minute I'll be pulled away from all this. My pager will alert me to a procedure in radiology and my dream will, poof, be gone but never forgotten. Pinch me, I must be dreaming."

He smiled, saying,

"I'm not going to pinch you. This is a better way to let you know it's not a dream. Come to me."

The colors of sunrise gave way to the blueness of day as her dream gave way to love. For now, it wasn't a dream, it was happening and she wanted to remember every moment."

They breakfasted on the Terrace before leaving for the airport. It was time to take Arlene back to North Carolina and return to the real world.

~ D ~

They arrived back in Miami a little after eleven a.m. After freshening up, they lunched on shrimp and crab salad in the Ocean House before going to the hospital.

"Is Dr. Marchez available? I'm Dr. Hardy."

"Yes Doctor, I'll tell him that you're here."

"He's coming for you, Doctor."

"Dr. Hardy, welcome back. You too, Miss Snell. Follow me."

He led them to a small conference room.

"Have a seat, please. Our patient is doing well. The stents are performing as we'd hoped. However, there has been no change in her comatose state but we did not expect any. The scan performed this morning indicated that the fluid buildup is beginning to subside. It will be a slow process but the procedure is working. Are you still planning to move her tomorrow?"

"Yes, Doctor. The modifications are complete and the team from Vidant Health will arrive at 6 a.m. tomorrow morning. They are flying in on my jet."

"That about wraps it up for us. We'll release the patient to you in the morning. Miss Snell, your sister is strong. I'm confident that she will fully recover. It will take time but in cases like this, that's normal. Would you like to see her?"

They followed him to a room finding Arlene, as expected, connected to five tubes. One entering her stomach through her nose and two others in each arm. Darlene walked over kissing her on the cheek saying softly,

"We're taking you back to North Carolina, tomorrow."

Her eyes were filled with tears when she backed away.

That afternoon, Ray worked hard trying to stave off the melancholy invading Darlene's entire being.

They had lunch in Little Havana again. This time, he introduced her first to sopato de platano (plantain soup) and then to bistec de pollo. filete de pollo a la pla saying it was chicken steak their way. She liked both but said they were very spicy.

"Ray, this is delicious but spicy!"

Afterwards, they spent the afternoon on the balcony sipping on wine spritzers. He suggested they walk on the beach or explore the resort but she begged off saying she'd rather spend the afternoon alone with him. The third drink brought a little hint of happiness with it and Ray added to it leading her into his bedroom.

She made love to him as if it would be the last time. She was so afraid her bubble would burst when they returned home, tomorrow.

A little after six, a cart with cheeses, crackers, dip, nuts, and wine arrived. There was still a hint of melancholy in her demeanor but she was trying hard to contain it. Ray knew what was going through her mind but saying something would not help. Only time could prove her misgivings wrong.

That evening, he suggested she wear her new dress. They would be dining at the Flagler Steak House on the resort property.

They began their evening with cocktails and blue crab dumplings for starters.

"Darlene, you're absolutely gorgeous in that dress. It's you."

As he'd done, too many times to count, he took numerous pics with his cell and asked the waiter to take several of them together.

"Thank you Doctor, you clean up pretty good too."

She'd never seen him in formal attire and what he did for the white dinner jacket, bowtie, slacks, and cummerbund was almost sinful. He looked like a movie star.

The waiter begged to interrupt asking about salads. They chose the iceberg lettuce wheels with chopped egg, bacon, tomatoes, sweet onions, croutons, and Point Reyes blue dressing. It looked so inviting.

"Ray, this is delicious, I wonder if it's available in Greenville?"

He laughed, replying,

"Probably not but then I found you there. Anything is possible."

He seemed to always have the right reply and how to say it.

She replied,

"One day, I'd like to open an upscale restaurant in Greenville. Maybe by the time I can, if I ever can; Greenville will be ready."

She looked into the eyes of her, Mr. Right. It's just another one of my foolish dreams."

"Your dreams are not foolish. Hold on to them. You can never tell what gifts providence will place on your doorsteps. Have you ever considered going to cooking school?"

She laughed softly,

"Ray, I have to work. As you can tell, I like to eat. That is a dream that will have to remain on the back burner for a long time. Yes, I'm saving for a restaurant but cooking school, I'd starve to death."

"We'll see."

The waiter was back, had they chosen their main entrée's?

"Have you decided yet?"

"The Pan Roasted Chilean Sea Bass looked good. May I have that with the grilled asparagus and the steakhouse onion rings."

"What are you having?"

He looked at the waiter,

"The linguine and top neck clams. I'd like a side of the butter roasted mushrooms.

She marveled at the fish,

"This is so good. I've never eaten roasted fish. They were always fried when I grew up…everything else was too."

"Did you go clamming back in Hyde Country?"

"Yes, what we didn't grow, we got from the sound. Daddy did deep a few hogs. All our neighbors did too. We had hog killings when it was cold enough. He'd take the pigs to a meat cutter in Engelhard and he'd cut them up and package all the cuts. Mama would render the lard from all the fat and that's what she used in all her cooking. They still press cracklings. Have you ever tried them?"

"No, I've been told that they are delicious in cornbread. Maybe you can fix some for me. I'd like that."

She was ready to fix anything for him. It would be another reason to be with him and she was afraid that her reasons were running out.

"Next time I go home, I'll get some. I make good cornbread. Arlene loves it."

Sadness suddenly ceased her but there was nothing she could do but let it go. She's visit her every day and when she awakened, she'd be there for her.

The waiter was back asking about dessert.

"Do you eat dessert with fish?"

"Not when I was growing up, milk either, but I do now."

"Waiter, bring us one serving of The Banana Split with vanilla, chocolate and strawberry ice cream, hot fudge, pineapple and strawberry toppings, topped with whipped cream."

She smiled at Ray, saying,

"I won't be able to get into any of my clothes when I get home. You're spoiling me."

"Oh, didn't I tell you? That's my intent. No, you'll be fine. A daily walk along the waterfront in Washington will take care of that."

Most of the huge dessert remained when they ordered coffee.

It had been a very special evening but they knew it must end, but not there. It would end in each other's arms back in their suite.

First, they sat on the balcony enjoying Irish Coffee he'd ordered when they left the restaurant. It was waiting when they walked in.

The waxing full moon shone brightly across the shimming waves. Only the sound of traffic interrupted the romantic setting. Ray pointed out a cruise liner, off in the distance.

"I'm sure its preparing to dock at Fort Lauderdale. That's one of the most popular points to embark and return from cruises in the Bahamas and Caribbean. I sailed on my first one from there a long time ago."

"It couldn't have been too long. How old were you?"

"Eight, our parents took us to Nassau. It was a fun cruise. Dan and I had run of the ship. We probably drove the staff nuts."

"I don't want to intrude, but you never talk about your parents. If I'm out of line, please change the subject and I'll apologize."

"There's nothing to apologize for. My father was killed in a helicopter crash near Ashville when I was ten. He was looking at a property near Brevard. His company was interested in developing it into a gated community with a golf course.

"Mother died when I was twenty-two. She was killed in a skiing accident in West Virginia. It was a freak accident, the lift chair broke and she fell 50 feet.

"It's been hard to accept but life must go on. Dan is two years older, He's married to Regina. They have two children, Dana is ten and Ricky is eight. They live in Cary but spend a lot of time traveling or their favorite place, the Sandpiper's Traceg Resort at Duck. When they're there they spend time at Ford's Colony Country Club in Williamsburg. They also enjoy dining in Virginia Beach and Norfolk. He has a helicopter there to ferry them around.

He has plans drawn up to build just north of the resort. I've asked that he check Ken out with the contractor he worked with on one of our projects. I want Ken to build it for him. It's 4,500 square feet. It would help Ken out of the gate.

"I'm sorry, I didn't mean to ramble."

She was trembling. *He lost both his parents in accidents. That was horrible.*

There were tears in her eyes.

"Let's go to bed. Please hold me."

"Arlene, we're going home!"

They began their last day making love before they showered and dressed. For breakfast they went down to Beach Club Restaurant having hand roasted Aztec blend coffee.

Ray suggested they have the macadamia crusted French toast that included Macadamia nuts and Bananas Foster

"I had it last year and loved it. I think you will."

It was and she did adding again to her worries about her weight

~ D ~

They arrived at the hospital finding the Vidant Health team making final preparations for transfer to the waiting jet.

They thanked Dr. Marchez for all he'd done.

Dr. Marchez, knowing there was a more than a doctor/patient relationship between Ray and Darlene, in parting, said.

"Dr. Hardy, please keep me in the loop on your patient's progress. I'm sure she will come out of the coma soon."

~ *D* ~

When they arrived at the airport, the team had already transferred Arlene into the jet. Ten minutes later they were inflight. In about five hours, they would land at PVG-Pitt-Greenville airport and Arlene would be taken by a waiting ambulance to Vidant Health.

The drama that had turned their lives upside down would still continue to but it would be monitored close by now, not from far-away Florida, but from Beaufort and Pasquotank Counties. Arlene would be close enough for Ken to keep a check on her, not every day but several times a week.

There was nothing to do now but wait for the fluid to drain and for Arlene to regain consciousness. No one could conjecture how long that would be. Darlene, Ray, and Ken, could only count the days.

After seeing Arlene in a room at Vidant Health, Ray drove Darlene to her home with all her luggage, she acquired two extra pieces, inside, it was time to say goodbye. Something she almost could not do.

"Ray, I don't even know how to thank you but somehow I have to try. First, thank you for what you've done for Arlene, and Ken too. You do for them as if they've always been part of your family."

Now tears were forming in her eyes and running down her cheeks.

"What you've done for me, there are no words. None that I have access to. There is such a chasm between you and I but you treat me as if there isn't. I didn't want to fall in love with you but I have and somehow, I'll deal with it. I have enough memories of being with you that will last me a lifetime.

"I know you must and will move on with your life. It's in your genes. I'll read about you in journals of medicine and probably in the wall Street Journal, no, I've never read one, but you'll be there. I know you will. My dream has been a wonderful one and I have no regrets."

He was wiping tears from her eyes and kissing her softly.

"Darlene, what we have is not a dream. I love you too. Time will prove that to you.

"Tomorrow, we'll be back at Pungo. It will not, it cannot be as it was. I'm not sure how it will play out but we're in this together. I knew it would be the first day I saw you.

"No we won't get married tomorrow, maybe not even next year. When I marry you, I want to be with you every day and right now, I have too many irons in the fire that won't allow it.

"I want to complete my study with Duke Marine. I have a year into it and I'm already making a difference. They want me to go to Australia and study marine life around the Great Barrier Reef and I almost committed to the year-long study before you came into my life. I want to go but now I want you with me. It's not logical though. I'll be living in a tent and spending a lot of time with the aborigines. While I'm there, I can look into the properties our company is interested in. That's no life for my lady but I promise to meet you in Hawaii once, maybe twice, during my absence."

"On the business side, Dan does most of that but I keep my finger on the pulse of our operation and the projects we're involved in and those we may become involved in. Flying all over the western hemisphere is one of the things I do for Dan. That's another reason it's so hard to keep track of me.

"Darlene, I love you, are you with me?"

Her tears appeared to be coming from a broken dam.

"Yes, yes, I'm with you. I love you!"

He kissed her tenderly and turned towards the door.

"I'll see you in the morning, Miss Snell, good night."

"Good night, Doctor, I'll be there."

"Back on the job"

"Good morning, Dr. Hardy"

The alarm broke the silence and her dream of being in his arms. Reality began to creep in. She was back in her apartment and it was Monday morning.

Showering first, she dressed and checked on Facebook. There was a message from Ray saying. *Wishing you beautiful dreams about us. I love you.*

Her day couldn't have begun any better unless she awakened in his arms. She was out of her apartment and on the way to the hospital at seven.

Inside the dining room, she joined Gail for coffee.

"Good morning, Darlene, you're back. How is Arlene?"

"She's still in a coma. No one seems to know for how long. It's so sad that all this had to happen on their honeymoon. Now, she's at Vidant Health and Ken's in Elizabeth City trying to carry on. Life can sometimes be a bitch."

She saw Ray get a cup of coffee and he spoke as he walked by.

"Good morning, Miss Snell."

"Good morning, Doctor."

Gail was smiling now.

"Darlene, everybody here knows you two have something going. Why be so formal?

Darlene was blushing,

"I don't' know. There's never any comingling between doctors and us common folks. You know that. Ray… Dr. Hardy prefers the formality and I guess I do too.".

Gail was in the query mode now.

"Is it serious? I mean are you two really in tight?"

"Tight enough, Gail. I'm in love with him. I tried not to be but I am. He's everything I ever dreamed, wished and prayed for. If there was ever a Mr. Right for me, it's him.

"I don't fit in his world; we were raised so different. His parents were so wealthy, they're gone now, both killed in accidents, and now he and his brother own a huge corporation with private jets, property everywhere…Like I said, we're worlds apart.

"I know it has to end, I'd be lost in his world, but right now, I'm going to live each day at the time. When the bubble burst, I'll have enough memories to last a lifetime"

"It's time to punch in. We'll get together later; I have to check on Arlene when I get off work."

~ D ~

Punching in, she saw nothing on the radiology schedule so she walked down the corridor to the dietary office. Nellie was talking to the bookkeeper when she walked in.

"Darlene, you're back. Come in my office and tell me about your sister."

"Nellie, it's been a nightmare. Arlene was apparently bitten by a mosquito while in Cozumel. The virus it carried caused fluid buildup around her brain and it caused her to go into a coma. She and Ken, her husband, were flown to Mt. Sinai in Miami and the CDC kept her in isolation for five days.

"Dr. Hardy and I flew down the day she arrived in Miami. There was nothing we could do but monitor her situation. He told them that he was her family doctor and was able to check the charts daily plus discuss the case with Dr. Marchez, the attending physician.

"A procedure was performed implanting stents to accelerate the fluid drainage and she was released to Vidant Health last Sunday.

"At least, now we'll be able to check on her daily. My family visited her Sunday evening and will most likely visit at least once a week. When she comes out of the coma, I'm sure they'll visit more often."

"Is Dr. Hardy your family physician?"

"No, he's just a friend that came to our aid. We flew down on his company jet and he arranged to fly Arlene back on the same jet."

She could easily see that Nellie had many more questions but politely ended her query.

At lunch, Ray spotted her and came.

"May I join you?"

She was a bit shocked but replied,

"Yes, doctor, please do."

She knew what the topic of conversation, in the hospital, would be for the rest of the day.

"What time are you going to check on Arlene, I want to take you. May I?"

"Of course you can. I'd like that. Six o'clock?"

He was almost whispering now,

"That's fine and I want you to spend the night with me."

Her eyes looked as if she'd seen a ghost when she replied,

"Ray, are you sure?"

"Of course I am."

When she moved about the hospital that afternoon, there was a slight grin on her face knowing all the whispering was about her and her, Mr. Right, Dr. Hardy. Yes, he was as long as she could hold onto him.

"I can't believe this is happening!"

But it is, I'm awake

"***Ray***, come in, I'm almost ready."

"What, no kiss!" He almost lifted her off the floor.

"Ray! Am I dressed all right?"

He stepped back pretending to do a complete once over. "Yes, you look great but you always do."

~ D ~

Arriving at the hospital, they took the elevator to the fourth floor stopping by the nurse's station first.

"I'm Dr. Hardy, Arlene Brooks' family physician. I'd like to see her chart please."

He studied the chart before inquiring if Dr. Kellenford was on the floor?

"No Doctor, she usually does her evening rounds after 10 p.m."

He thanked her, returning the chart.

They found Ken standing beside Arlene, talking to her as if she were awake.

They walked up beside him and Darlene placed her hand on his shoulder.

"Ken, Dr. Hardy says the charts don't show any change but the stents appear to be doing their job. She'll come out of it soon, we all pray she will. Mama, daddy, and the boys came by yesterday. They'll come as often as they can. How are you doing?"

By then, Ray and Ken had exchanged handshakes.

"I guess I'm as good as I can be under the circumstances. Dr. Hardy, I can never repay you for what you've done and now, with you help, it looks like I have a house to build near Duck. That's going to be quite an undertaking and I'm ready to get started. Your brother set me up with a line of credit. There's no way I could have gotten the permits and construction materials without it and I know I owe it all to you. Thank you, sir."

"Ken, don't thank me, your construction background in Raleigh got you the job. I only asked Dan to consider you. I was more than glad to do that."

Saying goodbye, they had dinner at CPW's enjoying cocktails and Burschetti Fresco and Calamari for starters.

"Have you eaten here before?"

Darlene looked at him, smiling.

"No, Ray; places like this are not in my pocketbook. I guess I'm more of a barbecue or fast-food person."

"The prices aren't too bad. You can run the ticket up pretty fast with booze but that's the same way anywhere. Have you looked at the main entrée's? I really like the Spaghetti Marinara. The tomato-basil sauce and meatballs are to die for. Would you like to try it?"

"May I have the Lasagna instead. It looks so delicious." She really wanted to try his dish but knew she'd be wearing the spaghetti before they finished.

As they enjoyed their entrée's, she watched intently as he very nonchalantly, took the noodles and using his spoon like a very small bowl twisted the noodles round and round until they were in a little ball and easily placed in his mouth. She knew she'd be cooking noodles very soon and try to master the technique.

After picking up her car. they arrived at his home on Teach's Cove a little after 11 p.m. His little cottage turned out to be a tri-level with parking garages beneath.

Inside, he led her to the elevator and up to the master's suite that occupied the entire third level. The setting was magnificent; the furniture was beachy but appeared to be very expensive.

He led her first to the alcove leading to the master bath saying she could leave her things on the dressing vanity. The entire opposite wall was filled with drawers and a door leading to a huge walk-in closet.

The bathroom took her breath. At the far end, a Jacuzzi dominated the space. Two steps led up to it and on three sides huge windows offered a panoramic view of Bath Creek. It also had a huge shower with several shower heads, a whirlpool tub, what appeared to be a compact refrigerator with glass shelves of stemware and glasses above. The other wall began with a separate area for the toilet and… she found out later that it was a bidet, She'd seen them in Miami and the islands but had no clue what they were. The rest of the space was taken up by a spacious twin-bowl vanity.

Back in the bedroom, he led her out on the deck. It commanded the same view as the Jacuzzi.

He was standing behind holding her in his arms.

"It's getting late; we should get to bed. I'll go downstairs and get the mail while you get ready for bed. I love you."

She showered and put on a pink nightie. He'd done it again. She was in another dream world. She was so out of place but so happy to be with him.

It was late but their desire to be one would not be denied. Next morning, they awakened like so many times before, in each other's arms. They showered together, that was a mistake, after thirty more minutes back in bed, they showered separately and rushed to get ready for work.

He was going to Beaufort and would back Thursday night.

"I want you to spend the weekend with me. I'll call you every day. Miss me please, I'll miss you."

She knew she would. He didn't have to ask.

~ D ~

When she had coffee with Gail, she was bubbling over with questions.

Darlene responded, saying.

"Come by about six. We'll go check on Arlene and share a pizza afterwards. I'll try to catch you up then."

There was one procedure scheduled for nine-thirty and then nothing until Wednesday afternoon. There was little to do in dietary so she passed her time away looking through the menu's from the past twelve-months. There was a lot of redundancy but she expected that. The patient load floated between twelve and sixteen while the retail customers remained pretty steady too. Usually sixteen or seventeen. She could almost tell the days her Mr. Right wasn't there.

~ D ~

Gail stopped by at six and they drove to Greenville checking on Arlene. The nurse said there was no change. In the room, Darlene held Arlene's hand and talked to her as if she was awake. Ray told her that studies were inconclusive but according to their findings, many times, comatose patients actually heard what was being said around them.

"Arlene, Gail's with me, remember her? She was in our graduating class. I told you before the accident that she'd working at Pungo now. We usually share lunch together. Tonight, we're going out for pizza, I wish you could come with us. I know that pizza is one of your favorite foods. You'll be able to soon."

She talked for another 10 minutes, including Gail in the conversation, while Arlene lay unresponsive in her comatose state.

Leaving, they took Arlington to Greenville Blvd and turned right stopping at Cici's at the intersection with Red Banks Road.

They ordered a pitcher of beer and a 12-inch thin-crust pizza with pepperoni, sausage, bacon, and cheese.

Gail was ready to hear the good stuff.

"All right, Darlene, fill me in."

"Okay, I already told you that I love him. When Arlene got sick, he insisted on taking me to Miami on his company's jet."

"Whoa, hold on. Company jet? What are you talking about?"

"He and his older brother own a huge corporation, Prime Properties, and have holdings all over the world.

"When we arrived in Miami, we were picked up in a limo and taken to the Breakers. You'll never believe how beautiful it is. The corporation has a lease on one of the penthouse suites. Gail, I was so lost but I loved it. He kept buying me clothes every time we went out. I didn't have anything to wear in places he took me.

"Gail, he even took me to St. Croix. He wanted to look at a property his corporation is interested in. It was so beautiful. It would take me all night to try describing it. Here, these are some of the pictures he took."

"My lord, Darlene, look at you! You're a knockout in that green dress. You look positively gorgeous and look at those heels, wow!"

"He saw it in one of the shops on St Croix and insisted that I try it on. Gail, I do feel beautiful when I wear it. That picture was taken at the Flagler Steak House. It's on the Breakers property. That was one upscale restaurant and the food... it was unbelievable!"

"That one was taken at Buck Island Reef National Monument. We took a boat over there when we were on St. Croix. Gail, it was just us and all the sand and the water, oh it was beautiful. We went snorkeling You have to see it to believe it. We were gone about four-hours, just he and I.

"That one was taken at a Cuban restaurant in Little Havana. Gail, he speaks fluent Spanish and ordered for all of us. Ken was with us that evening."

"Darlene, you're living every girl's dream. I'm so happy for you. Will you continue seeing him, I mean, you said it would probably end now."

She was smiling now,

"He says it won't. I hope it never does. I love him so much. He's going Australia soon for a year for Duke Marine Lab. He says he'll fly me to Hawaii so we can be together for a week sometime while he's gone. That will help. Who knows, if I still have him when he leaves, maybe I can keep him. I don't know how. His world and mine are so different. He says it doesn't matter. God, I sure hope it doesn't. If it ends, I'll probably go crazy."

~ D ~

Thursday drifted by and then it was Friday. He messaged saying he got in a little after 1 a.m. It was time lined at 1:15 a.m.

I'll see you at seven for coffee. Remember, you're spending the weekend with me. I love you.

See you at 7. I will if you want me to. I love you.

He was waiting when she walked in. Her coffee was already on the table. She could tell the milk had already been added; He never forgot anything.

"Good morning, welcome back. How was Beaufort?"

"About the same. I missed you."

"I missed you too. Oops, there's Mr. Fulcher. Are you picking me up?"

"I'll follow you home."

"Later."

She was going to spend the weekend with him. It couldn't get any better. Okay, it could, she could be living with him full time. She would if he asked.

Gail joined her for lunch.

"You two looked like lovebirds this morning. I can't tell who loves the other more."

Darlene was beaming,

"Me, I love him with all I have to give."

"Are you going to see Arlene after work? I'll go with you if you are."

"Sorry, he's taking me. We're going out to dinner afterwards."

"You want to do breakfast in the morning?"

She couldn't contain her smile. She whispered,

"I'm spending the weekend with him."

"Oh, I'll see you Monday. I know you'll have a nice weekend."

~ *D* ~

When they arrived at her house, all she had to do was grab her bag. She'd packed that morning.

They drove first to the hospital checking on Arlene.

Arriving, they stopped by the nurse's station before going to Arlene's room.

"Doctor, she has a little infection. Dr. Kellenford has her medications."

He asked to see the chart. Her temperature was up but nothing serious. Ken came in while Darlene was holding her hand and talking to her. It had become a routine. Both of them talked to her on every visit.

Ray and Ken talked about the project at Duck. Ken's remarks were all positive.

They left Ken alone to spend time with Arlene. He acted as if she heard every word he said.

~ D ~

"Let's go back to Washington and have dinner at Eli's Steak House. That okay with you?"

"Ray, you know anywhere you want to go is fine with me. I just want to be with you."

She really did want to be with him. It didn't matter where as long as they were together.

The steak house was located just across the river bridge where Carl and "Pig" Woolard's Riverside Oyster Bar operated for years. It reminded him of the Beef Barn in Greenville. Sadly, it had been closed for years.

He requested and they were seated in the grill room. The booths offered privacy and the dim lights added to the atmosphere.

"Darlene, they have a great salad bar and their steaks are usually grilled to perfection."

They began their evening with glasses of white Zinfandel and stuffed mushrooms.

The salad bar was next. It had almost anything anyone could possibly want including smoked oysters. After creating their salads, Darlene chose the rich Thousand Island dressing and Ray chose the creamy, Ranch.

That followed with ribeye's that were perfectly prepared as were the stuffed potatoes and broiled asparagus with cheese.

"Do you know yet when you're leaving?"

"Darlene, I not sure. I'll be in Durham Monday and Tuesday meeting with the research group. I should know when I get back. Right now, I guessing April."

"April! Ray! That's only a couple of weeks away. I'm going to miss you so much. A whole year, what am I going to do?"

"It will fly by; you'll see. It's not like we won't be in contact. Wi-Fi is already in place and there's a satellite connection for my cell. I'll be uploading reports once a week and we'll be in touch every day.

"Dessert?"

"Yes, our dessert."

~ *D* ~

Back in the cottage, they sat on the upper deck wrapped in a blanket. Bath Creek was so pretty bathed in the light from a waning full moon.

It was too chilly so they retreated to the Jacuzzi with the same scenery but is much more comfortable setting. The only light came from candles casting a romantic flickering glow around the enclosure.

Their dessert continued in bed as they entwined themselves in each other's arms. There was a mountain to climb and the night was young. Darlene was as close to heaven as she could possibly get on this side of eternity.

~ D ~

When she awaked Saturday morning, he wasn't in bed. Getting up, she walking over to the sliding glass doors and saw him on the end of the pier, drinking coffee. She quickly showered, dressed, and took the elevator down to the main level. She poured a cup of coffee and walked outside to join him. The air was chilly but she'd dressed for it.

"Good morning. You're up early. You slipped out without me hearing you."

He pulled her to him saying,

"It's too beautiful a morning not to enjoy it. How did you sleep."

"Like a log, your sleeping pill put me right to sleep. It is beautiful out here."

"Yes it is. This is my favorite time of day. Are you ready for breakfast?"

"Yes, are you?"

"Starving, let's put it together. Bacon, eggs, grits, toast?"

"Ray, that sounds delicious. Let's do it."

Back inside, he put the bacon in the toaster-oven and nuked the instant grits noting they were not nearly as good as stone-ground but this way was much faster. They set places at the counter, set the butter and jelly out and poured orange juice. When the toaster-oven timer dinged indicating five-minutes, Darlene began frying their eggs. Ray said he'd leave the hard part to her.

"I always break the yolks. You cook them."

Their breakfast was perfect and Ray's over-easy eggs were just right.

"You're a keeper. Anyone that can cook eggs like that must be and you are mine."

~ *D* ~

Back in their love nest, they enjoy a morning of love and relaxation. Being in his arms was the totality of her every wish.

As lunch approached, he suggested they take the Sea Ox out on the river.

Pointing to a weather monitor, he said,

"It's seventy-one and the wind is almost non-existent. We can even pack a picnic lunch. We'll cruise out of Bath Creek into the Pamlico River. We might even picnic at Goose Creek State Park. There's a nice sandy beach near the boat ramp."

"What will we take for our picnic?"

"Let's go check."

"We've got honey-ham slices, cheese, bread, potato chips, scoops, onion dip, pickles, and there are slices of carrot cake in the freezer. I love the one from Sam's and they freeze so well. We've also got wine and soft drinks. What is your pleasure ma'am?"

Their picnic basket was overflowing when they lowered and launched the Sea Ox into Bath Creek.

"You seem right at home on the water."

"Yes, remember me telling you about working for my uncle one summer? Arlie and I became old salts. It's wasn't any fun but we learned a lot about check lists, fueling, navigating, minor repairs. We even got our Boater Education Cards.

"My older brother, Dale, has a Sea Ox and we've taken it out lots of times. It's docked at Mackey's Point on Douglas Bay.

"Arlie and I went fishing in the Lower Middle Grounds near the target ships many times in the fall when the greys and speckles were running. Ray, we caught over two-hundred one time. We only did it once. Have you ever had to clean two-hundred trout?"

After an hour of cruising around Pamlico River, with her at the helm, they docked at the state park, and with picnic basket in hand, they strolled along the sandy beach finding the perfect place for a picnic.

Darlene spread the huge checkered tablecloth and began sitting their food out. Ray popped the cork on a bottle of Carolina Red pouring a taper for each. Facing the river, they sipped on the wine while remembering the beach on St. Croix.

"Ray, that was so much fun; I still can't believe I was there. You've given me so many unbelievable memories including this one. I'm spoiled; you realize that, sir?"

He reached over taking her hand.

"It's my intent to keep you that way. You've spoiled me."

Their picnic was to die for and of course, he took plenty of pics with his cell.

Back at the cottage, the coolness of the evening began settling in and they retreated to the living room. He lit the gas logs and they snuggled as they sipped on tapers of wine.

"How can you have all this and be alone. Ray, there must have been others before me. It's none of my business and I know what you told me but…"

"Darlie…no, for me it will be Darlene, there was another. It ended three years ago. I've never shared this with anyone. Are you sure you want to know?"

Now, she wasn't sure but she'd asked and already, wished she hadn't.

"Ray, if it hurts to talk about it, don't. I should learn to leave well-enough alone."

"Her name was Naomi. I met her in Aruba about five years ago. Dan and I were down scoping out a property. We met out by the pool. She was from South Africa and traveling with two of her sorority sisters. They were island hopping and leaving for Montserrat the following day.

"We clicked and I invited her to dinner. I was so taken by her beauty and charm, I offered to fly them there.

"I told Dan and he just shrugged saying,

"My baby brother finally has a date. Come get me when you're done.

"Four days later, I picked him up and we flew home.

"I couldn't get her off my mind and we continually texted and celled. A month later she texted saying she was going to spend a year at Duke in some kind of exchange program. Needless to say, we were together from the moment she arrived. No, I did not love her but I sure was infatuated. That entire year, I was useless. She was a party animal and we partied, big time, from Miami to Las Vegas and Hawaii.

"I don't think she was in class ten days the entire year.

"I was in Charleston looking at a property when Dan called. She had gotten into some drugs with some girls living in the condo complex where she roomed. She was in and out of a coma for six weeks before she died. She was cremated here and I accompanied her ashes to South Africa.

"I introduced myself to her parents as just a friend. It was apparent they didn't seem to be surprised by her death. Her life must have been comprised of one fling after another. Her sister, Jana, asked if I knew why she had been in a coma. I only replied that I wasn't sure. There was no way I was going to tell her although, in our conversation, it was apparent she knew what Naomi's lifestyle had been.

She wanted to know if we were more than friends? I replied,

"No, we only knew each other socially."

"I vowed that if that was what a relationship was all about; I was done and I was until I saw you and here I am. Only this time, I may be infatuated but…I am also in love!

"Thank you for asking, I feel better now."

"Ray, I'm sorry, I had no business prying into your affairs. Please forgive me."

"Done, let's grill a steak, I'm hungry. How about you?"

He defrosted a couple of ribeye's and found steak fries in the freezer. There was lettuce, tomatoes, a bell pepper, and Vandalia onion in the crisper. She dumped some of the fries into a pan and placed them in the 425-degree oven before assembling their salads.

"There should be garlic bread in the freezer."

There was, she took two slices out and placed them in a pan, ready for the toaster-oven. The slices only required 5-minutes on the toaster setting.

Out on the deck, the 48" built-in, Crown Verity grill was up to temperature 10 minutes later. He applied a thin coat of oil on the steaks before lightly sprinkling Tones Canadian Steak Seasoning on both sides. Now it was 4-minutes on each side and their steaks would be med. rare.

They were working together like a well-oiled machine.

With the Hatteras Red poured, dinner was served.

They finished their steaks about 7 p.m. and drove to Greenville checking on Arlene.

~ D ~

Their mother, father, and Ken, were there when they arrived. Ray checked the charts first, observing no changes in Arlene's status. They all walked to the cafeteria and visited about forty-five minutes before her parents said it was getting late and they had a long drive back to Hyde County.

Ken filled them in on the progress of Dan's house. He was ahead of schedule and hoped to have it "dried-in" by Easter. Dan's wife had been down twice and seemed to be very pleased with the progress.

They went back to the room and Darlene spent her usual 10 minutes talking to Arlene.

It had been over two weeks and Arlene had not shown any improvement but on the other side, her functions were all normal and she wasn't regressing. Time apparently, was the only cure and Darlene would just have to accept it.

~ D ~

The morning sun flooded the cottages along Bath Creek with an aurora of color. Mostly magentas, oranges and yellows. The palate would change with each passing minute. Somewhere between the yellows and blues, they climbed their mountain and remained there for a few splendid moments until little and little, they came down the other side.

She showered first and went downstairs to prepare breakfast. When he came down, all that was left to do was cook the eggs.

"Fried or scrambled?"

He kissed her first replying,

"Scrambled with cheese."

Tasting the eggs, he looked across at her saying,

"Perfectly prepared, I can never let you go, you belong to me."

"Yes I do, sir and don't you ever forget it."

"Church?"

"Do you mind?"

"Of course not."

They arrived at Woolard's Pond Church of Christ about ten of eleven joining her Aunt Bessie in the third pew.

When they were leaving, Reverend Latham spoke to Darlene and remembered Dr. Hardy from the wedding.

"Darlene, I'm so sorry about Arlene. I try to drop by for a visit two or three times a week. Our precious Lord will bring her through this. Dr. Hardy, It's nice to see you again."

She thanked him saying time was the cure and that belonged to the Lord.

Ray suggested brunch at Ironwood Golf and Country Club west of Greenville.

"They have excellent food. How does that sound?"

"Sounds delicious, of course, I haven't been there."

Forty minutes later, they arrived ready for a late lunch.

Seated with an excellent view of the golf course, they ordered the spinach salad with baby greens, topped with toasted pepita, sliced pear, and crumbled feta drizzled with a cranberry vinaigrette and the prime rib sandwich topped with Swiss cheese, lettuce and roasted red pepper. For sides they chose the sweet potato fries. A dark fruity red wine was the perfect accompaniment.

"Ray, the scenery is beautiful. Didn't we pass this place on Valentine's?"

"Yes, B**obb**y's is about half a mile from here."

~ *D* ~

Back at the cottage, it was too chilly to be outside, so they began the afternoon, relaxing in each other's arms, sitting on the overstuffed sectional couch

The sound system delivered Yanni's romantic music throughout every room. It seemed to infiltrate each amorous fiber of their hearts and ultimately led to a mountain climbing expedition than began in the Jacuzzi.

Afternoon was turning into evening and their weekend together was rapidly coming to an end.

For Darlene to return to her empty apartment was an exile she didn't want to face but knew, come morning, that would be her fate. He'd be gone until Wednesday and she'd only have him a little while before, poof! He'd be gone for a year. *A year! I don't know what I'm going to do!*

"Hey, where'd you go? Come back to me."

She looked into his eyes replying,

"I'm sorry, I keep thinking about you being gone a year. I can't stand the thought of us being separated that long. I just can't. I love you so much."

"It will go by so fast and we'll be back together again. I promise it won't happen again. If it does, you'll be with me. Now, come here woman, I love you."

~ D ~

Monday arrived much too soon but they'd been awake since five preparing for it.

Darlene left at six-thirty. "Call me, I'm going to check on Arlene after work. I love you."

"I love you too, I'll be back late Tuesday night and I'll be waiting Wednesday morning with a cup of coffee. Be safe."

~ D ~

Darlene found Gail in the dining room, "Good morning, I guess it's Monday again."

"Sure is, tell me about your weekend?"

"We had a ball. Dining, boat riding, picnicking, church… and other stuff."

"Other stuff, what other stuff?"

"Gail, bite your tongue."

"Oh, okay, you going to see Arlene tonight?"

"Yes, you want to go?"

"Sure, what about the doctor?"

"He'll be back Tuesday night."

~ D ~

After work, Gail followed Darlene to her apartment and they drove to Greenville grabbing a chicken biscuit at Bojangles on their way to the hospital.

There was no apparent change in Arlene. She seemed to be breathing normally and all the monitors appeared to be behaving normally. They took turns holding Arlene's hand and talking to her.

Darlene was surprised when Dr. Kellenford walked in. She'd seen her only once.

She nodded to them while she checked all the readings.

"I'm Dr. Kellenford, are you members of Mrs. Brooks' family?"

"Yes, I'm her twin sister. We met once when Arlene was admitted."

"Yes, I remember, you were with Dr. Hardy. There hasn't been any change in your sister since she was admitted. That's not unusual, I'm sure Dr. Hardy told you to expect it. The fluids continue to be reduced and the pressure level is almost normal. Mrs. Brooks could awaken at any time."

She left answering a page.

~ D ~

Back at her apartment, she answered a text from Ray.

I miss U 2 – D

She lay in bed with storm after storm of thoughts racing through her mind. *How can life be so wonderful one moment and so hurtful the next? I don't know how I got to this point in my life. I don't ever want to be without Ray. I probably don't deserve him but it doesn't matter. I love him, he loves me, he's mine! Australia for a year! Oh Lord, I'm going to go crazy!*

~ D ~

Tuesday just sort of happened. She picked up a three-pack at KFC on the way home thinking Ray might get home early and she wanted to be available if he called.

The chicken and 2 Bud Lights later, he texted.

Running late, C U a.m. I love U

I love U 2 – D

She fell asleep holding her pillow wishing the night away.

~ D ~

Wednesday morning finally arrived. She would see Ray in a couple of hours.

He was waiting with their coffee.

She wanted hug and kiss him but no way, doctors and staff just didn't do things like that. There was protocol that must be adhered to. She did squeeze his hand.

"You know I missed you…a lot."

He grinned replying,

"I missed you more."

There was no way that was possible. Being without him was akin to being in a jug without air. Without him, she felt almost like she was being suffocated. Her Mr. Right was sitting across the table from her. There had to be a way to keep him locked up and protected from all the females she knew must be after him.

"Would you like to spend the night with me? We'll visit Arlene, eat and the rest of the night will be ours."

"You know I want to. Your place or mine?"

"We'll do mine. Yours doesn't have a Jacuzzi."

She was seductively smiling now.

"See you at lunch?"

"I'll be waiting."

The day flew by as if she was in a dream, she was. There had been an afternoon procedure that she vaguely remembered and Nellie had said something about the diets. She couldn't remember.

~ D ~

They left her car at the cottage and drove to Greenville to check on Arlene. Ray looked at the charts before going into her room. The brain scan performed, on Monday, showed increased activity. That usually meant coming out of the coma was imminent. He wasn't sure if he should share that with Darlene. She would probably think that it would happen any minute and yes, it could, but not likely. He would tell her later.

They'd been there about thirty minutes when Ken arrived. After talking for a few minutes, they left Arlene to him and drove across Farmville Blvd to have dinner at the Seahorse Restaurant.

After ordering Michelob Ultras, they ordered, including the salad bar. Darlene chose the grilled chicken breasts with mushrooms, onions, and peppers. For sides, she chose the baked sweet potato and apple sauce. Ray ordered the 'Texan' ribeye, medium rare, with onion rings and green beans.

"Their Facebook page touts the best prime rib in Greenville. We'll have to try it sometime."

"Prime rib? I only had it one time. Arlene and I went to Myrtle Beach to see the "Alabama" show. We saw the matinee and had dinner at Chuck's. The waiter delivered prime rib plates to the table adjacent to ours. It looked too good to deny. Ray, it was.

"We wanted to spend two nights so we could eat seafood at Calabash but our pockets were not deep enough. One of these days, I'm going to eat at Ella's if I have to go by myself."

Seeing the cakes on display when they walked in, there was no way they could leave without sampling a slice the butter-pecan.

~ *D* ~

Back at the cottage, they spent an hour in the Jacuzzi sipping on Pink Magnolia spritzers. They said little, words were not necessary. Their magnetism was the driving force. Its intensity would not be denied. In bed, they were one. They climbed up and up, reaching the pinnacle, hovering there, before slowly, almost unperceptively, coming back down.

No, not completely. When they were together, coming all the way back down wasn't an option and it didn't matter where they were. Even when they had coffee in the dining room at Pungo, they floated above the clouds.

~ D ~

"Are you spending the weekend with me?"

"Yes, if you want' me too."

"Good, we're going to Bermuda."

"Bermuda, really?"

"Yes, we'll fly out of Greenville at five, Friday afternoon. We'll arrive about eight their time. They're an hour ahead of us. We'll be staying at the Grotto Bay Beach Resort and Spa. It's just across the causeway from the airport and only about a mile from the property I need to look at. That shouldn't take more than two hours at most.

"There will not be much time to explore but we will get a chance to visit the caves and maybe do some snorkeling."

"What should I pack?"

"Mostly casual but do take your green dress. We'll dine out formally Saturday night. If we need anything else, we'll buy it."

Thursday breezed by and they visited Arlene that evening. He saw more progress in her charts but wouldn't build Darlene's hopes up yet. Maybe when they got back from Bermuda.

She spent Thursday night at home packing. That would be taken care of when he stopped to pick her up. Later, she drove to Greenville checking on Arlene. Ken was there saying he could swear the he felt her finger twitch.

"It could have been involuntary, but I swear, it moved while I was talking to her. It won't be long now. She's waking up."

Finally, it was happening just like Ray said it would. Arlene was coming out of her sleep.

She texted Ray,

Arlene finger moved, happy! D

Great! B back Soon! R

After sharing that they'd be gone over the weekend, she picked up Chinese when she got back to Washington.

She rushed in changing clothes hurrying through the sweet and sour pork before calling her parents.

"Mama, it's me… Ken said he felt Arlene move her finger today… No, ma'am, she hasn't awakened yet but I'm sure it won't be long… No, ma'am we'll be in Bermuda… No, ma'am, it's an island in the Atlantic Ocean… No, ma'am, Ray's looking at a property for his company and I'm going with him… Mama, we'll be back Sunday night. I won't miss any work… No, ma'am, they'll contact Ray if there's any change… Yes, ma'am I will… I love you too, bye."

It was time for a beer, explaining anything to her mama was challenging at best.

~ D ~

"Bermuda"

Friday morning, she was up before five a.m. Excitement refused to allow more sleep. She was sitting in the dining room with their coffee when Ray walked in.

"Good morning. Are you ready for a romantic weekend?"

He took a sip of coffee watching her eyes.

"You know I am."

Excitement was written all over her.

"I guess my enthusiasm shows."

He was smiling now,

"Maybe just a little, I'm exciting too. We're going to have a ball. Bermuda is a little stuffy and totally different from the Caribbean. You'll see but you'll love it."

"I know you're excited about Arlene but please know that it will take time. That's normal and when she first wakes up, she may seem disorientated but that's expected and will gradually disappear."

~ D ~

Their flight took a little less than two hours and they were in their room about eight-thirty local time. Hungry, they dined at the Palm Court Restaurant beginning their evening with Bermuda Rum Swizzles.

As she nibbled on the cherry, pineapple chunk, and orange slice, she remarked. "This is really good. How many am I allowed?"

"It's one of their national drinks. It's got rum, orange juice, pineapple juice, a dash of Grenadine and Angostura bitters. You can only have two."

Then came ice berg and blue salads and for their main entree's, they enjoyed the lemon and herb crusted Mahi Mahi.

~ *D* ~

It had been a long and tiring day so after enjoying the evening view of the beach and Castle Harbour from their balcony, sleep followed but not before they entwined themselves in each other's arms and became one.

Darlene was in heaven. She was in the arms of her, Mr. Right, and every moment with him was like a delectable delicacy in time. It made no difference where they were as long as they were together.

~ *D* ~

She awakened next morning realizing that Ray was gone. The balcony doors were open so she scanned the property and beach. There he was, standing by one of the Cabana's with a cup of coffee.

Showering first, she dressed and found coffee in the lobby.

"You're up early. It is beautiful; no wonder you're out here. I'm starving, are you ready for breakfast?"

"What, no good morning kiss? I'm hurt!"

The kiss lasted more than a moment. She loved this man with all her heart.

He pulled her up close beside him saying, "Breakfast can't compete with you but if you're hungry, we'll eat first."

His breakfast was by far, more alluring than hers. They picked up hot coffee and a Danish on their way back to the room. He was right, his was better although by nine-thirty, they were starving. The breakfast buffet at the Hibiscus Restaurant was just what the doctor ordered. "My lady, this is what your doctor prescribes now"

Some of the entrées were a bit strange to her.

"Ray, what is this?

"Let's see, this is codfish and potatoes, this is johnny bread, corn beef cakes, that's cassava pie, egg sauce and avocado, and of course, Bermuda fried bananas. Darlene, try a little of each of them. You may find something you really do like. The corn beef cakes are delicious and the fried bananas are too."

She did like the bananas. The corn beef cake was okay but she preferred the scrambled eggs and bacon. She did try the johnny bread commenting that they called it flour bread back home.

~ *D* ~

After the buffet, they visited the property he'd come to see. They spent an hour leisurely strolling around the seven-acre expanse.

"This location is perfect but the renovations would have to be extensive. I don't think the numbers will crunch in our favor. Let's take a few more pics and I'll be done."

It was easy to see what his recommendation was going to be.

~ *D* ~

They spent the next two hours touring the Crystal Caves that were located only minutes from their resort. The pamphlet shared:

A BREATHTAKING NATURAL WONDER, THE CRYSTAL CAVES OF BERMUDA ARE AN UNDERGROUND WORLD OF DELICATE SPLENDOUR WITH MAGNIFICENT CRYSTAL FORMATIONS OF EVERY SIZE AND SHAPE, SURROUNDING AMAZINGLY CLEAR LAKES UP TO 55 FEET DEEP. 30 MILLION YEARS IN THE MAKING, THIS PRISTINE WORLD OF STALACTITES, STALAGMITES AND PURE WATER WAS DISCOVERED IN 1907. TODAY, THE CAVES HAVE BECOME ONE OF BERMUDA'S FAVOURITE ATTRACTIONS.

They were certainly that. Darlene had never seen anything so beautiful. The colors and shapes were indescribable, soothing, exquisite, and magnificent and the crystal clear water was so inviting.

"Ray, I don't have words to describe what I'm seeing. Thank you for bringing me. I love you so much."

"You're here because I love you."

They spent the next few hours riding a scooter around the island and walking along the waterfront in Hamilton. To, Darlene, the atmosphere seemed relaxed but much more formal than St. Croix.

That evening, they returned to Hamilton dining at the Harbour Breeze Restaurant. Yes, Darlene was wearing Ray's favorite green dress and he was in his white dinner jacket.

They began their evening with Coco Mojito cocktails.

"Ray, this is delicious. What's in it?"

"Malibu rum, Club Soda, Lime juice and Fresh Mint leaves. You may have two."

For starters, they chose Arugula Salad with a citronette dressing and shaved parmesan.

Afterwards, for their main entrées, she chose the Linguine Aragosta with morsels of tender lobster sautéed with sun dried tomatoes, crushed red peppers, asparagus & herbs in tomato cream sauce and he ordered the honey-mustard salmon served with market vegetables and the Chef's potato of the day.

"Would you like wine or iced tea?"

"Wine would be nice, thank you."

"Waiter, bring a bottle of La Scolca Gavi Dei Gavi Black Label, please."

He looked at Darlene,

"It's a white wine from Italy, I think you'll enjoy it."

"Ray, this is delicious and the wine is too. This restaurant is so nice. I'm still trying to get used to seeing men in coats and ties wearing shorts."

Ray chuckled, replying,

"It's a British thing. Would you like dessert?"

She grinned, replying,

"Here? You may want me to wear this again."

He smiled summoning the waiter,

"Waiter, one serving of the Tiramisu Italian coffee cream cake and two coffees."

~ *D* ~

Back in their room, it was a night of love as another chapter in her life was coming to a close. Come tomorrow, they'd return to North Carolina and seven days later, he'd be gone for a whole year.

"Ray, don't ever let me go, I love you so much." She held him as if she could feel him slipping away from her grip. She was so afraid that if he broke free, he'd be gone forever. A forever she felt she could not bear to be a part of. Being without him for a year would be almost unbearable but forever. Her heart would not, could not, endure.

Sleep finally came after midnight; it was a restless, fitful, sleep punctuated with moments of being half awake, looking to be sure he was still there.

Next morning, her eyes opened seeing him looking into hers.

"You did not have a restful night. Is there anything wrong?"

"You're going to Australia in a week. Yes, there's a lot wrong but there's nothing I can do about it. Ray, what am I going to do?"

He kissed her, replying.

"Do just like me, count off the days, one at a time, and before we know it, the year will be gone and we'll be back together again. Remember, I promised never to leave you again."

After a breakfast of coffee and Danish, they spent several hours snorkeling at Tobacco Bay Beach located near the historic St. Catherine's fort in St George. The water offered wonderful views of corals, fish and marine life. Darlene was much more comfortable snorkeling this time. Watching Ray, she'd found it to be relaxing and the sights were stunning.

There was nothing like it along the shores of North Carolina. Nothing she'd ever heard of. Maybe out in the Gulf Stream but there were no coral reefs.

For lunch they enjoyed grilled tuna fish sandwiches and local beer at the snack bar.

Later, they toured St Catherine Fort. One of the most impressive forts on the island, there were many historic exhibits, artifacts, and a well preserved interior to tour and explore.

~ *D* ~

It was time to leave Bermuda and enter the real world again. A world she would be alone in, come next Sunday. She still had one more week and was determined to savor every moment. Unless he said different, she would spend every night with him.

On their flight back, she asked?

"Will I be spending every night with you before you leave?"

He leaned over kissing her on the cheek,

"Of course, except Wednesday night, I'll be in Durham during the day and in Cary with Dan and his family that evening. The rest of the time, I belong to you."

They arrived back in Greenville about six-thirty that evening going straight to the hospital.

Checking the charts first, Ray saw more improvement and shared that as they approached the room.

Inside, they found Ken holding Arlene's hand. Her eyes were open but it did not appear that she was cognizant of her surroundings.

Ray whispered,

"Don't be alarmed, that's normal."

He could feel the tenseness in her hand.

Darlene was standing beside Ken now.

"Ken, how long have her eyes been open?"

He replied,

"They were open yesterday but she doesn't seem to be aware of anything. The doctor says that's perfectly normal. It may take a week or two but little by little, she'll be fully awake."

He looked at Ray,

"Dr. Hardy, what do you think?"

Ray responded, saying,

"I agree with Dr. Kellenford's prognosis. It's going to take some time. Remember, she's been comatose for a long time. I'm extremely happy with her progress. Soon, she'll begin putting bits and pieces back together. Her last brain scan indicated increased activity. She's coming out of it. I know you and Darlene are tired of hearing it but, time is in her corner. You'll see."

Darlene held her hand while talking as if she was listening to every word. Ray and Ken walked down to the cafeteria getting a cup of coffee.

"Ken, I'm leaving in a week for Australia and will be gone for a year. Please keep in touch with Darlene. She's having a rough time with it. My cell should still work and my email and Facebook too. Please let me know how she's holding up."

"Dr. Hardy, I will, you know I will."

~ D ~

They stopped by Darlene's so she could drop off her luggage and repack for the coming week. He went ahead saying he'd pick up Chinese and be waiting for her.

She knew she was rushing it but every minute away from him was a minute lost. It still took half an hour no matter how hard she tried to rush it.

By nine, they were enjoying, egg drop soup, egg rolls, Szechuan chicken, sweet and sour pork, beef with cashew nuts, and shrimp and broccoli. For a beverage he'd poured tapers of Sutter Home White Zinfandel.

After enjoying their sumptuous meal, they relaxed on the couch watching the flickering gas logs. She couldn't have been more content unless there were some way the torch could be passed to another but that wasn't going to happen. Her trial by separation was another day closer.

"Darlene, there are some things I want you to do for me while I'm gone. Do you mind?"

She had no clue what he was going to say but knew she wouldn't refuse anything for him.

"First of all, I want you to drive my SUV while I'm gone. I'll be much more comfortable knowing you're in it and not the Corolla you're driving. You can park it here in one of the garage sections. You'll be using my credit card for expenses. When it's time for it to be serviced, Crossroads Infiniti in Raleigh will contact you and they'll come get it, service, and return it. They'll leave you another SUV to drive. All the taxes, and insurance are paid for through the company. It's in the company's name, another tax thingy.

"Secondly, I want you to move in here. When your lease is up in July, I want you to put your furniture in storage. When I saw how much you liked the cottage, I bought it. All the expenses, utilities, insurance, maintenance, will be handled by one of the office secretaries. I'll put you in touch with her before I leave.

"That's not like having me here but at least, I'll know you're being taken care of. I don't want to leave you but I made the commitment before I met you and I'm driven to finish what I started."

She was almost too stunned to answer.

"Ray, I don't know what to say. I'll do whatever you say but I don't deserve any of this. I'm just me."

"And please don't ever change. The 'you' is what I fell in love with. I never thought it would happen but it has and I'm the happiest man in the world. When this year of separation is over. I'll prove it to you.

"Career wise, I don't know where you want your life to take you and I will not hinder or attempt to stand in your way. Mine, at this point, I'm not sure other than knowing that I definitely do not want a private practice. Maybe teach, I don't know. Maybe take a more active part in our company. I'll have a year to thrash it all out, over and over, until I come up with something.

"The only thing I'm very sure of, you'll be with me, whatever I decide."

After an hour in the Jacuzzi, they climbed their mountain, higher and higher, knowing they would never look back.

"Seven days and he'd be gone"

A whole year!

Monday, the morning arrived with a beautiful sunrise and they watched it unfold holding each other tightly. It was the morning of the first day.

After coffee and a pastry, they left for Pungo saying they'd see each other at lunch.

She had coffee with Gail filling her in on Arlene.

"She's waking up, little by little but she's coming around."

Gail was elated,

"I know you'll be with Dr. Hardy all week. I'll check on her after work. What time Sunday is Dr. Hardy leaving?"

"About five p.m., I'm dropping him off at the airport. I'll check on Arlene afterwards. You want to come over about eight? We can do a pizza and I'll tell you about Bermuda."

"Sounds good, let's plan on it."

There was one procedure at nine-thirty and nothing else scheduled until Wednesday afternoon at two.

Ray was waiting when she walked into to dining room about eleven. They had salads and he shared his thoughts for the evening.

"We'll check on Arlene and afterwards, have dinner at Moores BBQ. That sound okay to you?"

"She smiled, replying, it sure does, I love their food and I love you."

Walking in, they found Arlene mumbling mostly unintelligible phases. They understood some of the words but not what she apparently was trying to say.

When she saw Darlene, her face brightened and she began smiling and talking much louder. Her blood pressure rose significantly. She rushed to the bedside and took her hand.

Arlene calmed immediately and squeezed Darlene's hand. She still couldn't understand the jumbled up words but instead tried telling her how much she loved her and how good it was for her to be awake.

The nurse came in giving her a sedative saying she needed to rest. She'd been talking like that all day and was probably weak.

They stayed until the sedative kicked in and Arlene drifted off to sleep.

Ray squeezed her arm.

"She'll be fine; it just takes time. Another week should do it."

At the restaurant, they ordered a large barbecue combination plate, white meat, with potato salad and baked beans for her and the flounder/shrimp/oyster combination for him with potato salad and Cole slaw. Both wanted sweetened ice tea.

"Ray, eat some of this barbecue, there's no way I can eat all this food."

"Me, look at my plate. You eat some of this."

They asked for a small container and took some of the barbecue and flounder with them.

Back at the cottage, they spent an hour in the Jacuzzi sipping on wine spritzers and caressing each other. They were already dressed in their mountain climbing gear, so they began their assent upwards towards the summit.

~ *D* ~

The morning of the second day arrived with rain pitter, pattering softly against the windows and doors leading onto the upper deck. They snuggled and cuddled until six knowing another workday was just ahead.

"You're riding in with me. I don't want you driving in this mess."

"Ray, someone will see us."

"I don't care, I'm going to be gone, probably for good anyway and you, they can't easily replace you."

Of course, they were seen arriving together but like he said, it didn't matter. Replacing her would be a hassle and he'd be gone.

While drinking their coffee, Mr. Fulcher stopped by saying he was going to miss having him around.

"I know you're looking forward to continuing your research."

"Yes, I am, but I'm also looking forward to my return. I'm going to miss Darlene."

There was no look of surprise. He remarked, before turning to walk away,

"I'm sure you'll miss each other."

"See, I told you there was nothing to worry about."

The look on her face was almost amusing.

"Miss Snell, calm down. Doctor's orders."

She wanted to shake him but knew that would never work. Everyone in the dining room was staring at them.

That afternoon, they drove to Greenville to check on Arlene. She was asleep but checking at the nurse's desk produced favorable comments. She had asked how long she'd been there.

Ray remarked that she was almost there. According to the brain scan done earlier that morning, the activity indicated normal readings.

"When you check on her tomorrow, I'd be very surprised if she doesn't call you by name."

They left picking up a three-cheese pizza at the Pizza Inn in Washington on their way home enjoying it along with Michelob Ultras sitting at the kitchen counter.

That followed with an evening in the Jacuzzi and another mountain climbing adventure. They'd climbed before but each time the routes they chose seemed more and more familiar and that increased their excitement and enjoyment.

Later, in bed, sleep refused to come and Darlene was too restless to allow it to happen.

Ray sensed her restlessness and asked what was bothering her. He already knew but maybe talking it out would bring peace to her troubled mind.

"Darlene, what's bothering you? Arlene or me, or both?"

"Ray, of course I'm worried about Arlene. Once she's fully out of the coma, what then? Will she be in rehab or released? If she's released, will she need someone staying with her while Ken works? It all seems scary to me and with you leaving…you're my rock, I guess I'm just scared of the unknown. I can't stand the idea of you being all the way on the other side of the globe. Ray, I'll go crazy without you. You know I will."

He sensed tears and responded softly while holding her close feeling the tears on his chest.

"My darling, if Arlene is responsive tomorrow and more so on Thursday when we visit her; I'm sure Dr. Kellenford will move her to rehab for ten to fourteen days. At the end of that time, she should be fully recovered and ready to go home. I don't think she'll need anyone staying with her while Ken's gone. She'll be fully ambulatory and ready to get on with their lives.

"Remember, they were on their honeymoon. They have a lot of catching up to do.

"Us? Darling, you'll adjust after a few weeks, I'll be trying to adjust too. We'll be in constant contact every day. You'll have your work, family, church, and Gail to help the time pass.

The weather will be warming up too, by the first of May, you'll be able to spend a lot of time out on the deck and pier. You'll enjoy the river too. The Sea Ox will be at your beckoned call. You'll refuel it at the marina in Belhaven. You can have any service that's required performed there too. Just put it on the card.

"By June, we'll have set a date for our rendezvous in Hawaii and we'll be counting the days. You'll see, the days will fly by and the year will be over before you know it."

He sensed her breathing was shallow now, she'd drifted off to sleep.

~ D ~

Dawn of the third day found them still entwined in each other's arms. He dreaded awakening her but he needed to be in Cary by nine a.m. There was so much to be crammed into one day. After a jam session with Dan, he'd spend an hour with his lawyer updating his will. If anything happened to him, he was determined that his darling would be taken care of. Beneficiaries had to be updated on the personal and corporate level too.

"Good morning princess, it's another day. Should I sing to you?"

Darlene opened one eye first, replying,

"Sing to me? Really? Just hold me; I'm almost awake."

They shared a cup of coffee before going their separate ways saying they would talk later.

"Gail and I are going to check on Arlene and probably grab a burger. I should be home by ten at the latest, I'll wait for your call."

~ D ~

At Pungo, she had coffee with Gail then a procedure at ten. After a salad with Nellie at lunch, the afternoon melted away and by five-thirty. She and Gail were on their way to Greenville,

When they walked into Arlene's room. She was welcomed with,

"Darlene, it's you, where have you been?"

She rushed quickly to her twin's bedside hugging her tightly. Tears were flowing down her cheeks as she replied,

"Bill's Hot Dogs, where have you been?"

"And you didn't bring me one? Shame on you."

"Hey, Gail Gibbs, is that you?"

Gail reached out taking Arlene's hand,

"Yes, it's me, you look great!"

"Where's Ken?"

"Arlene, he's working on a project at Duck. He'll be by later."

"Duck? What job?"

Darlene knew it was going to be difficult but there had to be a starting point.

"You've been asleep for a long time. What's the last thing you remember?"

"I'm not sure, Ken and I were walking down a street in Cozumel. He said something about we shouldn't be there but I wanted to see how the real people lived. I think we ate something at one of the vender's stands…I'm not sure? Long sleep? What are you talking about?"

"You've been in a coma for almost seven-weeks. You got very sick in Cozumel and were flown to Miami. Ray, you remember Ray, Dr. Hardy, flew us down and about a week later flew you up here. It's a long story, one I'll share with you sometime but…"

"Ken!"

He raced to her bedside. Darlene and Gail stepped back.

"You're back, I can't believe it, you're really back. I love you so much!"

He looked at Darlene,

"Have you seen the doctor?"

"No, Ken, we haven't been here long. We're going to leave you two to catch up. Arlie, I'll see you tomorrow. I love you, Sis."

She walked over hugging her.

"I love you too, bring me a couple of Bill's Hot Dogs. I'm starving."

~ D ~

They stopped at McDonalds picking up Big Mac combos at the drive-thru on their way back to Darlene's.

Gail seemed as excited as Darlene saying,

"She seems perfectly normal to me. I don't think there'll be any rehab. If there is, it won't be long.

"Now, tell me about Bermuda."

"Gail, I still can't get used to flying on his private jet. It's like being somewhere in a dream. Can you imagine someone from Last Chance flying in a private jet? Anyway, it was beautiful, the people are kind of stuffy. Maybe they're not but after St. Croix, they sure seem that way. Everything's so beautiful. Most of the buildings are painted pastels and the whole island is so clean.

"The resort where we stayed was so nice, the restaurants, beaches, lounges. I tried so many different drinks and food. Some of their favorite foods will never be mine, especially for breakfast.

"I can't believe Johnny bread, corn beef cakes, cassava pie, Bermuda fried bananas. The Johnny bread is like our flour bread, corn beef cakes…no way, the fried bananas were okay. At least I tried them.

"Ray wants me to try so many things and lord knows, I'm making an effort. I admit their fish and chips were good but I still prefer ketchup on my fries, they put vinegar on theirs. Yes, I tried it, it's okay but I'll stick my ketchup unless I'm where the custom is vinegar, Ray say's it's the proper thing to do and when I'm with Ray, I want to be proper."

"We ate most of our meals at the resort but on Saturday night, we dined in Hamilton at the Harbour Breeze Restaurant.

"He wanted me to wear the green dress he gave me at St. Croix. Gail, I felt like a movie star. He was wearing his white dinner jacket and Bermuda Shorts with over-the-calf socks. From what I saw the other men in the restaurant wearing, he was properly dressed. We turned a few heads."

"She laughed saying,

"He always turns mine. I don't care what he's wearing. He said it was all me but no way, we were the couple.

"We did get a chance to do some snorkeling and toured the Crystal Caves. You won't believe how gorgeous they are. I've got a pamphlet."

She jumped up finding it and a few others, on the coffee table.

"They are unbelievable. Sunday, we toured St. Catherine Fort and spent the last few hours back at the resort before flying out late that afternoon."

She pondered on sharing her other news but it would have to wait. He might decide to do things differently before he left. She didn't care. All she wanted was him back in her arms. If she did move to Bath, maybe Gail would rent her apartment and maybe even pick up the lease. She'd let her rent it furnished and save having to put everything in storage. If Ray still wanted her when he came back, she'd have no use for any of her furniture.

Arlene would have first chance of refusal although she's said to keep it, she didn't need any of it. They were furnishing their new home with all new furniture. She'd wait and see what Arlene decided when she finally got to see her new home.

Gail left a little before ten and Darlene was walking up the stairs when Ray called.

"Hi, I miss you… Yes, you won't believe it, she's talking her head off like she just woke up from a good night's sleep… He came in about fifteen minutes after us… No, I knew they needed to be alone, we picked up McDonald's and came back here. She just left… You got it all done? Good, I know that takes a lot off of you mind… I'm sure I can if that's what you want… I'll tell them tomorrow… How can I guess, there's no way to even begin with you…Yes, I love you? All right, I love, love, love, you! Now it's your time… Thank you, Doctor… Yes, sir, I'll do that… What time are you coming back?... Okay, I'll drive straight to Bath… Good night, Doctor…I miss you, too!"

Sleep came easily, he would be back in her arms tomorrow.

~ *D* ~

The morning of the fourth day was greeted with a thunderstorm. The pyrotechnics and claps of thunder were hard to ignore. It seemed too cool but seeing the weather on channel 7, proved that wrong, it was already sixty-five and promises of upper-seventies were in the offering. Jim Howard said that Friday and Saturday would probably hit the lower-eighties and Sunday, maybe even the mid-eighties. She had no clue what Ray was planning but if it was in eastern North Carolina, the weather promised to be perfect.

She had coffee and a Danish with Gail saying she'd be off Friday. Ray wanted to go somewhere, she had no idea. "

I'll call you Sunday night after I drop him off at the airport. I'm sure I'll need someone to drink beer with. It probably won't be a good night."

She sent an email to Dr. Pulver saying she would not be in Friday and told Nellie the same. Nellie was all too aware of Dr. Hardy leaving and wished them a nice weekend.

"The weather promises to nice. Have a good time. I'll see you on Monday."

Four-thirty finally arrived and she rushed to meet Ray in Bath. He was waiting with open arms and she was more than ready to be in them.

"Put your car in the garage. You won't be needing it again. Come here lady, doctor's orders.

"You look like you could use a drink, let's go out on the deck." He had a pitcher of Mai Tai's waiting along with a tray of nuts, cheeses, chips, and dip.

"This will calm your nerves. Down the hatch. Doctor's orders."

Darlene, quickly put the first one behind her before settling in on the second one.

"It's beautiful out here...Oh, Ray, why do you have to go? I'm going crazy. What am I going to do?"

"He pulled her up close replying,

"Darlene, it's all going to work out. We'll get through it, you'll see. Have another one; doctor's orders."

The second one began settling her nerves and she calmed a little but not much. A few minutes later, she'd regained her composure, most of it anyway.

"Are we going to check on Arlene?"

"Of course we are. We can leave now it you'd like."

She was ready to be in his arms, climbing mountains, upstairs, in bed, in the Jacuzzi, anywhere as long as it was in his arms but she had to check on Arlene. She just had to.

"Let's go now."

~ D ~

They arrived at Vidant finding her parent's and Ken in the room. Arlene was like a six-year old, all bubbly and asking thousands of questions. All the tubes and monitors had been removed leaving only the pulse monitor attached to the pinky in her left hand.

She welcomed them saying,

"Come give your sister a big hug!"

Darlene couldn't believe Arlene came out of her coma so fast and apparently, so complete.

Ray checked the chart on the way to her room. She was scheduled to go home tomorrow morning. He'd been in contact with Doctor Kellenwood twice, She'd called Wednesday morning informing him of her decision and again today, before lunch. Had Ken been told, surely he must have been.

"Ken, can you step out in the corridor for a few moments and tell me how the project's coming along.?"

Darlene and the others were too busy to notice their absence.

"The charts indicate that Arlene will be released in the morning. Have they told you?"

"Yes, Doctor Kellenwood's office called about two. I'll be here in the morning at eight to take her home. I told Arlene when I walked in and she's been wide open ever since. They'll probably have to give her a sedative tonight. She'll never get any sleep if they don't."

"Did Doctor Kellenwood give you any specific instructions?"

"None, no medications, no instructions. It's as if she never was sick. It's got to be the hand of the Good Lord; it can't be anything else."

They walked back into the room and Darlene was all over him.

"Ray, she's going home tomorrow! I can't believe it, she's going home!"

She threw her arms around his neck kissing him wildly.

Her parents were concerned. Was she ready to begin housekeeping? Was she ready to cook?

"Isn't it too early?"

Her mother's mind was made up. She was going to spend a week with her.

"Owen, you and the boys will just have to fend for yourselves. Arlene needs me."

Ken was squirming now. Right when he thought they'd finally be alone, her mother was moving in.

"Mama Snell, it's not necessary. I don't have to be on the jobsite until next Tuesday and my secretary will transfer any calls or emails to me. We'll be fine. She'll get all the rest she needs and we'll walk around the neighborhood to build her strength back up. Dr. Kellenwood says she doesn't need someone looking after her. She'll be fine."

Gradually, Martha Snell acquiesced but she appeared to still have misgivings.

"I'm going to call you every day and if she's feeling the least bit poorly, I'm coming up there."

Ken had his wife back. Trying not to grin, he replied.

"Yes ma'am, Mama Snell, I will let you know if she gets to feeling down.

Darlene nudged up against Ray getting his attention winking and grinning. She knew where Ken was coming from.

About an hour later, they took their leave, picking up Chinese in Washington, and returned to Bath. There was a lot of catching up to do and she didn't want to waste a minute of it.

It was too pretty an evening not to be outside and they enjoyed their meal on the upper deck with glasses of wine.

"Ray, it's so pretty out here. I'm so glad you bought it. I love the places I've been to with you but this Hyde County gal still loves this setting the best."

He grinned to himself, thinking, *Boy is she going to be surprised tomorrow.*

She was pulling him up.

"The Jacuzzi is waiting and I am too."

Their evening of love began in the Jacuzzi and continued into the bedroom. Sometime in the quiet of the night, exhausted, they fell asleep with Darlene's head resting on his chest. What they had could only be described as love. It couldn't have been anything else.

~ *D* ~

It was the morning of the fifth-day. A beautiful sunrise filled Bath Creek with every imaginable color melting the dark of night into the light of dawn. First the magentas followed by oranges, yellows before blue washed all the other colors away.

Darlene awakened fully dressed in her mountain climbing gear and wouldn't be denied and there was no way he would even try. They were drawing closer and closer into one.

~ D ~

Later, working side by side, they prepared a breakfast of country ham, grits, the real stuff, red eye gravy, eggs over easy, toast, jelly, butter, milk, and juice.

With the last of the cleanup behind them, she was ready for her surprise.

"All right, Doctor; where's my surprise?"

He grabbed her saying, "You're not dressed for it. Put on shorts, a sleeveless top, Dockers, sunglasses, and a cap. Here, use this cap. The words, 'Captain Darlene' were embroidered above the bill.

She looked curiously at the cap.

"Have I been promoted?"

He laughed saying,

"Yes, you have, you'll see. Get dressed, I'll show you."

When they approached Washington, he turned left on Hwy 32 business.

She looked at him asking,

"Why are we going to my apartment?"

He laughed, replying,

"We're not, just wait."

When he came to the junction with River Road, he turned left and she was really confused but not nearly as much as she was when he parked in front of McCotter's Marina.

She followed him into the office.

"I'm Dr. Hardy, is everything ready?"

The clerk answered saying,

"Yes sir, follow me."

They followed him down one of the docks to a slip with a Grady-White Express 330 moored to it.

"This is it, Dr. Hardy. It's been thoroughly checked out, fueled and provisioned per your instructions. Have a nice cruise, sir."

Ray took her by the hand saying,

"Come with me, Captain; let's board your vessel."

She was really confused but obeyed and climbed aboard. They spent the next twenty minutes touring the sleek, beautiful craft, down below, the cabin was unbelievably appointed. All the boats this size she'd ever been on were working trawlers and looked the part. It seemed to have everything included a head (bathroom) galley with range, oven, microwave, sink, refrigerator and lots of cabinets and storage. There was also an entertainment center with a 21" LED-LCD TV-DVD player. Up forward, there was a V birth and a double births in the aft. It was air-conditioned too.

Topside even had a grill, plenty of seating, and storage. The cockpit was very impressive.

"Ray, she's beautiful, are we renting it?"

He pointed to the starboard aft; it was lettered, "***Miss Darlene***."

"No, Captain, it's ours."

"Ray! I can't believe it, she's beautiful."

In moments, the twin 300 HP Mercs were purring and they cast off and were cruising down Broad Creek into Pamlico River. He slowed as they approached Bath Creek.

"Do you want to stop by the cottage for anything? We won't be back until Sunday morning. I have all the provisions we'll need. You might want a bikini and makeup. I have everything else."

"Do you mind, there are a few things I'd like to take."

They moored on the dock opposite the Sea Ox and Darlene was back onboard fifteen-minutes later.

Before starting back out into the Pamlico River, they set a course for Back Sound and Shackelford Banks. The navigation/GPS system made setting and plotting a course easy but Ray wanted Darlene to be comfortable with it. They did three plots to help her get the feel of it and she plotted the last one without his help. Cruising at 25 knots, it would take about two hours to reach Back Sound.

"Captain, would you like to get us a beer or would you like to take the helm?"

"I'll take the helm, mate."

That was exactly what he wanted to hear.

"Aye Aye, captain."

At the helm, she didn't seem to tire, standing like a beautiful statue with her long blonde tresses trailing in the breeze. To him, she was the most beautiful woman in the world.

When they arrived on the sound side of Shackelford Banks, they anchored a hundred yards offshore with the Cape Lookout Light looming in the distance.

For lunch, they enjoyed BLT's with chips and beer. She couldn't believe how much food he'd stored onboard.

"We'll grill steaks tonight along with some of the five to seven count Tiger Shrimp. We can have a baked potato and a salad or just a salad. It's up to you. I love you, Darlene."

That led to a trip below and breaking in the forward birth. They lay in air-conditioned comfort reflecting their love for each other. Their time was disappearing and each passing minute was another one lost.

He was caressing her body and tracing the undulating sensual curves, valley's and mountains, with his finger as he shared his thoughts about how he felt.

"You came into my life and bowled me over the moment I saw you coming down the corridor. I can't believe it happened so fast. I was so determined that I would never let it happen again but it did.

"When I walked into your office asking about the pans. I didn't need pans. I needed you. My heart told me you were the one and you are. You are so beautiful, inside and out and there's not a deceitful bone or thought in your body. When I look into your eyes, I melt. I'm melting right now."

He leaned over kissing her tenderly, but long. It was as if he never wanted to let her go and it was getting harder by the moment. He toyed with the idea of giving her the ring he'd bought Wednesday but was determined to wait until Hawaii. She knew he loved her. She didn't need a ring to prove it. He'd wait.

"Ray, I've made some foolish mistakes in my life. Nothing mean or ugly…well maybe when Arlene and I went to the beach music festival and I got drunk out of my mind. No, I didn't do anything wrong other than…she hesitated but continued, I peed on a man's feet and got real sick throwing up all over me."

He was laughing so hard,

"You did that? I can't believe it. That must have been wild, no, not really; my frat brothers got me drunk one night and put me up to propositioning a nun. That's what they said and I was too drunk to remember. I got sick too and threw up all over me and my roommate. I guess we all do stupid stuff. How else do we ever learn anything?

"I know I was the first one for you. If I hadn't been, it wouldn't have made any difference. It really doesn't unless a previous partner makes the other look like a novice. Me?... I told you about Naomi. She'd already had more partners than she had fingers and toes. She didn't laugh so I guess I did okay. Do I?"

She hugged him tightly replying.

"You are wonderful. I don't ever want to climb a mountain with anyone but you.

They ventured back topside mid-afternoon. It was a gorgeous day. Temps in the mid-eighties, not a cloud in the sky, and the SW breeze was barely noticeable.

They weighed anchor and docked close to the Cape Lookout Light. As they approached it, Ray commented,

"It's not open to climb until May and maybe that's a good thing. 207 steps are a strenuous climb. It's as high as a twelve-story building. Maybe admiring it from down here below is enough."

Darlene chided him replying,

"I've climbed Pea Island and Cape Hatteras. It's not all that difficult, old man."

She was laughing now as he pretended to chase her.

From there, they docked on Shackelford Banks and enjoyed watching the wild horses move about the island. The scenery was so idyllic and soothing to one's soul. The horses moved around them, grazing here and there without a care in the world. The hustle and bustle of the mainland would never disturb them.

As the sun began sinking in the west, they weighed anchor and moved near Catfish Point anchoring about a hundred yards offshore.

About five, they enjoyed wine spritzers with a seafood dip, chips, cheese, and nuts.

"Ray, it's so gorgeous here. I could do this forever and never, ever, go back."

He responded,

"I agree with you, darling, but that can't happen. At least not yet but it can when I get back. Wherever you want to be, that's where we will be. If living on a yacht is your dream, that's what we will do. I'm committed to making you happy."

Hearing him say those things were dream enough. How could she have ever been so lucky?

"Ray, I don't know what to say except that I love you with all I have to give. I want to be with you forever."

"Hey, we'll never see our steaks unless we lighten up. Here, captain, have another spritzer."

Later, while Ray prepared their ribeye's for the grill, Darlene nuked the potatoes and tossed together a garden salad. While he grilled, she set the little table and lit a candle.

It was a perfect romantic setting.

"To us!"

When they went back topside, the last vestiges of the setting sun were fast disappearing and the quietness of Back Sound settled around them.

Below deck, their cabin was one of romance as the sound system filled it with one of Jim Brickman's CD's.

The gentle movement of the hull was like a rocking cradle that lured them into a blissful sleep after climbing their mountain. It was like a soundless lullaby luring them into the realm of peaceful dreams.

~ D ~

Next morning, day six, Darlene awakened to the aroma of coffee wafting throughout the cabin but no Ray. She quickly dressed finding him topside enjoying the cool morning air. Pod after pod of pelicans flew southward just above the water's surface. Some were already dive-bombing into the sound beginning their breakfast earlier than the others. Gulls were everywhere. They circled overhead hoping for a free meal that would not be forthcoming.

"If you start it, they'll drive you nuts."

Ray had been caught before and Darlene remembered her experiences with them from her days on her uncle's trawlers.

They breakfasted on 'day old' Krispy Kreme donuts brought back to their original freshness after a few seconds in the microwave. He'd offered to do a real breakfast.

"We've got bacon, sausage, country ham, eggs, grits, and I'm ready to cook for you."

Instead, they enjoyed the donuts with orange juice and more coffee.

"What would you like to do today. Where would you like to go?"

She leaned over, kissing him, before replying,

"Ray, I don't care. I just want to be with you."

They settled on Portsmouth Island. Ray had never been and it had been years for her

Weighing anchor, they cruised northward along Back Sound passing Harker's Island on their left and they entered Core Sound passing Marshallburg, Smyrna, Williston, Davis, Stacy, Sea Level, and Atlantic, before taking a north-northeastward course when they passed Cedar Island.

Minutes later, they docked on Portsmouth Island remembering the bug spray. The mosquitos were held at bay as they trekked towards the village stopping at the Methodist Church, and Salter-Dixon house that looked like it was still occupied.

Next, they stopped at the Portsmouth Life-Saving Station before picnicking back by the Salter-Dixon house just outside the picket fence. April brought indigo buntings to the island and they were beautiful to watch. Sparrow sized, the mating males where a beautiful shade of blue and their songs were full of gusto. Darlene said she'd seen a few back home but seeing so many at one time was special.

Seeing a tour group approaching, they walked leisurely back to **Miss Darlene** and took their leave of the thirteen-mile long lonely outpost.

They tied up at Shell Point dock on Harker's Island and visited the Core Sound Waterfowl Museum amazed by the intricate decoy carvings as well as those actually used for hunting. Some were detailed and very intricate while others were totally basic catering to the approaching ducks and geese, not the eye of the human beholder. The shorebird collection was just as interesting as were the other waterfowl.

Afterwards, they visited one of the shops and watched one of the carvers at work. It was difficult for Ray to understand his hoi toider brogue but Darlene understood every word. She still had remnants of it when she spoke. Especially when she became excited.

Her high school English teacher tried to pry it from her students saying they would be chided and picked on if they left Hyde County and she was right but remnants would always be there.

Ray loved it and said he hoped she'd never lose it but he was getting a full load here and managed to get the meat of the conversation but not the full beauty of the brogue.

From there, they sailed southward and dropped anchor off Lenoxville Point. The temps were in the upper eighties, cloud banks off to the east didn't seem threating and the winds from the sound were almost calm. They spent the first hour below exploring another route up their mountain.

They knew that tomorrow, Humpty Dumpty would fall and couldn't be put back together again for a long, long, year. Neither mentioned it but neither could put it out of their minds.

Back topside, they enjoyed spritzers while absorbing the warm sunny sun. About six, with plenty of sun left, they changed into shorts and tops, weighed anchor and sailed down Taylor's Creek to Beaufort docking at the Front Street dock.

Their reservations were for seven at Clawson's and they began their evening with Mango Margaritas.

"Ray, these are delicious. What's my limit?"

"No more than two; I want you to remember tonight. Cheers!"

For starters, they chose hot crab dip and cheddar bacon fries.

Seeing the one margarita had put a sparkle in her eyes, Ray suggested they switch to beer.

"Let's try the Buckshot Amber."

It tasted of toasted toffee and caramel.

Looking at the menu, they chose the shrimp and grits with grilled Mahi on the side.

The lively atmosphere encouraged them to have a second round of beer while they enjoyed the entrées. The grilled Mahi mixed well with the shrimp and grits.

Looking at the desserts, the death by chocolate was tempting but they chose Key Lime pie knowing where their real dessert would come from.

It had been a delightfully charming evening but it was only beginning.

Back on **Miss Darlene**, Ray pointing to the cockpit saying,

"Captain Darlene, lay in a course to the coordinates we moored at last night."

He couldn't believe how fast she accomplished it. He was confident that she could and would use and enjoy **Miss Darlene**. She piloted it all the way back just like he knew she could.

Arriving at the coordinate's, they dropped anchor and went below knowing it would be their last night together for a long, long time.

They lay in each other's arms repeating over and over again the words, *I love you.*

"Darlene, you have to know how much I love you. I keep thinking that I don't say or show it enough but please look into my heart, my whole being. I've lived every moment adoring and loving you from the first moment I saw you. I know that's redundant and I've said it so many times but I want to be sure you know."

They hugged tightly. Tears were flowing like rivers now. As they climbed their mountain, they held on with all their might but felt time pulling them apart. It was, but it wasn't forever although it already seemed that way.

"Ray, I don't know how a woman can possibly love a man as much as I love you. I only know that I do. If anything ever happens to you, my life will end. I may still breathe but the fire in my heart will have died with you. On the other side, please walk slowly because when it's time for me to leave here. I'll catch up with you and we'll be together in the circle of eternity that will never end. Oh! Hold me please, I don't know if I can do this."

~ D ~

The morning of the seventh day arrived with them still in each other's arms knowing what must take place.

Topside, they sipped on mugs of hot coffee watching the sun climb above the eastern horizon casting long shadows across Back Bay. It was a beautiful morning but neither saw, or could appreciate it. They were lost in their sadness knowing what must come.

They breakfasted on fruit and juice trying valiantly to keep the atmosphere cheerful but to no avail. Soon, by mid-afternoon, they would have to kiss and say goodbye.

The pelicans, gulls, and shorebirds were back just like yesterday but were almost invisible to them. Their hearts were hurting and the clock was ticking.

Giving in, they plotted a course back to McCotter's Marina and began their anguished trip back.

They stopped first at the cottage unloading all the provisions and personal effects. With Darlene at the helm, they continued on to the marina where she docked **Miss Darlene** perfectly.

"Ray, this is child's play compared to docking one of Uncle Russell's trawlers."

They went through the checklist before putting **Miss Darlene** to bed.

Stopping by the office, Ray introduced Darlene to the manager saying she would be the only one authorized to take **Miss Darlene** out.

"Provide her with anything she requires and send my company the bill."

"Dr. Hardy, will she need a pilot?"

He smiled replying,

"No, she's a better pilot than I."

Back at the cottage, they grilled burgers spending an hour on the deck before ascending to the master suite.

"Jacuzzi?"

"No."

She pulled him into the bed and spent their last hour showing him how much she loved him.

It was time. All his equipment and luggage were aboard Duke's chartered jet in Charlotte. He only had his briefcase.

"You drive."

She parked near the entrance and walked with him to the gate. That's as far as he would let her go.

"Darlene, always know that I love you and only you. I'll text you along the way and call when I arrive in Brisbane. It will take about thirty hours."

One last kiss and he was gone. She watched his private jet take off and reluctantly, with tears falling from her eyes, drove back to the cottage.

Tomorrow, she would begin counting the days until his return. She already was.

~ *D* ~

Back in the cottage, she opened a Michelob Ultra-Light and sat looking out across Bath Creek. Her heart was too full and spilled tears down her face splashing on her arms and blouse.

When she got up get another beer, she saw something unfamiliar on the fireplace mantel. She tentively took a few steps before realizing it was a framed photo of them in St. Croix. She in her green dress and he in his white dinner jacket. He'd taken, and had taken, many pics everywhere they went but she never expected this. She held the 14 x 18 pic close to her heart remembering the exact moment it was snapped. She held it at arms' length saying,

"Ray, thank you for doing this. I love you so much."

Her mood lightened a bit and she opened a second beer. Realizing that she was hungry, she made a BLT from the food they'd brought back taking it out on the deck. It was so quiet. Only the sound of a duck or crow intruded into the silence. She felt as alone as she'd ever been. Telling herself that she'd get through it helped but the emptiness and loneliness persisted.

Back inside, she spent an hour in the Jacuzzi finding another pic. This one was taken in Bermuda. They were in the Crystal Cave.

She put on her pajamas and walked into the bedroom seeing another framed picture on the nightstand. She remembered it be taken at Bobby's. They looked so happy together They were, she remembered it vividly. When they danced, they were as one. She was already in love and he was too.

It was going to be a sleepless night. Her mind, her heart, would not allow sleep to intrude on her loneliness. She felt so empty inside.

He texted about ten p.m.

Landed LA, I Love U!

Be safe. I love U 2!

The alarm shattered her fragile sleep. What little there was. She turned it off and stared at the picture saying,

"Good morning, my love. I miss you so much."

She showered and dressed before going downstairs and cranking up Mr. Coffee. She needed something to break the silence watching the early show on Channel 7. Afterwards, she listened to wakeup music on Sirius-XM. She had to put the melancholy mood behind her.

~ D ~

Arriving at Pungo at seven, she hoped Gail would join her for coffee. They arrived about the same time.

"You didn't get a lot of sleep. What happened?"

Darlene agreed saying she'd been up most of the night.

"He's gone, Gail. He's gone for a whole year. I can't believe how hard this already is. I took him to the airport yesterday and watched his jet take off. He texted me about ten last night from Los Angeles."

Gail wanted to hear about her weekend asking,

"What did you do over the weekend."

"Can you come by tonight? I'll try to tell you then. Oh, I'm living in the cottage at Bath. That's what he wants me to do."

She shared the address saying,

"Just GPS it and I'll be waiting for you."

Gail replied,

"Okay, six?"

"Yes, we'll cook some of the food we didn't use over the weekend…Don't ask, I'll tell you tonight.

Everyone knew that Dr. Hardy was gone and they treaded softly around Darlene. It was easy to see how much she already missed him.

Mr. Hicks asked if he could join her for lunch?

"Yes sir. Please sit down."

"Young lady, you look like you just lost your favorite doll. Don't look so sad, we both know he's coming back. A year's a long time but it too, will pass."

"Thank you, sir. I'll need your encouragement to get through it."

"You have it young lady. Anytime you want to talk, page me. I'll come running."

He looked down at his expansive midriff and laughed before continuing,

"Maybe not run."

~ D ~

Gail arrived about six with a look of awe on her face exclaiming, "Cottage? This is more like a castle."

Darlene led her up the steps replying,

"I know but that's what he calls it. He bought it because I said I liked it. Can you believe that? I can't."

Inside, she gave her the nickel tour beginning on the main level and out on the deck. Back inside, they took the elevator to the third level that opened into the master suite. The master bath blew Gail's mind and the Jacuzzi commanded her full attention.

"Darlene, I can't believe this. Do you actually use that?"

A bit embarrassed, she replied with a grin.

"Yes, every evening."

She opened the refrigerator door saying,

"We usually enjoy glasses of wine when we're in it."

In the bedroom, Gail picked up the picture on the nightstand remarking. There's no question that you two are in love. The look on your faces say that."

Out on the upper deck, Gail marveled at the view.

"It's so beautiful, I didn't know anyone lived like this."

Darlene replied,

"Me either until he showed it to me. It's so beautiful but it's very lonely with him gone. He wants me here and I'll do that for him but only because I love him. I'm so out of place in his world but he makes it easier to adjust."

Back down on the main level, they opened beers while getting thick bone-in pork chops ready for the grill.

"You want a baked potato or baked sweet potato?"

"I've never had a baked sweet potato. Let's do that. Darlene, do you put anything on it?"

"Yes, we put butter, cinnamon and nutmeg on ours."

She placed the sweet potatoes in the microwave and they walked out on the deck. Dusk was beginning to settle along Bath Creek when Darlene cranked up the grill saying,

"Ten minutes brings it to temperature and then it's ten minutes on each side and dinner will be served. Would you like a salad?"

Gail replied,

"Maybe lettuce and tomato. When are you going to tell me about your weekend?"

"Where should I start? Okay, Friday morning, we drove to McCotter's Marina on River Road beside the Country Club and he blew my mind introducing me to **Miss Darlene**. It's a thirty-three-foot cabin cruiser. When we boarded it, he said it was provisioned for the weekend. We sailed it back here and I picked up a few things before we cruised down the Pamlico River into Back Sound near the Cape Lookout Lighthouse. Gail, it was a weekend to die for. We went to the lighthouse, watched the horses, grilled steaks… oh, there's just too much to remember. Saturday, we cruised to Portsmouth Island with me at the helm. Afterwards we sunned along the sound and visited the waterfowl museum on Harkers's Island.

"That evening we dined at Clawson's in Beautfort. It was glorious, the drinks, food, atmosphere, him…him!

"Sunday we spent most of the morning enjoying each other…don't ask. We returned here about 1 p.m. and spent some time in the Jacuzzi,"

With a smile as big as Texas, she looked at Gail saying,

"Don't ask,

"I took him to the airport about three p.m. and he was gone. Gail, I miss him so much."

By the time she'd finished her story, their dinner was behind them and they were sitting on the deck, enjoying the serenity of Bath Creek, when her cell rung.

"It's him, I'll be right back." She rushed into the living room answering.

"Ray, I miss you so much…Where?... Brisbane?... It's what time? ...Nine a.m. Tuesday morning, that's unbelievable, I know you're tired…Hamilton Island Airport in the morning…Oh, Conway Conservation Park… Okay, I'll Google it… Low Rock Reef? I'll google it too… No, Gail's here, we just had dinner… Don't you tease me; I'll fly there tomorrow… I know but I miss you terribly… I understand, call me as soon as you can. I love you and I miss you."

She grabbed her laptop off the counter and rushed back outside, exclaiming,

"It was Ray. Oh, it was so good to hear his voice. He says it's already Tuesday morning in Brisbane."

She Googled Brisbane and pointed to the map.

"He's there but he'll be flying here shortly."

She Googled Hamilton Island Airport.

"Their base of operations will be here."

She Googled Conway Conservation Park. "

He'll be doing his study here."

She Googled, Low Rock Reef. "

It's part of the Great Barrier Reef. She Googled it. "See?"

"Gail, that's a million miles from here and it's looks like it's a million miles from nowhere too. I can't believe I let him go."

With symphony, Gail reached over touching her hand, replying,

"Darlene, it's going to be hard but he's got his heart into the study. When he gets back, you'll be waiting."

"Darlene, if you'll be living here, what are you going to do with your townhouse?"

"I don't know, Gail. He wants me to store the furniture and let the lease go when it comes due in July. He insists that I leave the utilities on. He's going to pay them. I tried to object but you know how far that got."

"How much is the lease?"

"$785.00 plus utilities."

"Darlene, I want to move out of Belhaven. Would you be interested in renting it to me? It would have to be furnished. Buying furniture right now is not in my budget."

"Let's go see Arlene next weekend, we bought the furniture together. If it's okay with her, you know it is with me."

~ *D* ~

Dear diary, there are 364 days left before he's back in my arms.

Tuesday was just another day as was Wednesday, Thursday, and Friday. Ray had called twice saying they were still trying to get everything set up. He was excited but missed her more than she would ever know. They texted every day.

Gail spent Friday night with her. They dined on Chinese and poured a few beers down when they returned.

Darlene called Arlene Wednesday and they were expected Saturday morning.

~ *D* ~

Dear diary, there are 360 days left before he's back in my arms.

Darlene had the coffee brewing when Gail came downstairs from one of the guest bedrooms on the second level. They shared a cup of coffee deciding on ham biscuits from Hardee's on their way to Elizabeth City.

They arrived at Arlene's a little after ten a.m. The GPS made finding her home so simple.

She welcomed them with open arms, hugs, and kisses.

To Darlene, she didn't look as if she'd ever been sick.

"Come in ladies, welcome to our home. Ken's out back puttering with the hanging baskets on our deck. I know, Darlie, it's probably too early for flowers but they're so pretty. Maybe Jack Frost will leave them alone. Yes, I remember what mama says but April 15th is only days away.

"Ya'll have a seat. Can I get you coffee or something else to drink?"

Darlene looked at Gail,

"We're good. Show us your home; we'd love to see it."

After the tour, Arlene led them out on the deck. It was spacious with two arbors. One had a swing suspended from it and the other had two weather resistant rockers with stuffed cushions. A table with six chairs occupied the center with an opened market umbrella.

"Ken removed the little deck that came with the house and added this. Don't you just love it?"

Darlene responded saying,

"It's so cozy and comfortable and you're right, the hanging baskets are beautiful.

Ken walked up the steps welcoming them. He'd been putting gardening tools in the garage.

Darlene looked at Arlene,

"So Arlie, you look all recovered, how do you feel?"

"Like brand-new. Honestly, I don't feel as if I was ever sick. Right now, I'm just enjoying our new home. Ken doesn't want me to go back to work until June. I have a position in Radiology waiting for me when I'm ready.

"Ken, tell them about your project at Duck."

He shared that it was on schedule. Dan's wife had been down last week and of course there were changes she wanted but that was normal and expected.

"I also signed a contract on a cottage in old Nags Head. It's a tri-level with 3,800 sq. feet. I'll come out of the ground with it next week. The Lord's been good to us."

Leaving them to talk, Ken walked back into the house.

"Arlie, Gail wants to rent my townhouse furnished. Half the furniture is yours. What do you think?"

"Rent your townhouse? Where are you going to live?"

"Oops, I don't think we've talked lately. Where do I start?"

She was still bringing Arlene up to date when Ken walked out saying,

"Ladies, it's time for lunch. Come with me."

The Cypress Creek Grill was located on Water Street across from Mariners Wharf Park that fronted the Pasquotank River.

Seated, they ordered iced tea and Ken suggested the crab and shrimp dip for starters.

"Ladies, lunch is on us."

Darlene queried Ken saying,

"It looks like all the old buildings along Water Street are being renovated, are they?"

He replied saying,

"Yes, almost all of them. Revitalization is finally reaching fruition. The Chamber hopes to make Elizabeth City a tourist destination and it appears to be working. As you can see, this location is busy and the other's along Water Street are too.

The change was sorely needed. All along this street looked like Washington Waterfront before it was transformed. It's also one of the reasons I wanted to come here. There's be plenty of work for contactors like me.

"Ladies, would you care for soup or salad?"

No, they were ready for their main course.

Darlene wanted the blacken Tuna, Gail ordered the New Orleans barbecued shrimp and Arlene chose the blacken chicken and pasta. Ken was last choosing the butterflied jumbo shrimp.

Their conversation continued mostly about what was happening in Elizabeth City and surrounding Pasquotank and Camden Counties.

Ken elaborated on the spectacular growth that was taking place north of the river. "

"Camden County is exploding in development. Subdivisions are popping up everywhere. It's rapidly becoming the destination of choice for folks moving into the area and it's only an hour away from the outer banks."

After lunch, Ken showed them his office across the bridge. Back at their home, he excused himself saying he needed to spend a couple of hours in the office.

"I'll see you when I get back."

Back out on their deck, it was much too pretty a day to be inside, Darlene continued chronicling her life since meeting and falling in love with Ray.

Her cell vibrated. It was him.

Hi, miss U. It's abt 5.m. Love U. R

Love U 2, Miss U most. D

"Where was I? Oh, that was Ray. You guessed that didn't you? He just got up. It's five a.m. Sunday morning down under."

Arlene was puzzled, "Down under what?"

Darlene laughed replying.

"That's what everyone here calls Australia. Everything there is opposite from here. When it's day here, it's night there. When it's summer here, it's winter there. When it's Sunday here, it's Monday there although where Ray's at, it's summer year round He's about half way between the equator and the Tropic of Capricorn. Confusing isn't it."

Arlene cocked an eye at Darlene saying.

"You didn't like geography in school and listen to you now."

They were all laughing as Darlene continued her saga bringing Arlene up to date.

"As someone said, 'That's my story and I'm sticking to it."

It was so good seeing Arlene and Ken, but the hour was growing late and Sunday would usher in another Monday.

"We need to get back, tell Ken how much we enjoyed seeing your new home and lunch. I may go home next weekend, it's been awhile. Love you, Arlie!"

After hugs all around, they pointed the Infiniti southward on Hwy 17 choosing to exit it at Midway on Hwy 45 picking up Hwy 32 in Plymouth, Hwy 264 in Washington and Hwy 92 completed their journey to Bath Creek.

They shared a salad and glass of wine before saying goodbye.

"See you Monday morning, I really appreciate your company."

It was still in the eighties so Darlene changed into shorts and halter top before walking out on the upper deck enjoying the view and another glass of wine. She missed Ray terribly but knew the loneliness had only begun. She was determined to be strong. He said he'd be back and she was determined to be waiting.

Right then, at that moment, she was so jealous of Arlene and Ken. They'd never have to go through what she was experiencing. What was she thinking. They'd just been through six weeks of separation. Arlene didn't remember any of it but Ken remembered every agonizing minute, every excruciating hour, every unbearable day, every heartbreaking week and there she was feeling sorry for herself.

After an hour in the Jacuzzi, she slipped beneath the covers in their bad and drifted off to sleep dreaming of being in Ray's arms and then climbing their mountain together.

~ D ~

Dear diary, there are 357 days left before he's back in my arms.

She awakened a little after seven as the morning sun streamed through the windows and doors. She hadn't drawn the curtains last night. Putting on her rode, she walked outside. It was already seventy-four degrees.

After making coffee, she came back to the upper deck enjoying the ambiance of the setting. Bath Creek could only be described as a place of serenity and beauty. The quietness and solitude of the morning was only interrupted by gulls flying overhead and someone's dog off in the distance. A Blue Heron flew noiselessly by.

Her cell broke her train of thought.

"Ray, good morning, I guess it's night there… I miss you too… Yes, we had a nice visit. Arlene and Ken are doing great… No, he took us to lunch and then by his office… Yes, he says that Dan's wife is very happy. She brings change orders with each visit but he's used to that… I'll probably go church and take Aunt Bessie to lunch afterwards… No, I think I'll go downhome and visit my family… Glenda who! I didn't know there were women in the research group, you didn't tell me you'd be down under with another woman!... Really, nobody's that ugly, you'd better be careful. I hate to have to go down there… I'm just kidding, you know that… With all my heart, Dr. Hardy… Yes, I'm counting them off, one by one… pics on Facebook? No, I'll check… I love you too. Dream about me, I did you. Bye."

Down on the main level, she fixed cheese toast and had a second cup of coffee while opening Facebook finding a dozen pics posted by Ray.

Okay, if that's Glenda, I'm in no danger. The compound appeared to be mostly tents except two buildings in the background. He'd tagged most of the pics. One person was assigned to each tent. One building was tagged kitchen and dining area. The other, showers and bathrooms. The very dark skinned men with gray unkempt hair were aborigines. They looked dangerous to her. The ones on the beach were beautiful. The emerald hued water appeared to be almost crystal clear.

She messaged a selfie wearing the red bikini tagging it as, "Come to me."

~ D ~

After dressing, she drove to Woolard's Pond Church of Christ finding Aunt Bessie in her familiar place, three pews back on the left.

Following church, she took her to K&W in Greenville for lunch. Aunt Bessie wanted the roast beef, stewed apples, and broccoli with a slice of peach pie. Darlene chose the baked chicken breast, no gravy, cabbage, and fried okra and the blueberry cobbler. Both chose water with a lemon wedge.

During lunch, she filled her in on Arlene and Ken and shared as much as she would about her and Ray.

"A whole year! That's a long time, Darlene. You're going to get mighty lonely."

Darlene smiled as she replied, "Yes ma'am, it will be but he's my Mr. Right. I can wait."

Aunt Bessie was prying now but she expected that.

"What are you going to do to occupy your time? There's going to be a lot of it."

"Aunt Bessie, I'll still be working five days a week and I'm signing up for some courses at Beaufort Community College."

"What are you taking, dear?"

"Ray wants me to take business management, bookkeeping, and a hospitality course. They also offer a course in culinary arts. I'm very interested in that. One day, I'd like to open a restaurant."

Aunt Bessie was all ears now.

"I can see the culinary arts class but business management, bookkeeping, hospitality? What in the world?"

"Ray and his brother own a huge corporation and he wants me to be able to understand some of the things he wants to discuss and share with me.

Aunt Bessie was digging in now.

"What kind of corporation?"

"It's called 'Prime Properties.' They buy property all over the world that is floundering and losing money. Property they believe can be turned around with an influx of new and creative ideas, and money. I've been with him looking at properties on St. Croix and Bermuda. He apparently has an eye and intuitive way of making the right calls."

"I thought he was a doctor?"

Darlene was grinning to herself as she replied,

"He is, Aunt Bessie, and he's finishing up his research project now. He feels that going forward, he'll devote more time with the corporation and wants me to be able to travel with him.

"I love him with all my heart and want to be with him wherever he goes."

Aunt Bessie seemed pacified replying,

"Darlene, honey, I've only met Dr. Hardy a couple of times but he seems like a fine gentleman. If he's your, Mr. Right, don't let him slip through your fingers. The right ones only come around once.

"Mine never did. No, that's not right. Darlene, he did but the war took him from me. Nobody ever turned my head like him. That's why I never married. Second best would have never worked for me."

Darlene was stunned. She had never heard anyone in the family ever mention a word about Aunt Bessie ever being in love and especially how it ended.

"Aunt Bessie, I never heard mama mention a word about your loss. I'm so sorry. I can't know how you feel or how life must have been for you."

"Your mother never knew, no one in our family did. When I graduated from high school. I attended East Carolina College on a limited scholarship. I got my room and board working in the cafeteria on College Hill.

"That's where I met Ira. He was in the men's dorm across campus from us. Like me, he was working his way through college too. We were cook's helpers doing any and everything the cooks didn't want to do or have time to do. Sometimes, we'd walk together to classes and as time went by we were together more and more.

"We didn't have any money so on weekends, we'd go to the library or attend some or the free performances at Wright Hall.

"I remember one Sunday, we walked down on first street and sat on the riverbank watching the traffic crossing the Greene Street Bridge. Neither of us had ever been north of the river and had no idea what was over there.

"We never went downtown either. Everyone that had money or could beg, borrow or steal any would be on Fifth or Cotanche partying at the Rathskeller, Fiddlers' Three, Attic, or one of the other clubs.

"I remember one time. We'd scraped up enough money to have breakfast one Sunday morning at the new Waffle Shop on Reade Circle across from one of the girl's dorms.

"Story was that every spring, as soon as the weather was warm enough, the girls would cover the hillside with bikini's making for some very hazardous driving. I'll bet it was a sight. I never had a bikini. Don't believe I'd have worn it if I had.

"Lord, I'm rambling, Darlene, I'm sorry. Where was I? Oh, the war was raging in Vietnam and boys were being drafted, right and left. Some even fled to Canada to evade the draft but not Ira. When he got called, he packed up and left. He told me before he left that when he got back he was going marry me and Darlene, I was ready.

"He didn't come back. We wrote letters for a year and then his stopped coming. After a couple of weeks, I feared for the worst and when I saw his name in the college paper's 'killed or missing in action' column, my heart died. It belonged to him and I still think about him every day. The bible says that we'll meet again if we believe. He was a believer, I know that in my heart and I'm waiting for the day."

There was a hint of tears in her eyes.

"Darlene, I've never told this to a living soul. Please don't tell anyone until I've gone to join him."

Darlene reached over touching her hand replied,

"Aunt Bessie, your secret is safe with me. I'm so happy you found someone and I know he's waiting for you. I'd like for you to spend the afternoon with me. Will you?"

Aunt Bessie, smiling now, replied.

"Honey, I've taken up enough of you time but I would really like to."

Arriving on 2nd. street in Washington, Darlene told her to change into something more casual.

"We'll spend most of the afternoon on the deck."

When they arrived at the cottage, if took a few minutes for her aunt to believe that she was actually living there.

"Darlene, never in my life have I ever seen anything like this. She took a seat on the couch saying she needed to catch her breath.

Darlene took the elevator up to the Master's Suite and changed into shorts, and a collared polo top.

Back on the main level she found her aunt holding the picture of them.

Realizing that Darlene was back, she commented.

"You look so happy together and I'm so happy for you."

Out on the deck, her aunt stood motionless taking in Bath Creek, saying,

"It's been years since I was this close to the water. I've never been on the waterfront in Washington It was not a place to go when I moved there. Last time I remember being on the water was back home. Lord, that's been a long time ago.

"Daddy used to take us fishing below the second blowout. We'd get oysters in Rose Bay too. That was before they clear-cut all that land between Belhaven and Swan Quarter. The fresh water runoff did away with the oysters.

Darlene wondered,

"When did you move to Washington?"

Aunt Bessie had to put her thinking cap on.

"Let's see, I graduated from college in 1963 and had my teaching certificate. There were postings on the bulletin board in my dorm from school systems listing available teaching positions.

"The closest one to home was Washington City Schools. Back then the county and city systems were separate. I got on teaching second grade at John Small School. It used to be just off Hwy 264 just east of Market Street. I moved into a boarding house across from the school.

"There were several other teachers living there. That's where I met Terzi Sawyer. She'd been teaching at John Small a year and had car. Best I remember, it was a nineteen-fifty-eight Chevrolet. It was black, not the expensive one but it was transportation. We became best friends and spent a lot of time together. When John Small School closed, we got positions at John Cotton Tayloe.

"There wasn't much teachers could to do back then, they were so strict on us. We would go to the Turnage Theater once a week and out to Mr. Ed's Barbecue Friday nights for dinner. There was a restaurant…Latham's, close to the school and the boarding house and we ate there after church on Sunday. In nineteen seventy, the house I live in came on the market and I managed to get a low-interest government loan. Terzi and two other teachers rented rooms, no meals, and thirty years later, I burned the mortgage. Terzi got married in nineteen seventy-eight, lord, I still miss her. I quit taking in boarders in two-thousand one.

"Now it's just me and memories of Ira. He's still waiting and one day, we'll be together again.

She looked at Darlene saying,

"You can't know how much I appreciate you listening to me. I've wanted to share my story for so long."

Darlene took her hand replying,

"Aunt Bessie, thank you for sharing it with me. Now I know you loved and were loved. I don't think life can offer anything better than that. Mine may be taken away from me tomorrow but like you; I have loved and I know I'm being loved."

"Come, let me show you the rest of the house."

She looked first at the elevator and then at Darlene.

"An elevator, I can't believe it. I climbed those stairs all those years, what next?"

Darlene stifled her smile knowing what would follow.

They stopped on the second level that opened into a hall with a bedroom on each side. Each had a full bath. The end of the hall opened onto the second level deck.

"Which bedroom is yours?"

Darlene bit her tongue trying not to laugh replied.

"It's on the next level."

She led her back to the elevator and continued up to the Master Suite. It opened into an alcove with the master bath and closets on the right and the Master bedroom directly in front of them.

She first led Aunt Bessie into the hall lined with drawers and the walk-in closet entrance on the right. The dressing vanities were on the left. When they entered the bathroom, Aunt Bessie froze. She'd never even seen pictures of anything like this in magazines.

"Darlene, is this real? Do you really live here?"

"Yes, ma'am, I do. Look at the Jacuzzi. I just love it and look at the view.

Aunt Bessie was looking but wasn't sure she was believing. When Darlene opened the refrigerator door, Aunt Bessie was sure she was dreaming.

Looking into the huge walk-in shower, she softly uttered,

"This is bigger than my whole bathroom."

The master bedroom was overwhelming too. She walked around the seating group seeing pics of them on the table and the nightstand. Out on the deck, she had to sit down.

"My heart's fluttering, Darlene. May I have a glass of water?"

Stepping towards the door, she replied.

"Yes you may. Could I get you a glass of wine?"

"Wine! Lordy, girl, I haven't had a glass of wine in fifty years. May I?"

Darlene brought tapers of white Zinfandel along with a small tray of cheese and crackers.

Her aunt timidly took a sip and commented.

"This is delicious and the color's so pale. It's not as sweet as the wine your father used to make. I really like this. What is it?"

Darlene replied,

"It's Sutter Home White Zinfandel. There are more expensive wines in the refrigerator and wine cooler downstairs but I like this one. Ray knows his wines and slowly but surely, I'm learning to appreciate the different kinds too.

"I remember Daddy's. Arlene and I got into it when we were eleven. We got so drunk and so sick. Daddy said there wasn't any reason to whip us. He was sure we had learned our lesson. I didn't touch another drop until I was out of college.

Her aunt laughed, replying,

"Yes, you and Arlene were a little adventurous. I remember the time ya'll got lost. Everybody in the community from Gull Rock to Nebraska were out looking for you."

Darlene was baffled,

"How old were we? I don't' remember that."

Her aunt replied, if my memory serves me correctly, you were seven. It was in the summer and ya'll slipped off while the others were loading watermelons. Somehow you found baby kittens in the hay loft over at John Cahoon's farm. How in the world you got there is a mystery? That was a good four miles away.

"You did get the belt that time but each of you got a kitten too. That's where all those cats around the farm came from.

Just as she was going to reply, she got a text.

Missing U counting days. R

Loving U 2. Aunt B here. D

"I apologize, Aunt Bessie. That was Ray."

"That's texting isn't it?"

Darlene replied,

"Yes ma'am, we do it once or twice a day. He's just getting up. It' Monday morning there.

Now on their second glasses of wine, they talked on until seven p.m. and the sun was being pulled down into the horizon.

They grilled chicken breasts and enjoyed them along with a salad on the lower deck. It had been a special experience for them. All those years and they knew so little about each other.

Darlene dropped her off about nine thirty that evening promising to see her next Sunday if she didn't go to Hyde County.

Back at the cottage she spent an hour in the Jacuzzi before going to bed. Remembering her day with Aunt Bessie and the memories they shared, she was asleep in minutes.

~ D ~

Dear diary, there are 356 days left before he's back in my arms.

Monday and Tuesday turned into Wednesday

~ *D* ~

Dear diary, there are 354 days left before he's back in my arms.

She had coffee and a Danish with Gail before punching in. They decided on pizza after work. Gail would drive over after work and they'd leave from there.

Arriving at the Pizza Inn, they chose the Everything Monster with a heart-stopping combination of beef topping, smoked ham, pepperoni, seasoned pork topping, savory onions, green olives, black olives, mush rooms, fresh green bell peppers and two layers of Mozzarella cheese and a pitcher of beer.

When the waiter brought it to them they were sure it was going to be a Prilosec night. They'd taken one earlier. They left with a box containing three untouched pieces. Gail said she wanted them. There was no way Darlene going to touch them.

Back at the cottage, they enjoyed tall pilsners of Michelob Ultra Lights and the serenity of the evening.

Gail looked at Darlene saying,

"I'd like to begin paying rent on your townhouse on May first if it's still agreeable with you."

Darlene smiled as she replied,

"Of course it is. You can move in now and begin paying the rent in May. The utilities are paid through the first. We can contact Washington Utilities the week of the twenty-seventh and request the change then."

Gail reached for her hand saying,

"Darlene, thank you so much. You have no idea how badly I want to get out of Belhaven. I'll move in Friday after work."

Darlene walked back into the kitchen removing a key from her purse.

"You'll need this, there is another one under a little rock by the stoop. If you can't find it, I'll show you."

~ D ~

Dear diary, there are 354 days left before he's back in my arms.

As if by magic, it was Saturday and she was going home. It had only been four months but so much had happened and it seemed as if years had passed.

Her cell rang just after six. It was him!

"What a pleasant surprise, I love you, Dr. Hardy… I hope you do, if you ever stop, it will break my heart… Nothing much, I'm going to visit my parents today. I may spend the night but I promised Aunt Bessie I'd see her in church tomorrow… Probably, she had such a good time…No, Gail's moving into my townhouse this weekend. I told her she could start paying rent on the first… Not yet, she and I may take **Miss Darlene** out next weekend… No, just for the day. How's

Glenda?... She what? I'll kill her… No, I haven't checked in lately… Oh, I will, I promise… All right, she'd better be… Dr. Hardy, if I could get my hands on you!... You know I miss you and I'm counting the days… You tell me when, I'll be ready…Okay darling, I love you too."

After showering and dressing, she rode the elevator down to the main level and brought Mr. Coffee to life. While the coffee was making, she opened her laptop and checked Ray's Facebook page. Glenda was… well, not in the running. The pics of the reef were beautiful. They reminded her of the ones near St. Croix. She'd be ready to go snorkeling again when he was.

After coffee and a bowl of cereal, she was on the road. Her trip was uneventful except when she crossed the high rise over the Inner Coastal Waterway. (ICW) It was one of her favorite places. The view from the old bridge was magnificent but the new view was much more impressive. She remembered so many times watching the boats, sailing under the bridge, north and southward, dreaming of a day when she would be on one.

I'm still going to see the bridge from the Alligator-Pungo canal, and it's going to be soon.

~ D ~

Arriving home, her mother was watering the flowers out front by the steps. They hugged and walked into the kitchen. There was something baking in the oven but she couldn't quite put her finger on it. It had to be a cobbler or pie.

"That's an apple pie in the oven!"

Her mother smiled nodding yes,

"I know how much you love them. We'll cut it after dinner (lunch). Your daddy, Evan and Billy are planting sweet corn and beets. They'll be up directly.

"Dale's gone to Engelhard. He's crabbing now. Doing good at it too. He's got a hundred-ninety pots and says he's going to add another hundred this year. He's doing about fifteen crates now. The crabs are selling so good, about everybody around's crabbing now. Russel buys everyone he can catch."

"How's life treating my little girl?"

"Mama, it's okay, with Ray gone I'm about as lonesome as I can be but time will take care of that.

"After church last Sunday, I took Aunt Bessie to lunch and then carried her back home with me. We had a real nice visit and she stayed for supper. That's the most time I ever spent with her, Mama, and I enjoyed every minute of it. I'm supposed to meet her at church in the morning."

Her mama, busying herself with lunch, replied,

"I haven't seen nor heard from her since Arlie was in the hospital. We don't ever get up that way and it's been a spell since she's been down here. I don't guess she drives that much either. Seems, anymore, it takes a funeral to get everybody together."

Darlene laughed replying,

"That or a wedding. Maybe I'll have one someday and we can all gather up somewhere."

She was ready right then, that moment, tomorrow, but her Mr. Right was down under all the way on the other side of the world.

Her mama replied as she removed the pies from the oven,

"Your day's coming, Darlie, I can feel it in my bones. Ain't no reason trying to rush it, you're still young and got your whole life in front of you."

"Mama, how old were you when ya'll got married?"

"I was almost eighteen. Back then, you either went off to college or got married and went to work. Down here, for most of us, it was farming or on water. Mostly some of both.

"Owen's daddy was farming more land than he could handle by his self, Russell had gone off and got a job on a trawler at Stumpy Point so his daddy told us we could farm on halves.

"We got married and moved in with them. Owen started on this house, two years later. It took us three years to get it ready to move in.

"I was pregnant with Dale then. We added on two years later when I was carrying you and Arlie.

"Evan was born two years after ya'll and we thought we were done but six years later, Billy was born. After him, I got fixed so there won't no more."

"Life's been good to us. We've had our ups and downs, farming and all. We lost most of the crop back in 1996. Hurricane Fran came through here that September. We lost all the collards, beets, carrots, and sweet potatoes. We'd just put some of the fall crops in the ground and lost all of that too. We would have had tomatoes at least until Thanksgiving but they rotted on the vines. We couldn't get into the fields. We survived it but it was hard."

She was interrupted by Darlene's father.

"Well, look at who's come to visit. Come here girl. Let me look at you."

Darlene hugged her daddy and kissed him on his stubbly cheek replying,

"Hey daddy, it's good to be home. You doing all right?"

"Yes, honey, your mama's taking real good care of us. What are you driving? Where's your car?"

"Daddy, it's Ray's Infiniti. He wants be to drive it while he's in Australia. It's a fine ride, daddy, you'd like it."

"How long's your man going to be in Australia? That a far distance from here."

"A year, daddy, he's working on a research project near the Great Barrier Reef. I brought my laptop so I could show ya'll some pictures. Here, look at these."

She set the laptop on the counter and brought us Ray's Facebook page.

"That's him the day he arrived. Those are Aborigines. They're like Indians over here. Ray says they've been in Australia for thousands of years. This is the camp. They sleeping in tents. This is the kitchen and dining room and that's the shower's and bathrooms. Oh, look at this, it's the reef where he'll be collecting samples."

She was interrupted when Evan and Billy walked in.

Evan spoke first,

"Hey Darlie (they all called her that and Arlene was, Arlie), That's some wheels you've got out there. Bet it drives like a million dollars."

She hugged his neck replying.

"It does, maybe I can take ya'll for a ride after dinner (lunch) if ya'll got time."

"Darlie, set the table please, dinner's ready."

Her daddy said grace and started passing the bowls and platters of cabbage collards, new potatoes, sweet corn, early peas, white side meat, fried pork chops, crab cakes, and corn bread, the thin crispy kind that Darlene loved. Sweetened iced tea was at each place with cayenne pepper vinegar, and butter on the table.

They talked mostly about Darlene's visit to Arlie and Ken's. They wanted to hear every detail and she enjoyed sharing every tidbit with them.

Her daddy wondered if she was all back to normal and Darlene assured him and her family that she was.

"It's as if she never got sick.

"Is she back to work yet?

"No, Ken wants her to wait until June. She's got a job waiting for her at the hospital.

His business is doing real good. The project he's doing in Duck is a big one. Ray got it for him and Ken's doing another cottage in Nags Head. He's a good contractor, daddy."

He wondered about Aunt Bessie. "When have you seen Bessie?"

Darlene shared what she'd told her mama earlier saying she was supposed to see her in church tomorrow.

"I'd like to take ya'll to Martelle's tonight. You boys are probably busy dating and all since it's Saturday but I'd love for you to come too."

Evan had a hot date but Billy was more than ready to go with the family.

Smiling now, Darlene replied,

"Okay, I know daddy likes to eat early. We'll leave about six. Daddy is that all right?"

He was already looking forward to it,

"Yes, that's fine, Darlie, we'll be ready."

After slices of apple pie, Darlene helped her mama put food away and wash the dishes.

Finishing up, she called Martelle's making reservations for four at six-fifteen.

That afternoon, she helped her mama in the flower beds while they touched on different topics. She knew her mama wanted to know about her and Ray so she opened the door.

"Mama, while Ray's gone, he wants me to live in his house at Bath. I moved in last week. Gail's moving into my townhouse this weekend. You remember her. She was in my graduation glass. She's Chester Gibbs daughter.

"Anyway, Ray says we're getting married when he comes back next April. Mama, I love him with all my heart and right now, I miss him terribly. Gail and Aunt Bessie are going to help me get through this year. I want you to keep me in your prayers too."

Her mama stopped what she was doing and hugged her daughter replying,

"Darlie, you know me and your daddy will. You'll get through it, if it's meant to be, it will be. It was for me and your daddy; it will be for you too."

~ D ~

They left about six, driving to Engelhard and Martelle's Feed House. Inside, they were seated at a table for four. Billy wanted a booth but his father nixed it saying,

"The chairs suit me and your mama better."

With their sweet tea on the table, Darlene looked at her daddy saying,

"Daddy, you order first."

He ordered the fried trout, oysters, and sea scallops with fries and slaw. Her mama wanted the fried flounder and shrimp with fries and slaw.

Billy want the large fried oysters with fries and slaw.

Darlene ordered the broiled shrimp and sea scallops with baked potato and slaw.

Her daddy looked at her asking,

"Honey, you remember that year you worked here?"

She remembered, especially Jimmy Balance. He wouldn't leave her alone and God! did he stink. All smokers did to her, and his stained yellow teeth, especially. Yes, she remembered.

"Daddy, that was my first job in the public. That first night, I was sure it would be my last but somehow, I got through it. It helped me when Arlie and I went to college. Aunt Bessie was probably the most help. She knew her way around folks and showed us how to act. Yes, sir, I learned a lot here and no, sir, I don't ever want to wait tables again but sometime in the future, I want to open a restaurant. I'm enrolled in the Culinary Art's class at Beaufort Community now."

When they finished, she paid the tab leaving a nice tip. It was time to go back to the cottage. It would be close to midnight when she got to her new home.

When she dropped them off, her mama insisted on her taking the second pie with her. She got little resistance from Darlene knowing what she would have for breakfast.

Hugging each of them, she waved goodbye saying she'd see them again soon.

~ *D* ~

Dear diary, there are 353 days left before he's back in my arms.

She awakened Sunday morning after a restful night of dreams intermingled between Ray and her family. It was a little before six and Ray usually called about that time.

Down in the kitchen, he called just as she cranked Mr. Coffee up.

"Good morning, I guess it good evening for you. I love you… I spent yesterday with my family and took them out to dinner last night… No, we had a nice visit. They're all doing good… Yes, I did and I told them we were getting married when you came back home. We are, aren't we?... Thank you, Dr. Hardy, I just wanted to check… Probably church with Aunt Bessie, I enjoyed her company last Sunday… Next Saturday, I want to take **Miss Darlene** up the Alligator-Pungo Canal to Alligator River… No, we'll turn about just before the bridge. According to the charts, there's no good anchorage along the canal. We may drop anchor near Frying Pan Landing and enjoy our lunch there… Of course, it's Gail. Is my man jealous?" She was grinning now… I know I'm pretty enough to be jealous over and don't you forget it. Keep your hands off of Glenda; you hear me?... Okay, I love you too. Bye."

After church, Darlene took Aunt Bessie to the Bonefish Grill in Greenville enjoying the Surf and Turf Eggs Benedict.

That afternoon, they spent more time together on the upper deck as her Aunt opened another door to her past; a more interesting life than anyone could have imagined.

~ *D* ~

Dear diary, there are 347 days left before he's back in my arms.

The next week just seemed to melt away and it was Saturday. Gail arrived a little after six and they breakfasted on eggs, bacon, toast, and coffee.

With their cooler packed with lunch and beer, they were ready. Darlene had called Wednesday saying she was taking **Miss Darlene** out Saturday.

They arrived at the marina finding **Miss Darlene,** fueled, and checked out.

Out in the Pamlico River, they cruised eastward and then into Pungo Creek before entering the Alligator-Pungo Canal. The manmade 'ditch' was twenty miles long. Traveling at twenty knots, it would only take an hour unless they spent time at the overpass bridge. Something Darlene wanted to do depending on the boat traffic.

As they approached the bridge, she slowed to five knots and drifted slowly under it. She'd taken one more 'to do' out of her bucket.

They arrived at the northern end of the canal and entered Alligator River cruising northwards toward the bridge. Not wanting to confuse the bridge tender, Darlene turned about and plotted a course into The Straights at Catfish Point. They moved into Babbitt Bay, passing Fowl and Crane Island. When they passed Crane Island Point on the Starboard side, they were in the Frying Pan.

Darlene didn't want to disturb the fishermen, and there were tons of them, so she brought **Miss Darlene** about and dropped anchor in Babbitt Bay. The weather was perfect and they enjoyed their lunch topside.

Gail was excited saying she'd never been on anything like **Miss Darlene**.

"A lot of our food came from the sound and we were out there a lot but never on anything like this. Lord, Darlene, if my daddy had ever been on a boat like this before he died, he would have thought he had already died and gone to heaven. To think that Dr. Hardy named it for you. This is so far above my upbringing; I don't even know how to act."

Darlene laughed before replying,

"Here Gail, have another beer. You think it's above your upbringing; what about mine?" I'm toying with the idea of tying up where Dale docks and taking daddy and mama out. Trouble is, I'm not sure he would even come aboard."

Gail was laughing now,

"If he thinks this is something, what would he do if he saw the mansion you're living in? He'd probably kill right over. Your mama would love it if you could ever get her inside. You know she would."

Darlene noticed the wind getting up out of the northeast.

"We'd better head back, the wind's picking up. I'll check NOAA's weather."

Nothing appeared to be making but they weighted anchor and plotted a course back down the Alligator-Pungo Canal. She'd done what she wanted to do and they could spend the rest of the afternoon anchored somewhere near Belhaven.

Next time, we'll overnight near Shackleford Banks. I like it there. You will too."

They arrived back at the marina and Darlene executed a perfect docking maneuver. After attaching the mooring lines, fore and aft, she dropped the keys off asking that it be serviced saying,

"I'll call about refueling and checking it out when I'm ready to take her out again."

Back at the cottage, they enjoyed wine spritzers with cheese, dip, chips, and nuts.

"We'll grill those porterhouses about seven.

Gail left a little after ten and Darlene spent the next hour in the Jacuzzi before curling up in bed, pretending the pillow she was clutching was her, Mr. Right.

~ D ~

Dear diary, there are 312 days left before he's back in my arms.

The month of April slipped into May and May became June. It was Sunday morning and time for Ray's call.

There he was, right on time.

"Is this my darling?... You know you are, I miss you more and more every day… I hope so… No, I rode back home yesterday and enjoyed the bountiful harvest…Dr. Hardy, collards aren't good this time of year, you know that. We had some of the best corn-on-the-cob I've ever eaten and soft-shell-crabs fried in bacon grease… No, they didn't buy them; Dale's got a molting shed now… Probably around $25 a dozen… Bring yourself back here sir, I'll fry them up just for you…Really? When?... You know I'm ready. July twelfth! I can't believe it!... Yes, I'm ready now. I'll tell them I'll be on vacation tomorrow; just tell me what I'm supposed to take… Of course I'll take the green dress, you dirty old man… You're right, I like you that way. Just wait until I get my hands on you, Dr. Hardy. I've got a prescription that will cure all your ails…. I know, it's only a month away. If I could just snap my fingers… I love you too, Bye."

She couldn't believe it. July twelfth, if she could only fast forward the calendar, it would be July eleventh right then. She'd finish packing and be out of there on the twelfth.

In church, it was all Aunt Bessie could do to keep her still. Afterwards, they had lunch at Ruby Tuesdays enjoying the grilled chicken and a trip to the salad bar.

Aunt Bessie knew there was no way to stymie Darlene's enthusiasm so she just let her bubble over. She'd never seen her so happy and so excited.

"Darlene, if you don't calm down some, you're going to explode. You know that don't you, honey?"

Darlene was in the clouds of happiness climbing higher and higher with each passing hour.

"Aunt Bessie, it's been so long and I love him so much. I'll die if July twelfth doesn't hurry up and get here."

"Where are you flying out of, Raleigh or Charlotte?"

"I'll fly out of Greenville on his private jet. He'll be waiting when I get there. I don't know which island or which airport. His pilot will know and I don't care. I'm so ready to see my man."

~ D ~

Dear diary, there are 301 days left until he returns, but, it's only 34 days until I hold him in my arms!

Monday morning when the sun peeped above the horizon, Darlene had already showered, dressed and was on the main deck drinking her second cup of coffee.

Excitement would not let her sleep. Gail would be the second one to know and then, Nellie. She was going to see her man.

Arriving at the hospital, she picked up a coffee and impatiently waited for Gail.

"Gail, get your coffee. I've got news!"

She almost got seated when Darlene started,

"I'm going to see my man on July twelfth! I'm so excited. I don't think I slept an hour last night. Can you believe it? I'm finally going to see him. It's only thirty-four more days"

"Hawaii?"

"Yes!"

"I'll come over tonight. I want to hear all about it."

"Good, come over about six, we'll drink a bottle of wine and grill some of the jumbo shrimp."

She punched in and filled out her vacation request handing it to Nelle. It was a formality but protocol had to be served. If it was denied, she'd simply walk out. Emailing, Dr. Pulver, was all she was required to do in radiology.

At lunch, Mr. Hicks asked if he could join her?

"You look like you just won the lottery."

"Mr. Hicks, I did, I'm going to Hawaii in July to see my man."

He chuckled knowing that winning the lottery wouldn't come close to making her as happy as seeing Dr. Hardy would.

"Miss Snell, that makes my day, the Misses will be happy for you too."

~ D ~

That evening, Gail arrived a little after six. Darlene was already on her second glass of wine. She didn't need it for the buzz, she was already higher than it could take her.

They went through one bottle and opened another. All Gail could do was listen. She knew if she ever found a man that could make her as happy as Darlene, all her prayers would be answered.

They grilled four of the five-to-seven count Tiger Shrimp and enjoyed them with a twice-baked potato on the side. By nine, Darlene was tired and close to being wasted. Gail wished her a good evening, knowing without a doubt, that she was having a good one.

"Darlene, get some sleep. I'll see you tomorrow.

~ D ~

Dear diary, there are 279 days left until he returns, but, it's only 9 days until I hold him in my arms!

The days and weeks were rushing by now and the long fourth of July weekend would begin today. They'd be off Friday, Saturday and Sunday. She was excited for the others but knowing how big the crowds would be, she chose to stay home. She'd thought about taking **Miss Darlene** down to Belhaven or maybe Washington for the festivities but Gail was going to Nags Head with her family and no way was she going alone. She chose to wait and celebrate the following weekend when she arrived in Hawaii.

What to do? The scales first, she hadn't gained an ounce over the past year. She couldn't believe it. No, her clothes fitted fine but she'd eaten tons of rich food and the cocktails, oh the cocktails.

Good, now I can have a big breakfast.

She began by putting a rasher of bacon in the toaster oven, 14 minutes at 425 degrees, prepared home fries from a left-over baked potato, put two slices of wheat bread in the toaster, and heated up the frying pan to medium low. She didn't like her eggs wearing skirts.

With three minutes left on the bacon, she cracked 2 extra-large eggs and gently opened them into the bacon grease. The ringer on the toaster-oven sang out so she removed the bacon placing the strips on Bounty towels to drain.

When the eggs were set just right, she gently flipped them over adding salt and pepper, and activated the toaster

With the, just right, over-easy eggs, crispy bacon, and home fries on her plate, she took the toast out and placed her breakfast on the sit-down side of the island counter. A glass of milk, juice, and Welches grape jelly in place, she was ready to breakfast in style.

Noon came and went, she had overdone it for breakfast and hunger wasn't even a factor.

She was sitting on main deck when her cell alerted her of a call.

Picking it up, she realized it was Dale, her older brother.

"Dale, this is a surprise. Is there anything wrong?... Of course you can. I missed seeing you when I was down… It's easy, just plug the address into your GPS (She gave him the address) Okay see you in a few."

Dale and his girlfriend were coming by. It was going to be a nice Friday.

"Hey Dale, ya'll come in."

They were standing out front, knowing he must have entered the wrong address.

Hugging her, he had to ask,

"Darlie, do you really live here?"

She responded,

"Yes Dale, and who is this?"

Dale was embarrassed,

"I'm sorry, where are my manners? Darlie, this is Sadie Guthrie. Sadie, this is my sister, Darlene, we call her, Darlie. Her twin sister's name is Arlene, we call her, Arlie."

She led them up the steps and through the main level out onto the spacious deck.

"Ya'll have a seat. What brings you up this way?"

Dale, responded saying,

"Sadie's never seen the Washington Waterfront so I'm taking her. You want to join us?"

Darlene replied,

"You do realize how crowded it's going to be? The holiday festivities are already underway and there will be hordes of people there. It will be like sardines in a can."

Dale replied,

"I know, but she really wants to see it."

Darlene replied,

"How about we see it from the river? It won't be nearly as crowded."

He was looking at Sea Ox on the lift.

"Is that yours?"

"It's Rays but I have the keys. There's another one at the Marina if ya'll would like to go out, It's much larger."

He looked at Sadie seeing a positive response.

"Yes, Darlie, we'd really like that."

She picked up her cell calling the marina instructing them to refuel and go through the checklist on **Miss Darlene**.

"How long will that take?... That's fine, I'll be there at two."

Dale was confused,

"**Miss Darlene**?"

Darlene laughed saying she would explain when they got to the marina.

"Are you hungry?"

They hadn't had lunch so she invited Sadie to help her make BLT's. Afterwards, she gave them the grand tour hearing nothing but oohs and aahs from them.

Dale and Sadie stood looking at the Jacuzzi and she knew what must be going through their minds. She vividly remembered what went through her mind the first time she saw it.

Out on the upper deck, Dale and Sadie were blown away by the scenic view of Bath Creek.

"Darlie, Dr. Hardy, must be rich."

She grinned, replying, Yes, very. Let's go for a boat ride."

Arriving at the marina, she picked up the keys being told everything had been taken care of.

They walked down dock to the slip where **Miss Darlene** was moored.

She first took them aft, proudly showing them the name.

Dale was almost speechless but managed,

It's named after you, Darlie. I can't believe it."

She responded saying,

"I couldn't either but here she is. Welcome aboard, let's cast off.

Onboard, she did the pre-check and brought all 700 horses to life. Dale cast off the mooring lines and watched his sister expertly back **Miss Darlene** away from the slip and out into Broad Creek and Pamlico River.

First, she took them to Pungo Creek and dropped anchor near the marina in Belhaven. From their vantage point, they could easily see hundreds of people enjoying the festivities along the waterfront. She remarked that they had a huge fireworks display.

"Arlie, and I came last year. We had a ball but the crowds were too much for us Hyde Country gals."

The harbor and marina were crowed with dozens of boats of every description, mostly sailboats, but many were also powered.

Weighing anchor, she exited Pungo Creek and made a starboard turn up Pamlico River towards Washington finding the waterfront equally as crowed as Belhaven if not more so.

She throttled back in the no-wake zone and dropped anchor about a hundred yards off the Estaurium. They enjoyed cold beers and snacks watching the throngs of humanity crowding the waterfront, streets, and parking lots filled with vendors.

Darlene looked at Dale, saying,

"I can find a find a slip if you'd like to get into the middle of all that."

Knowing before he responded, he looked at Sadie and she gave him that. "No way" look.

So much for the masses, after a couple of hours, they returned to the marina and back to the cottage.

It was about six and Darlene invited them to grill steaks.

They eagerly accepted and she took four ribeye's out and thawed them in the microwave.

Enjoying frosty beers on the main deck, she looked at Sadie asking,

"So, tell me about Sadie."

Sadie, noticeably nervous, replied,

"Darlie, there's not much to tell. I grew up in Stumpy Point. Daddy has a shrimp trawler and mama works at the crab factory. Us young'uns, Bonnie, Raeford, Dick, and me, went to W. R. Davie School and Mattamuskeet High School.

"Me and Dale graduated together. There wasn't any money to go to college so I got work cleaning cottages at Nags Head. The pay's good and I go, to and from, with three friends. That way, I only have to drive one week a month. The work's more than we can handle in-season but off-season, it's slow. We get paid by the cottage.

"Anyway, I started taking courses, online, three years ago and I'll get my associates degree in September. My degree is in hospitality. Getting seasonal work will be easy, but I want something more permanent. Right now, I'll stick with cleaning cottages."

"Me and Dale, we're steady."

She looked at him for agreement and received it.

"We've talked about it. He's doing real good crabbing and wants to stay put. If we, she reached over touching his hand, "continue hanging together, I'll stay put too."

Darlene looked them, remarking.

"I think you're lucky to have each other. Dale, you did good."

Sadie, appearing a little more at ease, replied,

"Thank you!"

It was after six, so Darlene cranked up the grill and put the potatoes into the microwave.

While Sadie put together tossed salads, Darlene lightly oiled the steaks and seasoned them with Tones Canadian Steak Seasoning.

The grill was ready so she handed Dale the steaks and turner.

"Chef Dale, do your thing."

She helped Sadie with the salads and got the dressings and condiments together.

"Sadie, would you like wine with your meal?"

"Darlie, I guess, all I've ever had was some daddy made."

Darlene knew all the boys had been in the wine back home. She and Arlie had been in it once or twice.

She opened a bottle of White Zinfandel and took out four tapers.

"Garlic Bread?

Sadie smiled, replying.

"Yes, please, Dale likes it."

Darlene took slices of Garlic Texas Toast from the freezer and put them in the toaster-oven.

Dale peeped in the kitchen door, asking,

"Darlie, how do you want your steak? Me and Sadie like ours, medium."

She responded, saying,

"Med-Rare, for me please."

While enjoying their meal, Dale asked how long would it be before Dr. Hardy came home?

She happily replied, "279 days but that's okay, I'll see him Sunday week."

He was puzzled,

"Sunday week, how?"

"We're spending a week in Hawaii. I'm flying out on his private jet."

They looked shocked.

"Private jet! He must be rich!"

"He sure is Dale, That's how Arlie got back to North Carolina when she was in the coma."

They liked the wine so she opened another bottle after the dishes were done. Sadie really knew her way around a kitchen sink.

About ten, Dale stood saying it was time for them to get back. He needed to be working his pots by sunup and Sadie had three cottages to clean.

"Darlie, we've had a ball. Thank you, gal. I love ya."

She hugged them both telling Sadie how much she enjoyed meeting her.

"Remember, when I get back from Hawaii, it's going to be awful lonesome up here till next April. Please come back often.

"Dale, tell the family I love them."

"Oh, are either of you on Facebook?"

Sadie responded,

"I am."

"Good, friend me and ya'll can see the pics I post. There's a bunch already there from Miami, St. Croix, and Bermuda. Ya'll take a look. Love you."

She spent an hour in the Jacuzzi reliving her day. Dale coming by was a surprise but a good one. She liked Sadie, they looked like they belonged together.

~ *D* ~

Dear diary, there are 277 days left until he returns, but, it's only 7 days until I hold him in my arms!

Saturday became Sunday and Darlene met Aunt Bessie for church.

Afterwards, they had lunch at the Warehouse Restaurant in Winterville. Mr. Hicks had recommended it saying they had a great Sunday buffet with some of the best fried chicken he'd ever eaten.

"They've got great salad bar too."

Darlene hadn't been but she was game knowing how much Aunt Bessie liked salads.

They placed their orders for iced tea saying they were doing the buffet. Darlene left her aunt at the salad bar walking into the room with the buffet. She chose, cabbage-collards, squash casserole, green beans flavored with country ham bits, hamburger steak with gravy over rice, and a luscious-looking golden fried chicken breast. She managed to find a little space for two hushpuppies but that was all.

She smiled to herself thinking, *this is just like carrying the groceries in, I try to make it all in one trip. Here, there's no limit.*

When she got back to their table, Aunt Bessie was placing her salad on the table but wasn't sitting down.

"Darlene, where's that chicken?"

She pointed through the double doors,

"Over there, just past the salad bar."

Aunt Bessie returned with cabbage-collards, a dab of the hamburger steak, and onions and just a smidgen of gravy. Of course, there was a chicken breast.

She could be a comedian when she wanted to.

"We've got to stop meeting like this, my scales are talking ugly to me."

Laughing in response, Darlene replied,

"I know what you mean. I love fried chicken but apparently it loves me more. It refuses to leave me."

They'd drizzled cayenne pepper vinegar on their collards. Without it, collards were like eating vanilla ice cream without chocolate syrup. It was okay but not nearly as tasty.

"Aunt Bessie, will you spend the afternoon with me? I'll be in Hawaii next Sunday."

She replied,

"Of course I will. Take me by the house and I'll change into something more comfortable."

After all the talk about scales, they couldn't leave without checking out the dessert line. The coconut cake was like a magnet. They couldn't leave without enjoying a slice.

Back at the cottage, they sat under the off-set market umbrella. Aunt Bessie had changed into Capris and a short sleeve top.

After a few minutes of enjoying the gentle breeze coming off the creek, Aunt Bessie wanted to share another of her, never told, adventures.

"Remember, Darlene, never tell anyone, never!"

"Terzi got married, I think I told you. She married a local business man, Thorton Phillips. He'd made a lot of money and built a fine house on a farm he owned over on Cherry Run Road. They lived there about ten years then he sold his business and they moved to Florida.

"Anyway, right after they got married, she invited me to go with them to a club located up on Highway seventeen about five miles north of town. I think it was called the Brentwood Lodge.

"Darlene, that was one swanky place. First, he took us into the lounge. I'd never seen anything like it. On the left, there was a huge horseshoe shaped bar that must have seated thirty people. On the right was a large fireplace with seating groups of tufted-leather furniture and tables for two and four people. He said there were game rooms beyond the far door and a swimming pool out back.

"Back in those days, there wasn't any such thing as 'liquor-by-the-drink.' The members brought their bottles in brown paper bags or like Terzi's husband, had a locker in the lounge

"He ordered drinks, and ice and mixed his liquor with Coco Cola, Ginger Ale, or water.

"First, mine was too strong so he poured about half of it out and put more Ginger Ale in it.

"Everybody in there, men and women, seemed to be smoking and I won't comfortable with it but because of Terzi, I put up with it. We stayed in there about an hour before a waitress came and got us for dinner.

"Darlene, he ordered steaks for us and let me tell you, that was the finest and most tender steak I ever had, then or now. Mine was, at least, 2" thick. We had salads first and then the steaks with baked potatoes and asparagus. I guess that was the first time I ever had butter, sour cream, chives, and bacon bits on a baked potato. Your mother can tell you, we ate a lot of potatoes fixed about every way you could imagine but butter and salt and pepper was the only thing on the table.

"When we finished, he said there was a live band in another room playing '40's' music. Would we like to go in?

"I don't remember the band's name but they could really play '40's' music. He and Terzi danced to ***'string of pearls'*** and when they started playing ***'in the mood,'*** he asked me to dance.

"Darlene, when I first bought my house, Terzi and I would dance to some of the old 'LP's.' We loved Glen Miller. I never went to a dance though. When he asked me, Terzi pushed me out on the floor and ***we cut a rug***.

"If a member of the board of education had seen us, we would have been fired the next day.

"That was the only time I ever danced with a man but it was enough. I still remember it like it was yesterday."

She was looking off into nothing now, remembering.

"It's so nice to have someone to share my memories with. It makes them seem so real again. Thank you, Darlene."

Darlene knew her aunt's memories were being relived now. One day, she'd looked back and relive hers.

~ D ~

Dear diary, there are 271 days left until he returns, but, it's only 1 day until I hold him in my arms!

The next few days seemed to disappear into thin air. She'd texted and talked to Ray each day and was almost too excited to contain her happiness.

Suddenly, it was Saturday. Everything was hanging in the dressing alcove or on the vanity tops. It would all fit into one suitcase and a clothes bag. She'd gone over her list three times.

Her cell rang out, it had to be him, it was. "Hello sweetheart, I'm so excited…you're where?... 30,000 feet?... When will you arrive?... Good, get a good night's sleep, you'll need it… Yes, Dr. Hardy, I know there are two climbing our mountain. I'm ready for you, sir… Ten in the morning?... I'll be there… How long is my flight?... nine hours, three p.m. Hawaii time… Yes, you be there, I'm coming for you… Yes, until tomorrow, I love you!"

The hours grudgingly drug by, one by one and by eight p.m. she was in a tizzy. There had to be some way to calm down. In the bar, she poured three-fingers of Jack Daniels Black on ice cubes. The first sip took her breath. Little by little the drink disappeared and along with it, her nervousness. An hour later she was more than relaxed. The Jacuzzi beckoned and then as if by magic, it was Sunday morning.

"I can't believe it, I'm in Hawaii!"

***Dear** diary, there are 270 days left until he returns, but I'll hold him in my arms today!*

The jet was waiting when she arrived and by ten a.m., they were airborne after being welcomed by the pilot and a stewardess. She brought a copy of Nicholas Sparks, **Nights in Rodanthe**, to help pass the time. She also had her laptop and cell phone.

An hour into the flight, the stewardess asked if she'd like anything, coffee, soft drink, water? "

We also have three entrées to choose from for lunch, fried chicken, meat loaf, or crab cakes.

"You can choose now or I'll check back with you later."

Darlene responded saying,

"A cup of coffee would be nice, 1 cream, please."

"Yes ma'am, the Krispy Kreme glazed donuts are still warm. Would you care for one?"

Yes, she would but only one.

About noon, her time, she lunched on the crab cakes with a baked potato and garden salad. Seven more hours to go.

She got interested in the book and time began to fly by. Six hours into the flight, the stewardess brought a soft drink and chips.

Eight hours into the flight and only about an hour out, the stewardess was back with Mai Tai's saying Dr. Hardy suggested that she could have only two.

They both laughed as Darlene replied,

"I'm sure he's right."

At ten of three, HNL time, the pilot announced, "

We're approaching LiHue airport, the temperature is eighty-five degrees, the skies are clear and trade winds are about 5 knots.

"Dr. Hardy says, 'Welcome to Paradise.' He's waiting on the tarmac."

She thanked the pilot and stewardess before departing the jet.

It seemed as if it had been forever but now she was back in his arms, kissing him over and over. Tears were streaming down her cheeks. It was real and not a dream. They were together again.

He placed two blue orchid leis around her neck leading her towards the waiting car. Her luggage had already been placed in it.

The ride to the resort took about an hour traveling along HI-56 N. but she remembered little only wanting to see, touch, and be held by him.

Arriving at the resort, it was only minutes before the covers and clothes were scattered helter skelter. They climbed their mountain taking several routes until exhaustion finally conquered the moment.

After showering, they dressed, and spent an hour on the balcony with tapers of champagne, enjoying the beauty of the Pacific Ocean and the Bali Hai mountain range to their right.

Looking into her eyes, he commented, "Back in the fifties, there was a Broadway play and movie named, **South Pacific**. Did you, by chance, see it?"

She, still mesmerized by his countenance, replied,

"Yes, Arlie and I watched it on HBO. We loved it, especially the love scene with Bloody Mary."

He pointed over towards the mountain range, saying.

"That's where it was filmed. I'll take you there before we leave. You must be hungry. Are you ready to eat?"

Yes, she was hungry but hadn't noticed until he asked,

"Yes, I guess I am."

"Dress casual tonight, maybe a sundress, tomorrow night's green dress night."

She gave him her sexy smile, replying,

"You dirty old man."

A few minutes later she came out of the bedroom wearing the red sundress he gave her in Miami.

"Will this be all right?"

"You know it is." He loved her in that dress. It wasn't the green one but it was close enough for their first meal together in months.

~ D ~

Arriving at the Kai, they were seated with a view of the shimmering sea. Tiki torches created the romantic ambiance of the evening.

Ray ordered a bottle of Hagafen Riesling and they chose to share the Cast Iron Sizzling Shrimp in garlic butter with local bread for starters.

"Darlene, I've tried so many times since I arrived in Australia to remember what as absolute joy it is to have you sitting across from me. I've repeatedly dreamed about it and now, finally, here we are."

She looked into his eyes, replying.

"Ray, I've daydreamed about you every day and dreamed about you every night. I've missed you so much. Gail and Aunt Bessie have been with me constantly and I survived but I miss you more than words can say."

They sipped the wine and enjoyed the shrimp although neither could have commented on either the next day.

For her main dish, she ordered grilled Ahi Tuna steak with lemongrass coconut sauce with sides of roasted yams and garlic herb spinach. He chose the Mahi Mahi baked in a Ti leaf with sides of roasted sweet corn and the coconut rice steamed in a banana leaf.

Later, they enjoyed Kona coffee before walking out onto the beach. The trade winds wafted softly through the palm fronds and tropical flora, as it brushed almost imperceptibly by them. He stood behind her with his arms around her waist.

"I love you Darlene with all my heart."

She turned to him, brushing her lips against his, replying.

"Ray, with all my heart, I love you. There can never be another. God forbid that once your research is over, that we'll ever be separated again."

They walked, hand-in-hand, back to their suite hearing soft Hawaiian music off in the distance.

Picking up where they left off earlier, they were in each other's arm, climbing their own personal mountain over and over again until exhaustion overcame and sleep conquered them.

Next morning, the warm trade winds billowed softly through the open balcony doors ushering in her first Hawaiian sunrise.

Her man was standing in the opening sipping on a cup of coffee with an aroma that beckoned her.

Realizing she was still nude, she picked up a robe and joined him.

He kissed her on the nose saying,

"You looked too peaceful to disturb. Coffee still with one cream?"

He poured a cup from the carafe on the tray cart that contained several pastries along with pineapple, kiwi, and papaya.

"Would you like to walk along the beach before breakfast?"

She was more than ready and in minutes, they were strolling, hand in hand, along the sandy shore. There was so little activity along the beach. They only saw one other person and he appeared to be practicing Yoga and they did not disturb him.

Ray, where are the gulls? I can't believe I can't see or hear them."

"There aren't any and no pelicans either. There are shorebirds and there are no snakes either. That's why some call the islands, paradise. Having you here makes it paradise for me."

"You always say the nicest things. I love you, Dr. Hardy. I'm ready for breakfast, are you?"

They breakfasted at the Hanalei Wake Up Café enjoying their King's Reef Omelets that included tomatoes, onions, cheese, ham for him, bacon for her, and bell pepper with hash browns on the side.

Afterwards, their driver returned them to the resort.

It's your first full day in Hawaii. What would you like to do?"

She was clueless and didn't really care. She was there to be with him.

"I usually follow you. You choose."

That was easy, they rented a thirty-eight-foot catamaran and spent the day off shore sunning topside and climbing mountains below. The view of the island was so beautiful, really indescribable, you had to be there. Nothing like the shorelines back in North Carolina and neither were the almost crystal clear brooks.

For lunch, they enjoyed the picnic basket prepared by the resort. It contained wine, different fruits, nuts, boiled shrimp, buffalo wings, potato salad, and key lime pie.

That afternoon, they snorkeled alongside the catamaran and then sailed back and forth offshore until a little after four. Docking, they returned to the resort.

On their balcony, she enjoyed wine spritzers with cheese, crackers, and dip.

"Tonight, my lady, we're dining formally and I get to see my favorite lady in my favorite dress. It can't get any better than that. Tomorrow, We're going to tour Pearl Harbor, Waikiki Beach and Diamond Head. I think you'll enjoy that."

Before getting ready for dinner, they climbed their favorite mountain knowing there'd be more dessert after dinner.

~ D ~

They were seated on the Makana Terrace beginning their evening with Hawaiian Margaritas.

For starters, they chose Papaya and cucumber salad and a Sushi roll. She'd never tried Sushi but knowing her man enjoyed it, she was game finding it nothing like she would have guessed. Actually, it was pretty good.

He looked across the table, and while drinking in her beauty asked,

"Tell me about Aunt Bessie?"

She chuckled, replying,

"Aunt Bessie is phenomenal. Arlie and I always had her pegged as stuffy old maid. Oh, we love her but until lately, I thought she'd led a very boring and noneventful life. I couldn't have been any more wrong.

"Ray, she's lived, loved, and experienced life to its fullest. No, not in years and years but in microbursts. She made me promise not to share her life with anyone so, she looked at him, smiling, I shan't."

He grinned, replying,

"So be it, when you ask about my past again, I'll refer you back to this moment. We have our life to build stories on. One day, our children and grandchildren will have our stories to enjoy."

The sweetness of his statement, our children, grandchildren,

"Ray I want so much to be the mother of your children. I love you so much."

"I love you too, Darlene. Our day will come soon."

For dinner, they chose the Teriyaki Prime Rib with fried garlic and ginger and for sides, they chose the potato Au Gratin.

Later that evening, they enjoyed flutes of champagne on the balcony while exchanging stories about how they made time go by wishing to be back together every moment.

His research sounded exciting. Her life was boring compared to his. Gail and her family filled most of her boring existence. Taking the college courses helped fill the gaps but each time she arrived back at the cottage, loneliness would engulf her.

"I check off each day knowing I'm one day closer to having you back in my arms. Your texts and calls help and the pictures help fill in the void, but Ray, nothing can come close to being in your arms. I love you so much."

He was holding her in his arms.

"Darlene, you are my all and I love you with all my heart."

"Tomorrow, We'll be spending the day on Oahu and overnight at the Royal Hawaiian."

Dessert was served as they climbed their mountain before drifting off into dreams of each other knowing tomorrow was going to be a busy, but exciting day.

~ *D* ~

Next morning, they breakfasted on coffee, juice, and fruit that room service delivered just before six a.m.

Packing lightly, their driver ferried them to the airport where his jet was waiting.

They boarded along with their driver and thirty minutes later, arrived at Honolulu International. The driver exited first, their rental car was waiting. He unloaded their luggage drove them to Pearl Harbor. Their tour was memorable, especially the battleship Arizona memorial.

For lunch, they enjoyed salads the at the Surf Lanai Restaurant before checking into their suite in the Mailani Tower. Early registration had been requested.

Standing on the balcony overlooking Waikiki Beach with Diamond Head in the distance to their left, they sipped on wine spritzers and climbed their mountain once before exploring the island.

He remarked, as the driver opened the door for them.

"We'll skip Honolulu. You may as well be in the middle of Miami. Driver, take us to Diamond Head."

Arriving at the state park, they hiked the Diamond Head Summit Trail. It was strenuous but the view was worth the ninety-minute round trip. They spent thirty-minutes on the summit and Ray took dozens of pictures, instantly posting them on his Facebook page.

From there, they went to the north shore and spent an hour watching the surfers attack the biggest waves in Waimea Cove. According to Google, the biggest waves occurred in the winter months but the ones they were seeing seemed huge to her.

Ray pointed out Sunset beach and the Banzai Pipeline asking if she wanted to try it. She couldn't believe anyone in their right minds would attempt riding those monsters but there they were, trying, time and time, wipeout after wipeout. They could, her, no way!

After visiting pineapple and sugar cane fields, they returned to Honolulu and shopped at the Ala Moana Shopping Center finding several dresses he wanted her to have. She chose a flowery Hawaiian shirt for him.

The next hour was spent walking along Waikiki Beach.

"It's too commercial now and the tourists are thick as flies. You have to get off Oahu to find a secluded romantic beach."

It was crowded but at least, she'd walked the walk and he'd posted several pics of her being there.

In their suite, they enjoyed wine spritzers and cheese before dressing for the Aha'aiha Luau at Pikake Terrace Restaurant at the Royal Hawaiian's sister property, the Sheraton Princess Kaiulani.

It started at five-thirty and featured prime-rib, crab legs and dozens of other delicious entrées from the islands. The Te Moana Nui evening was very enjoyable and they would remember it for many years.

Later, memories were made as the they came together as one. She had no idea what he'd planned for tomorrow, it would be a day she'd never forget. One he'd been planning and dreaming of every day since they'd parted. She would be a part of him for the rest of his life.

She looked up at him.

"Ray, you left me. Where did you go?"

He smiled down at her, replying,

"Not far, my love, just dreaming of the time we'll be together to stay. Never to part again."

She was too excited to sleep. They walked out on the balcony and enjoyed the trade-winds as the palm fronds and flowers swayed gently in the warm evening breeze. The beach was still crowded as lovers searched and hoped to find a special moment on Waikiki Beach. There were older couples too. Perhaps reliving a visit, a moment, from years before. Maybe it was their honeymoon and being back on the beach rekindled memories and ignited the cooling ashes of time.

She wondered where they would be in ten, twenty, thirty years? Would they have married, had children, grandchildren?

~ D ~

Next morning, they breakfasted on their balcony enjoying the fabled scenic beauty of Waikiki Beach. Not nearly as crowded now, it seemed so serene and peaceful.

"Ray, is this somewhere you would like to live?"

Taking another sip of coffee, he replied,

"Darlene, not here, maybe on the Big Island or Maui. This is much too commercialized now.

"In times past, right after the second world war, this would have been perfect. Even in the 50's, 60's and 70's. Once the tourists discover a place, they ruin it.

"I think if left to my choice, I'd choose Australia. It's as if they are living fifty years in our past. I much prefer that to our present.

"Operating a business like ours would be very impractical from there but a hideaway, maybe in the outback, would be perfect.

"I want to visit Alice Springs and Ayers Rock before I leave Australia. That's about as far away from civilization as you can get except places like Papua, New Guinea.

"Now that's the ultimate getaway. No, you don't want to go there.

"One of the outer Islands in the Tahiti group would be perfect too. Bora Bora is beautiful but already, it's too commercialized."

He reached over touching her hand.

"Darlene, as long as I'm with you, it doesn't matter where we are."

After a seafood salad lunch at Trader Joes, they flew back to their resort.

"Darlene, will you marry me?"

"***Remember*** me asking you about South Pacific? Let's walk down the beach and I'll point out the place that was the background for Bloody Mary's **Bali Hai**.

The walk took a little over an hour but time seemed to fade into nothing when they were together. They stopped often, sitting under a palm tree or on the sandy beach near the almost becalmed ocean. They watched catamarans seemingly floating just above the waves, sail to and then away from them.

With each step, the spot he repeatedly pointed to, loomed closer and closer.

The sun was dipping towards the western horizon. Another day in paradise was beginning to turn into evening. The sun dropped closer and closer to the waves and then as if by magic, King Neptune seemed to reach up and pull the fiery orb into the deep but not without a struggle. The western sky filled with color. First yellow, then orange and finally, hues of red and purple filled the sky. There wasn't a sound, it was so majestic and peaceful.

"Ray, it's so beautiful." She turned towards him. What was happening? He was on one knee…was he proposing!

"Darlene, I love you with all my heart and want to spend the rest of my life with you. Will you marry me?" He was slipping a ring on her finger.

Almost numb with tears flowing down her cheeks, she managed to say,

"Yes, yes, yes! I love you so much."

They stood in each other's arms. Unlike the scene in South Pacific, their love would continue to wax strong. Yes, they would be separated again until next April but after that, their promise to each other was, **never again**.

Back at the resort, a romantic table for two awaited on their balcony.

The waiter poured champagne and they began their evening with grilled curried pineapple. Seafood salads followed and then bowls of she-crab soup.

She hardly noticed any of the food. Her mind and heart centered on him. Her, Mr. Right, was going to be her husband. The five-carat solitaire on her ring finger would tell the world. It already had as he flooded Facebook with pic after pic.

"Would madam care for more champagne?"

The spell wasn't broken but for a moment she came back down, replying,

"Yes please."

They dined on Mahi Mahi with twice-baked potatoes, grilled asparagus, and spears of pineapple.

"Darlene, we need to set a wedding date."

A little surprised, she looked across into the eyes of the man she was going to marry.

"A date? Yes, we do."

She was still somewhere above the clouds, up above the stratosphere.

There was another surprise coming as he continued,

"We can be married here or wait until I return in April. What would you like to do?"

Her sanity almost escaped her,

"Here, now? Is that possible?

He was smiling now,

"Yes, we can be married Saturday."

She was confused.

"What about the marriage license?"

He handed it, along with a copy of her birth certificate to her saying,

"All we have to do is get you signature on it tomorrow and we'll be set."

Her mind was swimming,

"Saturday? Oh Ray, yes, yes, but what about our families?"

"It will be live-fed to them and we can have another wedding when I get back. Oh, by the way. Dan and Regina are here. Your mother and father are too."

She almost swooned,

"My parents are here! How?

"Yes, they're in suite eight. Will you marry me on Saturday?"

She was in a complete tizzy but,

"Yes, Ray, you know I will."

He was beaming now,

"You've just made me the happiest man in the world. We'll see them for breakfast in the morning."

Their first dessert was bananas foster following by their special dessert.

There would probably be little or no sleep for Darlene. Her mind continued to flood with memories and dreams of their future.

~ D ~

Friday morning, the rising sun filled their suite along with fragrances from the tropical flowers outside wafting in on the morning trade winds.

She was wide awake and had been for over an hour. Too many things were happening and she was having trouble keeping up. Her parents were here, in Hawaii, how in the world did Ray accomplish it. Her daddy rarely left Hyde County. She wasn't sure he'd ever been out of the state. Now, her parents had flown all the way here. How did Ray accomplish it? How?

They joined the others in a private room at the Makana Terrace Restaurant.

She couldn't believe her eyes. Aunt Bessie was there too. That was how Ray got her parents there.

She hugged each of them and greeted Dan. He introduced her to Regina as her future sister-in-law.

She had to look at her parents twice. He was dressed in slacks and a colorful Hawaiian shirt and her mother, and Aunt Bessie, had on Capris and colorful tops.

Dan was in shorts and a collared polo, as was, Ray. Regina and Darlene were attired in colorful sundresses.

Seated around an oval table, Ray began, "I guess you're all wondering why I invited you here."

There was soft laughter and smiles around the table.

He continued,

"In case you haven't heard, there's going to be a wedding here tomorrow and you're all invited. Seriously, as you already know, we're getting married and want you to be a part of our wedding. I know it seems a bit unorthodox: short notice, location, timing, but I don't want to wait until next April. Our wedding will be very informal. We'll be married on the beach and there'll be a little reception afterwards."

"Mr. and Mrs. Snell, Aunt Bessie, I hope you're enjoying this little corner of paradise. You'll all accompany Darlene back to North Carolina on Sunday. Dan and Regina will be flying with you too. I'll return to Australia on Monday."

~ D ~

After breakfast, Darlene joined her family in their suite.

"Mama, Daddy, I can't believe you're here. How in the world did Ray ever get you on his plane?"

They looked at Aunt Bessie.

Smiling, she began.

"Ray, he insists I call him that, called me Monday and told me what he was planning. Was there any way to get her parent's there. I told him I'd try. It had been years since I'd driven back home but I was determined to try but I didn't have to. He sent a car for me.

"Talking to Martha was one thing but Owen, that was another thing. He had excuse after excuse but Evan and Billy insisted they could manage without him. By the time we got on the plane, he'd had two nerve pills and Martha had taken one. It was their first time flying and let me tell you, when they started up in the air, well, you wouldn't have believed it. Me? I was like a school girl again, ready for another adventure.

"When we arrived, Ray had a driver and hostess waiting. She took us shopping suggesting different outfits we could choose. When we walked into this suite, your father kept walking around not understanding all these rooms were just for us.

"Darlene, we're so excited for you. You make a very handsome couple and it's so apparent how much you love each other. It's sad you won't be able to have a honeymoon."

"Aunt Bessie, this week is our honeymoon and it's been just that. It's been so wonderful but anywhere with Ray is wonderful."

She walked with them out on the balcony.

"Daddy, did you like flying?"

He was grinning, "Darlie, it wasn't no fun to start with but after a while I got used to it. The pilot kept telling us where we were naming off states and cities. Most of em' I'd never heard of but some like Denver, Salt Lake City, and Los Angeles, I had. The food was real good too. Martha and Bessie especially liked the salmon. I liked the hamburger steak. Them drinks she gave us right before we landed were mighty good. I had two, your mama and Bessie had one. When we landed, I felt good. Kind of like having a good day fishing."

Her mother looked at her with a sly grin.

"Owen liked them drinks. I wish I knew what they were. I'd keep some in the house. There's days I'd feed him a couple of them."

"Mama, I'll get you some,"

Darlene was laughing now. Her daddy had gotten high. *I'll bet that was a sight.*

Her cell alerted her of a text from Ray.

Meet me on the Terrace for lunch. R

C U then. D

She spent the next hour trying to help her parents understand what the past months had been like without Ray admitting defeat on almost every adventure.

Aunt Bessie understood but she'd shared them with her in a very different setting. She would just have to bring them to the cottage and try explaining it there.

Maybe she'd take **Miss Darlene** to Hyde County and take them for a cruise. No, the cottage would be better. Maybe not the Jacuzzi on the first visit but by then, she'd be married. It was all so confusing but right then, confusion didn't matter. She was getting married tomorrow.

~ D ~

On the terrace, they hugged and kissed before he assisted in seating her.

A smile covered her face,

"Dr. Hardy, what in the world are you doing. I'm running as hard as I can, but I can't keep up."

He was beaming like a star-struck teenager.

"We're getting married tomorrow. Remember?"

"Yes sir, but playing cards with you is beyond difficult. You've got most of the cards and I'm just trying to hang on."

More serious now, he replied,

"Darlene, I don't wait any longer. I want you to be my wife now, not next April. I know I'm rushing things and I realize that I seem to be plotting a course without consulting you but. Darlene, there wasn't time. Please don't be upset. I'd hate for you to be upset on our wedding day."

"Dr. Hardy, I don't mind you taking the lead. There's no way I could have accomplished what you have. Getting my parents here is tantamount to going to Mars. Using Aunt Bessie was brilliant. I love you so much, I'm just going to try to hang on and see what's next…What is next?"

"We'll have a little party for them tonight and after the wedding tomorrow, we'll have a small reception.

"We'll have each other until nine, Sunday morning. Remember the time difference? It' will be eleven p.m. when you get back to Greenville. You can drop Aunt Bessie off and my driver will be waiting to take your parents' home.

"The pilot will drop Dan and Regina off in Raleigh. A second pilot will fly back here and take me back to Australia, Monday.

"Oh, you're not expected back at work until Tuesday. I called Mr. Fulcher. You'll need Monday to get over the jet lag. You haven't experienced that yet and it can knock you on your knees."

"Now, my wife to be, let's enjoy lunch."

After salads and wine, they parted.

~ *D* ~

She, her mother, and Aunt Bessie visited a couple of boutiques looking for her wedding dress. His words, very casual, nothing fancy,

"Remember, it's going to be on the beach."

Finally, she settled on a white knee-length dress of Tulle and Chiffon. The bodice was adorned with vintage lace and the V neckline was scalloped. The sleeves were sheer lace. There would be no veil or trailer and her shoes were white flats. It wasn't even close to what she'd dreamed of. A dream she'd carried since her twelfth birthday but never in her wildest dreams or fantasies, could she have believed that her Mr. Right would be standing beside her, saying "I do" in Hawaii. The dress no longer mattered; only him.

Something old, something new, something borrowed, something blue, would probably come from her mother and Aunt Bessie. She was ready.

Back in their suite, they were in each other's arms wishing tomorrow would come.

"Ray, I don't know how to put into words, how I feel. You swept me off my feet the moment I saw you and I haven't hit the ground since. I love you so much. I wish I had the words."

He pulled her to him, replying,

"You don't need words, I can see it in your eyes and if you look, you can see the love I have for you in mine."

The next hour dissolved during an expedition up their mountain.

~ D ~

It was time for the luau. the roasted pig, Kalva Pua'a in Hawaiian, was the honored guest. The chef explained,

"It's cooked in the ground in a tradition that goes back to the arrival of our people from Polynesia over a thousand years ago. It's a long process, 8 hours in fact. As you can see it's skin is a golden brown and eating pieces of it is a highlight for many of us. Next is Teriyaki beef and chicken, then Shoyu chicken, baked Mahi-Mahi, Lua Lua, and chicken long rice. As you can see, there's also barbecued shrimp and crab claws too.

"This is poi. The Tara root has been a Hawaiian staple forever. Poi comes from it. Yes, it's an acquired taste but you have to try it. It you don't, you can't go back home saying you've been to Hawaii. Try it, you eat it with your fingers like this."

They watched and then imitated him licking it off their fingers like it was banana pudding until they tasted it. Darlene wanted to spit it out but wouldn't. Her parents and Aunt Bessie, swallowed it fast like a pill but their faces told the real story. Dan and Regina had been baptized a few years back on Maui. They stood quietly by trying not to laugh but it was almost impossible.

The chef smiled saying they'd done well. Now they could say they'd been to Hawaii. He continued down the long line of buffet tables pointing out poke saying it was raw fish marinated in lemon juice, Lomilomi Salmon followed, then Pipi Kaula, potato salad, squid Luau, baked sweet potatoes, pineapple chunks, Papaya slices, watermelon, grapes, cantaloupe, strawberries, mangos, bananas, Lychee, apples, and coconut.

Her father found something he remembered from the plane. Mai Tai's, he was going to enjoy his evening if Martha would let him.

During the feast, authentic Hawaiian music filled the background and was punctuated with hula dancers and later, wrapping up their evening, Polynesian dancers performed the **Hawaiian War Chant**.

At ten, the party broke up, each knowing brunch would be served on the terrace at eleven.

Her father had enjoyed three Mai Tai's. When he returned to Hyde County, he'd be a teetotaler again. Most times anyway unless her mother deemed it necessary to bring out her stash to calm Owen Snell down.

~ D ~

Back in their suite, Darlene lay in the arms of her, Mr. Right, tomorrow he would be her husband. Tomorrow, she would become, Mrs. Raymond Albert Hardy. Ray would belong to her and she to him. Few, if any fairy tales could compare to the one she was living. She closed her eyes wishing for tomorrow and blinking once, it was.

They stood on the balcony welcoming their wedding day. There were tapers of champagne waiting.

They tipped their glasses and Ray began,

"To this, our wedding day, may our hearts feel this way every day, until death we part. I love you with all my heart, body, and soul."

"Ray, I don't have the words but I do have the love. To us, I'll love you forever and ever."

~ D ~

She couldn't believe her eyes. Her father was walking along the beach in shorts…shorts, he'd never worn shorts in this life and his farmer's tan attested it. He seemed relaxed and contented. Tears formed in her eyes. He, her mama, and Aunt Bessie were going to see them get married. Her whole family would. Ray had set it up with the resort to live-feed their wedding on Facebook and You Tube.

The clock was ticking.

At brunch, everyone seemed excited. Ray and Darlene were by far, the most excited.

They ordered shrimp and grits along with pineapple spears and Macadamia nuts. Everyone was offered champagne while most chose juice or coffee knowing there would be champagne after the wedding.

It was informal, no speeches except Ray chiding them about not forgetting the wedding.

~ *D* ~

At two o'clock, everyone was in place. Darlene checked her dress one last time, ***Something New.*** She held her blue ***Something Blue*** orchid bouquet in her hand along with a lacy handkerchief Aunt Bessie wanted her to carry. ***Something Old.*** A lone steel guitar began playing the ***Hawaiian Wedding Song*** and the bride, accompanied by her father, walked towards the flower covered trellis. The minister was waiting to receive them. Ray, with Dan by his side, stood waiting. He was wearing vanilla colored slacks and coat with an open collar, white Italian shirt.

He stepped forward, taking her hand. Dan remained to his right. Aunt Bessie was on the left.

The minister began,

"We are gathered together to join this man and woman in holy matrimony. Who gives this woman, Darlene Snell, to be wed?"

Her daddy cleared his throat,

"Her Mama and I Do." Then he stepped back several steps and took a seat beside her mama.

"Is there anyone present that knows of any reason why Darlene and Ray should not be joined together in holy matrimony? If so, let them speak now or forever hold their piece. There was total absolute silence.

Now, Reverend Maxie faced the couple,

"Let me charge you both to remember, that your future happiness is to be found in mutual consideration, patience, kindness, confidence, affection and undying love. Ray, it is your duty to love Darlene as yourself, provide tender undying love, and protect her from danger. Darlene, it is your duty to treat Ray with respect, support him, and create a healthy, happy home. It is the duty of each of you to find the greatest joy in the company of the other; to remember that in both interest and affection, you are to become one and undivided."

Then Reverend Maxie looking toward Jerry began,

"Will you, Ray Hardy, have Darlene Snell to be your wife? Will you love her, comfort and keep her, and forsaking all others remain true to her as long as you both shall live?"

Ray looked into Darlene's eyes,

"I will"

"Ray repeat after me, "I, Ray Hardy, take you, Darlene Snell, to be my wife, and before God and these witnesses I promise to be a faithful and true husband."

"Will you, Darlene Snell, have Ray Hardy to be your husband? Will you love him, comfort and keep him, and forsaking all others remain true to him as long as you both shall live?"

Darlene looked into Rays eyes,

"I will"

"Darlene, repeat after me, "I, Darlene Snell, take you, Ray Hardy, to be my husband, and before God and these witnesses I promise to be a faithful and true wife."

Reverend Maxie looked to Dan,

"May I have the ring please?" Dan placed it in Reverend Maxie's hand and he blessed it before handing it to Ray.

At Reverend Maxie's prompt,

"I, Ray Hardy, take you, Darlene Snell, to be my wife; slipping it on Darlene's ring finger he continued,

"With this ring I take you for my wife, and all my worldly goods I endow to you. In sickness and in health, in poverty or in wealth, 'til death do us part."

Darlene was almost trembling, ring? she'd forgotten the ring. Everything happened so fast. What now?

Reverend Maxey looked to Bessie Snell,

"May I have the ring please?" She placed it in Reverend Maxie's hand and he blessed it before handing it to Darlene, saying,

"This ring belonged to their father. Dan requested that it be used here."

Darlene could breathe again. ***Something borrowed***

Prompted by Reverend Maxie, she began,

"I, Darlene Snell, take you, Ray Hardy, to be my husband, slipping it on Ray's ring finger she continued,

"With this ring I take you for my husband, and all my worldly goods I entrust to you. In sickness and in health, in poverty or in wealth, 'til death do us part."

Reverend Maxie joined their hands together;

"For as much as Ray and Darlene have consented to join together in holy wedlock, and have witnessed the same before God and these witnesses, and thereto have pledged their faithfulness each to the other, and have pledged the same by the giving and receiving each of a ring, by the authority invested in me as a minister of the gospel according to the laws of the State of Hawaii, I pronounce that they are husband and wife together, in the name of the Father, and of the Son, and of the Holy Spirit. Those that God has joined together, let no man put asunder.

Smiling Reverend Maxie looked at Ray, saying,

"Ray, you may kiss your bride."

After a tender kiss, they walked hand-in-hand, into their new life as one.

Only You played in the background as everyone congratulated them.

~ *D* ~

Back in their suite, they had an hour before the reception.

"Ray, I still can't believe this is happening. Is this real? Am I really your wife?"

He pulled her close, replying,

"Now and forever, we are man and wife. My dream of finding you has been fulfilled. I love you, Darlene."

~ *D* ~

During the reception, which was very informal, Ray introduced Darlene to Reverend Maxie and his wife.

Darlene, this is Donald Maxie and his wife, Dee. I met him a few years back at a retreat in West Virginia. I was coming out of a crisis, and he encouraged me to put my past behind and live for the future, my future. When I left the retreat, I felt reborn and I'll always be indebted to him.

"Dee, Donald, my wife, Darlene Hardy. I like the sound of that."

There were a few toasts but mostly, the congratulations were informal and the atmosphere was relaxed as their guests mingled while enjoying hot and cold hors oeuvres and finger foods A champagne fountain was the centerpiece but a punch bowl of Mai Tai's was the most popular beverage.

The new, Mr. and Mrs., made their rounds thanking everyone for attending before beginning their, very brief, one night, honeymoon.

~ D ~

Their evening was one of love. As they truly melded into one, they climbed their mountain but this time, it was different. In God's eyes, they were one. A new life that would have to take a break until next April but they could wait; they were one.

~ D ~

Next morning, everyone one flying back to North Carolina, breakfasted on the terrace at seven a.m. They had to leave the resort at eight and be in the air by nine.

A waiting limo took them on the hour drive to the airport.

With one last kiss, Ray and Darlene parted, pledging their love forever.

"I love you, Darlene, my wife, I'll see you in April."

"I'll be waiting, my husband; I love you."

Tears were streaming down her face as she, and the others, boarded the waiting jet.

Ahead, was nine hours flying time and five hours' difference in time zones. The flight back was radically different from her flight over. This time, she was accompanied by her mama, daddy, Aunt Bessie, her new brother and sister in law, and her new-found friends, Reverend Donald and Dee Maxie.

"Alone Again!"

Dear diary, there are 263 days left until he returns.

She didn't awaken until eleven a.m. Still tired, Darlene went to the kitchen and put life into Mr. Coffee.

She'd been a dream world for a week but for now, her dream was on hold until April. The rings on her finger brought a smile across her lonely face. That part was real, they were married and would be until death took one of them away.

The coffee made, she poured a cup and walked out on the deck but quickly retreated. The temperature was already in the upper nineties and there was no trade wind or ocean breeze on Bath Creek. She was back in North Carolina and it was July.

Tossing a salad together, she escaped to the upper deck finding just a hint of a breeze but not enough to enjoy her salad. There was nothing to do but eat her lunch at the island counter. On her laptop, she brought the wedding festivities up on You Tube and for a few moments, was happy again but her joy lasted only moments. Ray was flying away from her and tomorrow, he would be half a world away.

Her only salvation was jet lag. It arrived like a bolt of lightning and she was out until eleven that evening. Feeling refreshed, she spent an hour in the Jacuzzi nibbling on boiled shrimp and dip.

By one a.m., she was asleep again. When she awakened about five a.m., she was ready to go back to work knowing Gail would be there. Someone had to be, she was lonely. She missed her man and talking to Gail would help.

~ D ~

Dear diary, there are 262 days left until he returns.

At two minutes of seven, she walked into the dining room and was immediately surrounded by everyone there. Gail had made sure that they'd seen the video and congratulations were in order. Even two of the doctor's and Mr. Fulcher offered their congratulations. Being married to a doctor apparently made all the difference.

Gail finally waded through the crowd.

"Well, Mrs. Hardy, congratulations. Let me see that ring."

Darlene held her hand out.

"It's beautiful isn't it?"

Gail was wide-eyed,

"Darlene it's positively stunning. Can I come by tonight? I want to hear all about it."

Nellie was waiting when she walked into the dietary office.

"Darlene, that was a beautiful wedding. One of these days, Hiram's going to take me to Hawaii and it's probably sooner then he thinks. It was easy to read between those lines. Hiram Wiggins probably needed to get on the ball.

Darlene was all smiles now, responding,

"Nellie, it was beautiful. Just as advertised. Unlike here, the temperatures stay in the eighties and there's always a cooling breeze. The food and beverages, I'm scared to get close to the scales. You've got to go."

Mr. Hicks found her at lunch.

"Miss Snell...ah, Mrs. Hardy, that was quite a wedding. I shared it with the Misses last night. I was stationed at Hickam Field back in the late seventies. I loved it."

~ D ~

That evening, Gail lifted her spirits knowing she probably wouldn't hear from Ray until tomorrow.

Over glasses of wine, she shared many details of her dream-like week.

"Gail, you should have seen me when he proposed. I had no idea and was caught completely by surprise but that was only the beginning. When he told me he wanted to get married last Saturday…No one can ever know the feelings that surged through my body. Oh yes, I wanted to marry him but that quick?

"From the minute he proposed, we were in the fast lane. Picking out my dress was probably the hardest part. He said to keep it informal because the wedding was on the beach. What did you think of my dress? I've always dreamed of a full-length dress with veil and trailer but marrying him was far more important that what I wore.

"Daddy did good giving me away. I was so proud of him. You ought to have seen him the day before in shorts. That was some sight. You could tell by his farmer's tan that he never wears them but there he was in Hawaii, walking on the beach in shorts.

"Gail, I forgot the ring. I know you couldn't tell it in the video but I did. When the minister mentioned rings, I almost died but thank goodness, Dan wanted to use their father's.

"It went from one surprise to another. When he told me that mama, daddy, and Aunt Bessie were there, I almost fainted. I would have never believed daddy would ever have gotten on a plane, mama either but Aunt Bessie made it happen and she said they loved it. Maybe not the first hour but they came around.

"When they served Mai Tai's, about an hour before landing, that was it for daddy. He loved them and after two, he was a happy man. Mama's got two bottles of pre-mixed ones. She says there are times when he can use a couple of drinks and now, she'll be ready."

Sleep came easily that evening, she was sure Ray would call in the morning. He did.

~ *D* ~

Dear diary, there are 261 days left until he returns.

When she awakened, her cell was ringing; it was him!

"Is this my husband?... Yes, I am, you know I am. I love you… Yes, you were right, Monday, it hit me like a hammer, I was still a little tired yesterday but now I'm fine… Everybody in the hospital apparently saw it. I got so many congratulations yesterday… I don't know, I may call Arlene and drive up for a visit… You did what?... Yes, I know I'm your wife but… Yes, sir, Dr. Hardy, thank you very much… I miss you too. I love you. Bye."

He was direct depositing a $1,000 a week into her checking account. No, she was instructed to continue using the bank cards for all expenses. What next, she was part of the *rich folks* and might as will get used to it.

~ *D* ~

Dear diary, there are 258 days left until he returns.

Saturday, she invited Gail to drive with her to Elizabeth City. She'd called Arlene earlier and they were expected late morning.

Arriving, Arlene suggested they drive to Virginia Beach and spend a few hours shopping.

"We can have lunch there. I know just the place. Ken took me there a couple of weeks ago."

Arriving at Waterman's Surfside Grill, at the waiter's suggestion, they chose the Original Waterman's Orange Crush for their beverages and for starters, they chose the crab dip and steamed shrimp.

Between starters and salads, Arlene wanted to hear all about the wedding.

"Ken and I have watched it on You Tube a hundred times. Darlie, you looked so happy and Dr. Hardy did too. Did daddy really wear shorts on the beach? I can't believe it and he drank alcohol? What's this world coming to?"

Darlene was laughing now,

"Arlie, everybody was happy but none were as happy as Ray and I. I was in the clouds until we kissed goodbye Sunday morning. I know he'll be back in April. That seems like forever but I'm counting the days.

"Daddy in shorts? That was unbelievable. I had to look twice but he really did. I don't know how many Mai Tai's he drank but he was a happy man and when he gave me away… you saw it, he was perfect."

Arlene, curious now, asked,

"Will you try to get together over the holidays?"

"Arlie, I don't know, I guess I'll just have to wait and see. His research keeps him pretty busy working six days a week and any trip will take at least a week plus the jet lag. He hasn't mentioned it. I'll just have to wait and see."

For salads, they chose the Waterman Salad of assorted greens with pecans, golden raisins, cucumbers, tomatoes, sliced red peppers, Granny Smith apples and Gorgonzola cheese, finished with balsamic vinaigrette.

"How's Ken's project coming?"

Arlene replied,

"It's dried in and the drywall's going in now. Regina wants it finished by Christmas but I don't see how. It's a huge project. I'll take you down when the drywall's finished."

She looked at Darlene,

"Are you still going to work, I know you don't have to now."

Darlene was smiling now,

"For now yes, with him gone, I'd go nuts if I didn't. We haven't talked about it but he puts money in my account every week. I don't know what I'm supposed to spend it on. All the expenses are paid for through the corporation. I guess we'll get it all figured out when he gets home. Oh, by-the-way, this is my treat, I insist."

For their main entrees, they chose the Just Seafood plate. It was a combination of jumbo shrimp, sea scallops and lump crabmeat, broiled in a lemon butter, white wine sauce and served with mashed potatoes and sautéed vegetables.

Darlene wondered,

"When are you going back to work, Arlie?"

"August third and I'm ready. Ken's gone most of the time and I'm getting a little bored. I'm totally ready."

After lunch, they visited several clothing shops. The season was winding down and there were sales galore but nothing really caught their eyes.

By five, they had dropped Arlie off and were en route back to the cottage.

It had been a nice visit but wine spritzers and the deck beckoned.

~ *D* ~

Dear diary, there are 257 days left until he returns.

She was up early and having coffee on the deck when he called.

"And how was your Sunday, my dear husband?... I'm sorry, that sounds very boring to me… Gail and I visited Arlie… No, we went to Virginia Beach and had lunch… Waterman's, the food was delicious… Arlie says the drywall's going in now… Probably not, something like that can't be rushed… Of course I want to rush you home. How can I?... That's what I was afraid of… Church with Aunt Bessie… I will, Love you too, bye."

Spending Sunday with Aunt Bessie was no longer considered boring. She wondered what she would share with her today.

~ D ~

After church, they drove to Goldsboro and enjoyed the buffet at McCalls. The fried chicken, barbecued chicken, pork barbecue, fried fish, shrimp, collards, string beans, corn, mashed potatoes, fries… the list went on and on. There was no way they could try it all but they tried choosing banana pudding for dessert.

While eating, Aunt Bessie remembered the time that Terzi and Thorton took her to Hub's Rec near Belhaven.

"Arlene, you've never seen such a rundown place in your life but it was packed with customers from all over. We had to stand in line for nearly an hour but Thorton assured us that it was worth the wait and it was. I didn't want to see the kitchen but loved Hub Keech's food. He had a way with it, especially shrimp. Arlene, I've never tasted anything like them. We went back a couple more times before they moved to Florida."

On their way back, they stopped at the mall in Greenville spending an hour in Belks before visiting two shops in Arlington Village.

~ D ~

She dropped her aunt off a little after five and drove to Hyde Country to visit her family.

She couldn't believe it, her daddy had on shorts and he must have been wearing them every day. His legs were tanning up quite a bit.

Her mama laughed, saying,

"Darlie, you ought to see him without his shirt. I guess he wants to look like those folks in Hawaii. I don't mind, ever since we got back, he acts ten years younger." She was blushing now. "He's hard to keep up with anymore."

Darlene smiled to herself thinking, *They're only in their forties, why not?*

Her mama offered leftovers for supper saying,

"Darlie, you know we always have a big dinner on Sunday. She remembered but hungry, she wasn't. McCalls was still with her.

She shared her visit with Arlene saying she was going back to work on August third.

"She's getting bored at home with Ken being gone so much."

She left a little after ten knowing she'd be ready for the Jacuzzi and a glass of wine when she got home.

~ D ~

Dear diary, there are 242 days left until he returns.

The next couple of weeks drifted by. She'd almost gotten used to being alone again. Not completely, she missed Ray so much.

It was Saturday again. Her cell alerted her to a call from Dale.

"Dale, anything wrong?... Oh, good. Come on by, I'd love to have some company... Okay, bye."

~ *D* ~

When they arrived, she knew something wasn't quite right. Her intuition was right.

"Darlie, we've got a problem. Can we talk to you about it? We can't go to our parents."

She was pretty sure she knew.

"Go ahead, Dale. What's wrong?"

He wouldn't look at her but uttered,

"Sadie's pregnant."

"How long?

"Five weeks."

She was treading softly now.

"What do you plan to do about it?"

She did not want to hear, abortion, no way.

He was holding Sadie's hand now.

"We want our baby but Darlie, there ain't no way we can get married. We don't have anywhere to stay and not a whole lot of money. What are we going to do?"

"First things first. There's always somewhere to stay. There's nobody in our old room. Evan and Billy have their own rooms. You need to get married now and fess up to your parents. They'll be hurt some but you'll be doing the right thing and they'll love you for it. That plus, you're going to give them a grandchild.

She was smiling now.

"Your preacher or mine?"

Dale was uneasy again,

"Darlie, you know we ain't got one. Sadie's family goes to church but ours don't.

Darlene looked at Sadie.

"Your preacher or mine?"

Sadie, her eyes wet with tears, replied.

"Mine, we'll go talk to him tomorrow when Dale gets done with the pots. I'll be back from Nags Head by then"

Darlene's fears were lifted; they were going to do the right thing.

"Good we've got some celebrating to do. There's going to be another wedding."

~ *D* ~

Later that evening, they parted ways. Darlene felt for them but there wasn't anything she could do. She thought about calling her parents but chose not to. It was up to Dale and Sadie to pop the news. Her family thought a lot of Sadie and a grandchild, that would be something special for everybody.

~ D ~

Dear diary, there are 235 days left until he returns.

The following Saturday, she drove to Hyde Country and took her family to the wedding at Soundview Church of Christ in Stumpy Point. Like hers, it was a small wedding with only the families present.

After the wedding, she handed Dale an envelope with ten one-hundred dollar bills inside.

"Congratulations big brother, I love ya'll."

There was no honeymoon, they moved into Darlene and Arlene's old room. It was bigger than Dales. Life would be good. Sadie would be a big help to Martha and she welcomed her like a daughter.

~ D ~

Dear diary, there are 132 days left until he returns.

August, September, and October, slipped quietly by. Darlene had adjusted with the help of Aunt Bessie and Gail and more importantly, with the almost daily contacts via cell, voice and texts, plus Facebook, and emails from Ray; she was holding it together. The family was going to gather downhome for Thanksgiving and Darlene was so ready to see them all together again.

Thanksgiving day, she picked up a cooked ham, carrot cake, pumpkin and sweet potato pie from Sam's before stopping by Aunt Bessie's. They arrived downhome a little after eleven. Everyone was there. Mama, Daddy, Arlene and Ken, Dale and Sadie, Evan and his girlfriend, Nance, and Billy.

The table was set and delicious aromas of roasted turkey, oyster dressing, collards, mashed potatoes, giblet gravy, string beans, candied yams, cranberry sauce, crackling cornbread, and biscuits filled the house. Evan introduced Darlene and Aunt Bessie to Nance saying they were hanging together.

With all the sumptuous food on the table, her daddy yielded to Ken for the blessing.

"Heavenly Father, on this day of thanksgiving, we ask your blessings on our family, our friends, our homes, our health – and on the food we are about to receive. We thank you for this time together and the many gifts you have given us. Help us to remember in this time of bounty those less fortunate than ourselves. May your love encircle us all that we may share in your glory. Amen."

Darlene thought to herself, *Arlie is so lucky to have Ken. He's perfect for her. From what I can see and hear of Sadie, She's a blessing for Dale and our family too.*

If there was one thing her daddy could do, it was carving a turkey and he was doing a magnificent job on that. The light and dark slices were passed around per each one's request. The whole meal was a bountiful blessing and it was evident that everyone was going to take full advantage of it.

Between bites, Darlene asked Ken about Dan's project.

"Darlie, we're doing cabinet work now. There's so much of it on every level; I have three crews doing only that and it will still be after new year's before they're done. I'm hoping to finish it up in February. Next time you're up, I'll take you on a tour."

"I'm looking forward to seeing it, Ken, maybe mid-December."

Arlene asked about Ray,

"When have you heard from Ray?"

"This morning, we talk, or text every day. He posts pics on Facebook at least twice a week."

Arlene replied, asking,

"How many days left? I know you are keeping count."

"One hundred, thirty-two. I mark them off each day."

After dessert that no one needed, the men went into the living room and the women into the kitchen.

Darlene worked beside Sadie at the sink and it gave her a chance to ask how things were going?"

Sadie glanced at her with a smile.

"It couldn't be better, they accepted me with open arms. I'm so blessed."

"When are you due?"

"March 25th." I hope it's a couple of weeks late but it doesn't matter, everybody already knows."

"Sadie, Dale loves you, we love you. That's all that matters."

"Boy or girl?"

She was beaming now, "Boy, he's going to be, Dale Jr."

It didn't take long before all the food was put up and the dishes done.

Darlene and Aunt Bessie left at eight. She had chosen to work on Friday so that Nellie could be with her family. It wouldn't be nearly as lonely working.

~ *D* ~

Dear diary, there are 129 days left until he returns.

Sunday, after church, Darlene took Aunt Bessie to the Three Steers Restaurant in Greenville knowing that she was probably in for another good story, she was.

Woody and Janie Smith had one of the best salad bars in town and that was exactly what Aunt Bessie wanted. The restaurant was crowded but after a fifteen-minute wait, they were seated in the back dining room.

After making their salads, Aunt Bessie sailed into the time Terzi and Thorton took her to "The Switch" in Williamston.

"This was back before the Town and Country Restaurant opened their lounge and the Holiday Inn hadn't been built yet. Thorton said that back during the second world war, it was a hot spot. They called it The Chitlin Switch back then probably because it was beside a meat packing company.

"He said that the lady that owned and operated it was the prettiest thing in Martin County in her younger days. Anyway, it was another one of those brown bagging clubs but Darlene, they put out some mighty fine food. The steak I had was delicious.

"They danced there too but I just watched them. There wasn't any way for trouble to start, the sheriff was there. Miss Effie Sparrow ran a tight ship."

After lunch, she took Aunt Bessie home and spent the afternoon looking at pics Ray had posted and messaging him about Thanksgiving and how nice it was to see the family together.

~ D ~

Dear diary, there are 115 days left until he returns.

Two weeks passed and she, and Gail, drove up to Arlene's. They were going to tour Dan and Regina's house.

The house was huge. The first level contained three-garages, storage, and a shower. The main level contained a kitchen large enough to prepare for fifty people.

In the kitchen, all the appliances were either Wolf or Sub-Zero. There were two cooking centers, both with copper hoods, forty feet of counter space containing a vegetable prep area with a huge "farm" sink; a dishwashing area including a 2 compartment sink, dishwasher, disposer, and compactor. The separate refrigerator and freezer were huge and built into the wall.

The twenty-foot island contained the second cooking center with a 2" solid hard rock Maple cutting surface extending the entire length with sinks, under counter refrigeration and tons of rollout cabinets. Overhead, a twenty-foot wrought iron pot and utensil rack dominated the view. A hall opened beyond the freezer with a twelve-by-twelve pantry on the left. The specs indicated it had commercial four tier, twenty-four-inch-deep, seventy-six-inch-high epoxy coated shelving throughout. Beyond it, an eight-by-twelve wine cellar including a Sub-Zero 27" wine cooler with a 132 bottle capacity.

The other side of the hall opened into a laundry, next it opened into another room labeled banquet service and linens. Out in the hall on the left, was a built-in desk with cabinets and beyond was a complete bar that included a Perlick draft beer tower, bar sink, cocktail unit, blender station, ice machine and Perlick back bar equipment, including under counter refrigeration. Above, extending the entire length were mirrored glass and bottle storage displays. The bar itself was sixteen feet long with pleated and rolled black leather on the front and arm rest. The top was Italian marble. Above the soffit dropped down 24" from the ten-foot ceiling and its facing was covered with the same pleated and rolled leather. Mounted below were stemware display racks highlighted by recessed pot lights. The eight barstools were dark oak with swivel bases; the seats and backs were tufted red leather. He related that Regina planned to entertain often and the kitchen and bar were designed to support her.

There was a huge dining space that could readily accommodate fifty people, and the living area was enormous. Ken explained that Regina wanted four seating groups. The largest in front of the fireplace, centered between built-in bookcases and one that faced the ceiling to floor windows offering a view of the sound and two smaller ones separated by a planter.

She had retained a firm from Norfolk to do all the planters and they would also be doing the extensive landscaping outside.

Two elevators were located on opposite sides of the house. One led to the three lower levels and the other to all four levels. The fourth level was restricted.

The third level had three bedrooms, each with a full bath, there was an exercise room and a game room. A seating area with a glass wall looking out into the sound dominated the end of the corridor.

"See, I told you it was huge."

Darlene replied,

"Yes, Regina's really going to enjoy entertaining here."

Alene looked at her sister asking,

"Darlie, when are you going to start on yours?"

Darlene laughed while replying,

"Arlie, I have no clue. I'm not doing anything until Ray is back in my arms. I don't even know where we're going to live yet."

~ D ~

Arlene was grinning now,

"You haven't seen the master suite yet. You won't believe it."

The restricted fourth level contained the master suite with a very large master bath, complete with Jacuzzi, refrigerator, and wine cooler. Cedar lined walk-in closets were on one side of the alcove leading in. One the opposite side a dressing area comprised a third of the wall and cabinets and drawers populated the rest of the wall.

~ D ~

Back down on the main level, Arlie and Ken led them through huge French doors that opened into the sunroom with a twelve-twenty-foot pool.

Doors also led from the main area and sunroom onto a massive deck with steps leading to the boat slip and patio that contained a covered cooking center complete with a built-in 60" Crown Verity gas and an oven, deep-fat fryer, over/under refrigerator-freezer and under counter wine cooler.

The boat slip could easily moor a sixty-foot Hatteras. Just behind it was the helipad. It had been finished early in the project offering the opportunity for Dan and Regina to check on the project often which, Regina did often.

~ *D* ~

Dear diary, there are 102 days left until he returns.

Sunday morning about ten, a special delivery of roses arrived. She couldn't believe they delivered all the way to Bath on Sunday. The card simple said, *For my Love, Ray*

They arrived every day until Christmas. On Christmas day, three dozen arrived along with a special Fed-ex delivery. It was a beautiful diamond necklace, matching bracelet, and earrings.

For My Wife on Christmas Day. I love You. Ray.

Tears streamed down her face. She missed him so much. All she could do was count the days. There would be no celebration until he returned. She'd called Regina asking what to do about a Christmas present. She consoled her saying to just tell him how much you love and miss him. He knows your hands are tied.

~ *D* ~

Dear Diary, it's 95 days until he returns

She knew the holidays would be lonely but they were even more lonesome than she could have ever imagined.

He called at the stroke of midnight on New Year's Eve telling her how much he loved and missed her.

Darling, it's less than a hundred days now. We'll never be apart again, I promise. That's my new year's resolution to you.

She did as he asked and opened a bottle of Champagne pouring two tapers. *Now darling, walk out on the deck and take a sip from your glass. Then*

slowly pour mine into Bath Creek. Put both tapers in a special place and when I get home, we'll drink out of each other's glass.

She worked New Year's Day and invited Aunt Bessie over for dinner that evening. Somehow, someway, the days had to pass.

Dear diary, there are only 60 days left until he returns.

January became February and Valentine's was only weeks away. She'd just gone to bed when her cell alerted her to a call from Ray's brother, Dan. It couldn't be good news. He rarely ever, almost never, called.

"Dan, what's wrong?... Oh lord, Dan, tell me you're joking." She knew he wasn't "What's being done, who's searching for him?... Please call if you hear anything… No, I'll be all right. Please pray, Dan, please."

It couldn't be happening but it was. A bush pilot had picked Ray up at the little airport near the research compound to fly him to Alice Springs. They never arrived. There were no cell towers in the outback and

communications were sketchy at best. That's all anyone knew at the moment. Search planes had been dispatched but as of yet, nothing. The small plane wasn't equipped with transponders or other ID devices. Bush pilots flew by the seat of their pants.

Ray had mentioned more than once about his desire to see the outback. He wanted to visit Alice Springs and Ayers Rock before he left and danger never entered his mind.

~ D ~

Dear diary, there are only 59 days left until he returns...If he returns?

All Darlene could do was pray. Friday, she was like a walking zombie. Gail finally squeezed the story out of her over lunch and insisted they go to the cottage notifying Nellie of the situation saying that they were leaving.

"I don't know when she's coming back, I'll email or text you."

Gail following her to the cottage and poured a very stiff drink as soon as they arrived. They both had one and then another. The hours ticked slowly by with no word. That was the hardest part. He was 12,000 miles away, lost and probably injured, maybe worst, and she had no way of finding out. Gail mixed a third drink for Darlene and began putting together a pot of soup. She knew Darlene didn't eat lunch and probably no breakfast either.

By six p.m., she'd gotten a little soup into her before calling Arlene.

Can you stay with her tonight? I'll drive down early in the morning.

Gail replied,

"You know I will."

The Prozac, combined with copious amounts of Jack Daniels's Black Label, put a restless, and very despondent, Darlene, to sleep and she slept undisturbed until seven the next morning.

Gail would not leave her side. She drifted in and out sleep, in the recliner, throughout the night only leaving her side about six a.m. to make coffee.

~ *D* ~

Dear diary, there are only 58 days left until he returns...If he returns?

The coffee was almost ready when Darlene walked, very groggy, out of the elevator asking,

"What in the world did I drink last night. I'm going to die."

Gail smiled, replying,

"No more than it took to put you asleep and it took a lot. Here, try this Bloody Mary, the coffee's ready too."

She sipped the coffee then took swallows of the Bloody Mary before saying,

"Please tell me yesterday was a bad dream."

Gail could only reply,

"No Darlene, it really happened but until we know different, we have to believe that Dr. Hardy's isn't hurt. I don't know anything about flying but from what I've seen on TV, those outback pilots are very tough men. We just have to trust in God that they're fine; they just have to be rescued."

Darlene's cell interrupted their conversation. It was Dan.

"Dan, have they found him?... She listened quietly and the minutes ticked by.

"That's all I can do, Dan. Please call when you hear anything. Thank you. Bye."

She took several sips of coffee before beginning,

"They haven't found him yet. The, what did he call them, The Air Guard, searched all day. It's night there now. The bush pilots are searching too. They are concentrating their search in the White Mountains National Park. Dan says it's dominated with rugged and heavily forested areas. It will just take time before Ray can be found. Oh God, give me the strength and protect my husband."

Arlene arrived a little after eight bringing Aunt Bessie with her. Both had overnight bags. It was just the right potion Darlene needed.

Aunt Bessie and Gail prepared breakfast while listening to Darlene explain to Arlene all she knew, which sadly, wasn't very much.

"Arlie, Dan says they probably went down in a huge national forest and from the way he described it. Spotting the wreckage from the air will be difficult at best. It could take days, even weeks. Arlie, what am I going to do."

Tears were streaming down her face.

Arlene put her arms around her twin trying to soothe her.

"Remember when I was in the coma and you wondered if I was going to make it? God answered your prayers then; He will now. We just have to put our trust in Him."

After a breakfast of scrambled eggs, bacon, grits, toast, juice and coffee. They grouped around Darlene by the fireplace Each tried in their own way to cheer Darlene. She knew what they were doing and tried, very hard, to smile but it was hardest thing she'd ever been confronted with.

By noon, she was a nervous wreck. She took a Prozac but refused anything else. If the call came in, she wanted to receive it.

That evening, Gail drove to Washington for pizza. She returned with a twelve-inch Philly cheese steak pizza and a Cali chicken bacon ranch pizza. She also had bread sticks and chocolate lava crunch cakes.

Darlene's spirits were lifted just enjoying the aroma when Gail unboxed their dinner. Darlene, Arlene, and Gail had pitchers of frosty Ultra Lights while Aunt Betty enjoyed glasses of the Chardonnay.

After their pizza feast, they sat around the fireplace listening first to stories about how Washington and Beaufort County used to be. Darlene, now very relaxed, wondered if Aunt Betty had imbibed enough wine to

share one of her real-life stories. No, she didn't but there were plenty others she was willing to share.

"Girls, you're not going to believe this but back in the sixties, I think it was 1961, the local TV station, WITN, put their new tower to work. It was the tallest one in North Carolina.

"They called it, **The High and Mighty**. Thorton took Terzi and me down there, it was near Grifton, and we rode the elevator to the top. When we got to the top, I was shaking all over.

"I looked down once and almost fainted. The cars didn't look an inch long. It was quite an experience back then. They say the new tower is two-thousand feet high. It sure looks like it is."

Her story lightened the atmosphere and Darlene seemed less nervous but she still hurt and it was evident to everyone.

Dear diary, there are only 57 days left until he returns...If he returns?

Sunday morning, Darlene was up at five a.m. She switched the intercom on hearing someone in the kitchen. After showering, she dressed and took the elevator to the main level.

Aunt Bessie was sitting at the island counter, sipping on a cup of coffee. She looked up and said.

"Darlie, the coffee's made. I'll fix you a cup. Did you sleep any at all?"

Thanking her for the cup, she replied.

"Somebody slipped my a "mickey. I don't' think I turned over."

Hoping, she had to ask,

"Did I miss anything."

Aunt Bessie replied,

No, honey, we would have awakened you, maybe today."

Asked about church, Darlene replied,

"I know I should but no, I'm going to stay here until he calls."

~ *D* ~

Dear diary, there are only 54 days left until he returns...If he returns?

Monday, and Tuesday slipped by and not a word. Wednesday morning a few minutes after nine, Dan called. Hoping against hope, Darlene answered,

"Dan, please tell me he's been found... I'm trying to be patient but it's hard. The hardest thing I've ever done... No, but thank you. Aunt Bessie and Arlene are still here. Gail had to go to work. She'll be back tonight. Should I go to Australia or would that just create problems?... I understand but, Dan, I have to do something. I'll go crazy not knowing what's going on or if he needs me... Thank you, Dan, please keep me in the loop. I have to know."

They were all huddled around her.

"Dan says that the wreckage hasn't been located yet. They now have two helicopters searching the gorges and ravines. He says they can do a much more thorough search and land if they find anything. Aborigines are searching the park on foot. They know every inch of it. He says that if the plane's there, they'll find it and if it isn't the search will be expanded.

"I want to go to Australia but he advises against it. He says he may send Regina and I to Hawaii next week if Ray hasn't been found by then. When they find him, if he needs me, I'll only be nine hours away. That's some comfort but not a lot, right now, it's all I've got except you. God bless you both for being with me. Lord knows how much I need you."

~ D ~

Dear diary, there are only 50 days left until he returns...If he returns?

Valentine's fell on Sunday. She wanted to be alone for a few hours so Aunt Bessie, Arlene, and Gail, went to church leaving her surrounded by the framed pics of Ray and her.

She also brought up the pics taken in Hawaii and their wedding. Tears of sadness, mixed with tears of joy, streamed down her face as she talked to the pictures.

Ray, my darling Valentine. You'll never know how much I love you. I don't have the words but look into my heart. You are my one and only love.

I Don't know why this happened but I do know that it only makes my love for you stronger. Happy Valentine's, darling. I love you with all my heart.

Somehow, she felt better, maybe putting her feelings into thoughts was a magic elixir.

She ringing cell brought her back down to earth. It was Dan.

"Dan, do you have good news?... They can't be far, can they… Yes, I'll be there at two. Pray for him, Dan. I am."

The badly damaged plane had been found in a deep, heavily forested gorge but neither Ray or the pilot were there. That was probably a good thing. If they walked away, their injuries couldn't be too bad.

Ray wanted her to meet Regina at the airport at two. They'd fly to Hawaii. By then, maybe Ray would have been found.

She texted Arlene and Gail saying she would be in touch. *Pray for us.*

She hurriedly called Aunt Bessie and quickly packed.

~ *D* ~

"The Plane's Been Found."

He can't be that far away!

They arrived in Honolulu at six p.m. local time and were taken to the Royal Hawaiian.

Dan called Regina about an hour later. Nothing yet but the aborigines were expert trackers and were following what must be their trail. He'd call tomorrow unless he heard something before.

Regina suggested they walk on the beach.

"Sitting in here will drive both of us crazy."

There was a wedding near the hotel so they walked down and watched. Darlene, misty eyed, watched the ceremony and almost lost it when the couple kissed.

Regina took her by the hand and led her to the beach bar in front of their hotel ordering Jack Black's with a splash of water. On the second round, Darlene's nerves eased giving them a chance to talk. Yes, they'd talked on the plane but Darlene was so guarded but now she began to open up a bit and Regina did too.

"Dan has never been quite as adventurous as Ray. He's more of a number cruncher but, like Ray, if they see a property they like, he can be crazy too. For the most part, we get along fine. I'm from Asheville. Friends introduced us at a party in Raleigh. I don't know, we just seemed to know immediately that we belonged together. I knew nothing about his background. All he really told me was that he and his brother had a business in Cary.

"When I found out how rich he was, I panicked and broke off the relationship. I wasn't a gold digger and was sure I wouldn't fit in. If their parents had been still alive, I probably wouldn't have fitted into their social structure.

"My parents are far from rich. My father's a banker and has done quite well but Dan and Ray's entrepreneurial instincts puts him in the basement.

"I tried to warn Dan that I wasn't close to his social status but he let me know, very quickly, that there was no social ladder in his life. His, and Ray's friends, were *new money.* He admitted his parents were very well off but he and Ray didn't travel in their circles. They formed their own.

"We have a great circle of friends now and we're comfortable with all of them. None have any business interests in Prime Properties.

"Darlene, he went after me the same way he did properties. I didn't stand a chance. Whenever I faltered, or panicked, he picked me up and ran. It was hopeless, I was his. Now, I'm glad I am. We have two wonderful children. Dana is eleven now. She's such a loving and kind child. Ricky is eight. They attend a private school and are excelling there. We couldn't be more proud."

"Now, you know my story. How did Ray hook you? I'm sure I can guess."

Darlene laughed as she began.

"He swept me off my feet before I could even catch my breath. He invited me out on Valentines but my twin sister was getting married that afternoon. He invited himself, showed up, met my family and didn't run. I was sure he would.

"After dinner, he took me home. I was already in love, I thought, until he kissed me goodnight. Then I knew what love really was. I had no idea about how rich he was.

"Doctors usually drove very nice cars so I didn't have a clue. He told me he'd rented a little cottage near Bath. It turned out to be the biggest house I'd ever seen.

"When Arlene got sick and was in a coma, he flew me to Miami and that's when I realized that I was in over my head but it was too late. I would have followed him to the end of the earth. My feet haven't touched the ground since."

That evening, they dined at Dano's Steak and Seafood in the Ala Moana Shopping Center across from the Royal Hawaiian.

After ordering Blue Hawaiians, Regina asked if Ken had taken her on a tour of the house near Duck?

Darlene responded,

"Yes, last week. Regina, it's beautiful. I know you'll enjoy it. The kitchen is unbelievable. You must really enjoy cooking and entertaining."

Regina, beaming now, replied,

"Yes, I really do. I guess the year I spent working in the kitchen at the Angus Barn started it all. Back then, before I met Dan, my dream was to operate a restaurant.

"Mother and Father dined out often, she didn't really like to cook but could hold her own.

"There are several great restaurants in Ashville. My favorite was the Admiral on Haywood Road. Their presentations blew me away. They didn't just place a plate of food in front of you, they presented it.

"My sophomore year, I managed to get into the kitchen. My father knew Thad Eure, that was the only way I ever got in.

I was a gofer but that was fine. I learned so much and as soon as the chef realized I was there to learn. He opened door after door.

"When I left at the beginning of my junior year, I was hooked for life. I have a large kitchen in our home and we entertain often allowing me to enjoy my hobby.

"I've attended dozens of mini-cooking schools both in the states and abroad. When Dan goes out of the country, I usually accompany him and wherever we go, I try, by hook or crook, to get into as many restaurant kitchen's as I can."

After ordering salads, she continued,

"Now, I spend my days taking care of my responsibilities first, then I cook. Dan wants me to write a cookbook. I've given it some thought and probably will, why not? I don't have a theme yet, but I'm working on it."

When their salads arrived, they ordered the 8 oz. filet Mignon's, med-rare, along with the shrimp Newberg. For sides, they chose the sautéed Maui onions and grilled asparagus.

"Darlene, are you happy with what you're doing or do you have other aspirations?"

Regina was trying very hard to keep Darlene's mind off of the situation and to some extent, it was working.

"Regina, I don't know. Before I met Ray, my life was pretty much laid out in front of me. Now, I don't know. I don't know what Ray wants or what he expects of me.

"Now he's my number one priority. I want so much for him to be proud of me. The last thing I ever want is for him to be ashamed of something I've done or didn't do. I could never live with that. We haven't talked about it. I hope and pray we can soon. Oh, Regina, what am I going to do?"

She wondered if she should mention wanting to open a restaurant. No, now wasn't the time.

Regina took her hand, replying,

"You'll be fine. We just have to take this one day at the time."

Back in the suite, Regina took a call from Dan while Darlene was out on the balcony.

She was remembering a year ago on Valentines. It was the happiest day of her life.

Arlene had married the man of her dreams and she was having dinner with her, Mr. Right. Little did she know that evening, what would transpire over the next twelve months. Her dream had come true and she'd married Ray.

The whole year had been like living a dream. A dream that was far too fantastic for her to even ascribe to. Even in wishes and dreams, there normally were limitations especially when she had no clue about places and things she knew nothing about.

Now, a year later, on Valentine's day, she was in Hawaii not really knowing if she'd ever see the man of her dreams, her husband, alive again.

"Dan called, no they haven't found them yet but it appears that one of them is trying to leave clues. Someone is leaving torn pieces of paper behind. It's only a matter of time now."

~ D ~

Dear diary, there are only 49 days left until he returns...when he returns?

Darlene was up before dawn walking along the beach. All she seemed to be able to do was cry and pray. *Oh God, please keep Dan safe. I love him so much. Our life together is just beginning. Don't let it end now. Grant us some time together before you take one of us. Please God, please!*

Back in the suite, she joined Regina having coffee and a pastry. In Australia, it would be night and she was sure the search would not continue until dawn. It was going to be another long day.

"Did you hear from Dan?" She wished she hadn't asked but it was too late now. If Regina had good news, she would have already shared it.

"He called a few minutes ago. They found another scrap of paper. The trails leading deeper and deeper into a gorge. When they find them, Dan's afraid they won't be able to air vac them out. They'll find and bring them out, Darlene. We just have to be strong and wait. That's the hardest part."

"Why can't we go to Australia now? At least we'll be close by when they find them."

"Dan says they may send Ray directly to the states. If they do, it will be on the company's jet and they'll pick us up on the way. He says if we're there, They'll have to backtrack to get us. I know you're hurting but we need to leave the decisions in his hands."

Darlene knew she was right. Her heart was asking the questions, not her mind.

~ D ~

Dear diary, there are only 48 days left until he returns...when he returns?

They spent another day in paradise not appreciating a minute of it. Darlene's mind was in Australia and Regina's was trying her best to keep her stable. It was becoming more and more difficult with each passing hour.

For lunch, they had conch burgers, fries and Mai Tai's at Don's Crab Shack. On any other occasion, it would have been an enjoyable experience.

The clock seemed to move slower and slower. Before dinner, Darlene called Arlene, Aunt Bessie and Gail. She didn't have any news to share but needed to hear familiar voices.

Her conversation with Arlene put a sparkle in her eyes and lifted her spirits up higher than they'd been in days.

"You're what?... Arlie, that's wonderful…when?... August fifteen, wow! Do you know yet?... A little girl, Arlie, I'm so happy for you and Ken… No, they're following a trail but nothing yet. I guess that means the injuries are minimum. I hope so anyway. Regina and I are counting the hours… Okay, I love you too… I will, bye."

Arlene was pregnant. If she could have only gotten pregnant. She would, at least, have his baby but she didn't, if it was the Lord's will, she would.

That evening, Regina suggested Mori's.

"We can walk there. I met the chef a few years ago on one of our island hops. The food's great and you'll love the atmosphere."

When they were seated, Regina suggested that she order for them. There are some entree's I want you to try."

Looking at the menu, Darlene was more to ready for her to choose. Like most of the places she'd been with Ray, she was lost. They started with Mai Tai's and "King & I" Rolls. She explained that it was soft shell crab, Thai style Hamachi tartar, garlic cream cheese

Darlene liked the roll. If it contained soft shell crab, she couldn't taste it. The texture was there but there was no way it could have come out of Pamlico Sound.

Their soup course followed. Regina ordered Moloka'i Sweet Potato Bisque with coconut milk, Kaffir-lime mango and goat cheese crème fraiche.

"I served this last Christmas and got rave reviews. Let me know what you think."

If she was trying to keep Darlene's mind occupied, she was doing an excellent job. So far, the food was delicious although she had no clue what some of the ingredients were.

The wine she ordered was bit on the tart side. Actually, it had a woody taste. It seemed to go well with the seafood. The red would have probably been too sweet.

For their main course, Regina ordered the black peppered Kampachi served with gingered risotto, oxtail & local cremini, soy mirin, and a spicy truffle palm salad.

It was delicious as were all the entrée's.

"What do you think? I'm considering this for our Memorial Day celebration. I hope we're in moved in by then. Ken say's we're on schedule. If that's the case. We'll be in by late April."

After a cup of Kona coffee, their dining experience was over. Regina had done an excellent job keeping Darlene's worried mind corralled but the rest of the evening was ahead of them.

Regina's cell interrupted their conversation. It was Dan. Although she could only her one side of the conversation, she knew Ray had been found.

Regina looked at her saying,

"He'd been found; it will take at least day to get them to a point where they can land a helicopter. Dan says they were in a cave. Responders had to parachute in. He's safe now. We'll be there tomorrow.

"Would you like a drink, I would?"

For the first time since Darlene received the dreaded news, she began to relax. Not completely. That would only happen when she saw Ray and knew he was going to be alright.

It had been a nightmare but maybe in a couple of days, it would be over and she's have her man back in her arms.

"We're in Australia now"

I'm close to Ray!

Dear diary, there are only 48 days until he returns...He's been found!

The private jet picked them up at seven a.m. HST. It would be nine hours before they reached Brisbane. They would arrive at noon AEST time on Tuesday.

Darlene's excitement was off the charts. He was hurting but he was safe. Her prayers had been answered.

It didn't matter how long it would take to make him whole again. She had her entire life to wait. She texted Arlene and Gail. *Please let everyone know he's safe.*

They arrived at BNE in Brisbane and were met by a waiting driver. He took them to the Stamford Plaza Brisbane. They were led to their suite on the top floor. The suite was spacious, well appointed, and the view was stupendous.

After calling the hospital and being told not to visit until tomorrow.

"He's still being processed and there will be tests until late in the night"

They lunched at the Brasserie on the River enjoying their buffet.

That afternoon, they explored downtown Brisbane and visited the MacArthur Museum finding it very interesting. Darlene remarked,

"Grandpa Snell fought under General MacArthur in the Pacific. He got a purple heart on Guadalcanal."

Their tour helped to pass the time away. Darlene's nerves were almost stretched to their limits. Being so close but not being allowed to see him was almost too much.

She knew the rules. The doctors were there for a reason and appeasing the patient's family was not on the top of their list. She'd have to wait it out. After all, she hadn't seen him since Hawaii. Another day wouldn't be the end of the world.

~ D ~

That evening, Regina suggested they have dinner at George's Paragon Seafood Restaurant.

"It's Greek and looks like a great restaurant. We'll get to see a little of Brisbane's nightlife.

She made reservations for seven p.m. Just after four so they had wine spritzers with brie cheese and wafers. It was Darlene's first experience tasting brie and she really liked it. The woody Chardonnay complimented the cheese. She could add another cheese to her growing repertoire.

Arriving at the restaurant, they were seated with a view of Eagle Pier.

Regina suggested the 2012 Heytesbury from Vasse Felix in Margaret River Chardonnay.

"It's got a great flavor. I think you'll like it."

It was different from what she'd expected but she liked the mineral taste?

For starters, Regina suggested the Greek salad with a vinaigrette dressing.

Now on their second glass of wine, Darlene was more relaxed but wondered what Regina would suggest for their main course.

She'd never had a Greek anything except the time she and Arlie drove to Kinston and ate at the Olympian Restaurant. One of the worker's at Vidant Health raved on and on about the food. They tried the Gyro's. They were okay but not for them. It was another experience in life but was no longer on either of their bucket lists.

"What's going through your mind? I'm not trying to pry. I've never been away from Dan more than a week and it was hard. You, it's been months. How have you survived?"

Darlene smiled replying.

"Regina, It's the hardest thing I've ever done. At first. I cried myself to sleep every night but after a few weeks, I knew that had to change. I would have been a basket case.

"I was very lucky. One of my classmates works at the hospital. We really enjoy each other's company and she's beyond supportive.

"Gail and Aunt Bessie have been by my side almost daily. Arlie checks on me too. Without their support, I could not have made it.

"Unlike you, I don't really have any diversified interests. I hope to have when our lives settle down. I thought about going back to school. Ray wants me to take bookkeeping and management courses. I'm sure I'll try to do what he wants me to."

For their main course, Regina suggested the seafood crepes with prawns, scallops, calamari, mussels and barramundi.

"It's a French dish with béchamel sauce. It's no more than a white sauce with nutmeg. I tried it last year at one of my luncheons and, Darlene, it was a hit."

Regina was taking her all over the globe. Why not?

"Yes, let's try that."

Regina's cell alerted her to a call from Dan.

"Dan, where are you?... Oh, we'll see you back at the hotel… Probably an hour, we are just ordering our main course… Love you too."

"She smiled saying,

"Dan's at the airport. He'll be at the hotel when we get back."

Darlene enjoyed the crepes. It was a first for her but she'd probably try them again, especially those presented as desserts. Regina made them sound so delicious and they were.

~D~

When they arrived back at the suite, they found Dan on the balcony enjoying the evening view of Brisbane.

He welcomed Regina with a kiss and gave Darlene a hug.

"Ladies, how was dinner?

Regina replied,

"It was nice. We had a Greek salad and the seafood crepes. Darlene really liked the crepes and the wine. It was a Margaret River Chardonnay."

He replied, Sounds like a nice evening.

"Let's get a good night's rest. Tomorrow will probably be a long one. Depending on how the tests went today, they may release Ray tomorrow and we can take him back to the states.

"Remember, it depends on the tests and if Ray's up to the trip. He may need a few days to recover from his experience. He had what must have been, a very harrowing experience."

He laughed before continuing, "

My little brother might not want seconds on this one."

Darlene was sure she didn't want him to go back again. She wanted him back home, wherever that might be. She didn't care as long as she was with him.

"Dan, if they release him, where will you take him?"

"Darlene, that's really up to the trauma team. They'll know his needs and make the recommendations. I brought Dr. Ingrid Cox with me. She's heads the trauma department at Duke. She's conferring with the trauma team now. Hopefully they'll release Ray to her. We want him as close by as possible."

"In the morning, we'll have breakfast here and Dr. Cox will join us."

"Darlene, rest well. We'll see you in the morning. Breakfast at eight good for you? I'll have coffee, juice, and pastries sent up about six."

She thanked him knowing she'd probably be waiting when the coffee arrived. She thanked Regina for her support and Dan. He was definitely the captain of their ship.

"Dan, I can never thank you enough."

Dan smiled,

"Darlene, you don't have to thank us, we're family. Good night."

Darlene was asleep as soon as her head hit the pillow. Her body clock was so confused but it didn't matter. Physically and mentally, she was worn out. The whole experience was exacting a heavy toll.

~ D ~

Dear diary, there are only 47 days until he returns... but! I'll see him today!

The sun was up before Darlene, but barely. Hearing the coffee being delivered, she showered and dressed before entering the common area. Dan was already up reading a paper. He looked up saying,

"Good morning Darlene. I hope you slept well."

She smiled replying while pouring a cup of coffee.

"I did, Dan, I guess I was tired. Did you?"

"Yes, thank you. I'm a little more adept at bouncing all over the globe than you but, at times, it still takes its toll."

"Try one of the rolls or a piece of toast. Down under, they're more into rolls or toast. There's one sweet pastry if you, like me, prefer it."

"Later, at *brekkie*, that's what they call breakfast, we'll have a more American style menu."

Regina entered the room, already dressed. After a cup of coffee, she would be ready for breakfast.

Dan texted Dr. Cox asking her to meet them in the hotel lobby.

After introductions, he led them outside and down the street to Harry's Restaurant and Bar.

Waiting to be seated, Dan observed,

"I'm told this is one of the best breakfast places in Brisbane. They have a buffet and an Ala Carte menu too."

After being seated with coffee in front of them, the consensus was the Ala Carte menu.

Dan suggested Dr. Cox order first. She chose the Eggs Benedict,

"I'd also like orange juice."

Dan looked at Darlene. She chose Three-egg omelet,

"I'd like tomato juice, please."

Regina chose the Eggs Florentine,

"I'd like orange juice also."

Dan ordered the Three-egg omelet,

"I'd like orange juice too."

Dan asked Dr. Cox to share with them what she'd found out in her meeting with the trauma team.

"Mr. Hardy, ladies, from what I can determine after meeting with them and your brother. My synopsis is this. Dr. Raymand Hardy suffered a major trauma. It's complex with many different and varied avenues. Until I can study his case further, it would be frivolous to form a definitive prognosis at this time. I will say that he remembers little of his ordeal. He does not know who he is or anything about you, his family.

"Over a period of time, he will gradually regain his memory. It may be days, weeks, or even months. There is no way to postulate on that at this time.

"From my experience, I find that seeing, you, his family, especially his wife, will trigger reactions deep within his brain. The more time spent with him, the quicker he will regain his memory.

"Physically, it appears that he was very lucky suffering only bruises and contusions.

"Again, I cannot be sure on anything I'm telling you until he's, hopefully, released to me and I can get him back to Duke."

Dan and Regina were concerned but Darlene was stunned. He wouldn't know her. How was she going to deal with that? She wasn't remotely prepared for what she'd just heard.

~ D ~

When they approached the cubicle, Dr. Cox reminded them again, that he would not know who they were but please tell him who you are and share highlights of your life with him.

"That will begin the process of remembering."

Darlene walked up to his bedside first. He was staring directly into her eyes.

"Who are you? Do I know you?"

"Ray, I'm your wife, Darlene. I'm the lady in the green dress."

It was easy to see that something registered. Fleeting, but still, very noticeable.

He was smiling now,

"Darlene, I don't remember you but something inside my heart tells me that I do know you. You must be part of my life."

He looked from her to Dan and Regina.

"Do I know you?"

Dan smiled, replying,

"Ray, I'm your brother, Dan, and this is my wife, Regina. Ray, we operate a business called *Prime Properties.* It's located in Cary, North Carolina."

Ray seemed puzzled, it was very apparent that he was trying desperately to assimilate what he was being told.

Still looking at Dan, he asked?

"North Carolina, where am I now?"

Dan took it slowly sharing that he was in Brisbane, Australia.

"You are a doctor and you have been doing a study along the Great Barrier Reef for the past eleven months. You are doing the research for Duke Marine Labs. You have been associated with them for the past two years."

It was agonizingly apparent to everyone that Ray was very confused but he was too curious to relent from his queries.

"What happened to me? Why am I here?"

Dan, very carefully, explained what happened and why,

"You wanted to visit Alice Springs and Ayers Rock before leaving Australia. You and a bush pilot crashed on your way to Alice Springs. You crashed in The White Mountains National Park in very rugged and heavily forested terrain. The search took over a week to find you.

"Now, we're here to take you back to the US, hopefully North Carolina and Duke University Hospital."

It was easy to see that some of the key words were familiar but still, very confusing. He was trying desperately to make sense of the conversation. He was also tiring rapidly and Dr. Cox suggested they leave so he could rest.

Darlene eased up beside the bed reaching over touching his cheek. He looked deeply into her eyes. He smiled before saying,

"You are my wife? The green dress in my life?"

She leaned over, kissing him on the cheek before replying,

"Yes I am, Ray. There are two green dresses. I love you."

She started to back away but he reached for her hand.

"I know you are very important in my life and I want so much for the fog to be lifted."

He was exhausted. It was so apparent to everyone. They slipped quietly out of the cubicle as his eyes closed and sleep overtook him.

Darlene wiped at the tears from her eyes as she followed the group out of the hospital and back to their suite. Dr. Cox remained at the hospital to confer with the trauma team.

~ D ~

Ray suggested they have room service bring lunch and ordered three chef's salads.

During lunch they talked about their visit. The consensus among them was that Ray saw something familiar in Darlene. She would be the key to expedite bringing him out of his state of amnesia.

Darlene knew that she would share pictures in her cell with Ray on their next visit. There were several of her in the two green dresses. She knew there were at least four of them together.

She felt deeply that he remembered her. Now, all she had to do was open the door and he would walk back into her life, their life.

~ D ~

The next morning, they entered his cubicle hoping the curtain separating Ray from them had parted. Dr. Cox had warned them at breakfast that the transition would slow.

"Just be prepared for it."

With her cellphone in hand, Darlene approached Ray. He held his hand out saying,

"Good morning, Darlene. You're the lady in the green dress and you are my wife. No, I don't remember yet but I really want to."

She leaned over kissing him tenderly on his lips, replying,

"Yes, Ray, I am your wife and here are pictures of the green dress. Remember, I told you there were two of them.

"This one was taken on Valentine's last year. This was on our first date. This picture is of us at Bobby's Restaurant in Greenville, NC.

"This is the green dress you picked out for me in St. Croix. This is the one you really like and here we are together in St. Croix.

This one was taken in Bermuda and this one was taken in Hawaii the night before you proposed. We were married two days later."

He was squeezing her hand now. In the mist of confusion, there was recognition too. He looked back and forth from the pics to her saying,

"I'm getting little blips. They all contain you. I want so much to remember…and, I will. I have to because I so much want to be your husband."

Still holding her hand, he looked at Dan and Regina.

"I know you are part of my life. The fog is beginning to lift. I guess I'll just have to be patient. I'm not sure being patient and waiting is part of my personality."

He smiled saying,

"I guess, this time I'll have to."

He looked back at Darlene asking,

"Wedding? Tell me about our wedding?"

For the next fifteen minutes, she paged through the wedding pics explaining what and who was in each pic.

He was too tired to continue but didn't want Darlene to leave his side.

"I have to rest now. Will you stay with me?"

She looked at Dan and then the nurse that had just walked up.

"May I?"

The nurse responded, saying,

"Yes, he's going to have to sleep but you may stay."

Leaving, Dan said they would check on her later.

"We'll see you then. Ray, get some rest. We'll see you a little later."

Ray refused to let go of her hand but drifted off to sleep almost immediately.

Mid-afternoon, he still was sleeping peacefully but hadn't shown any signs of awakening.

She slipped out of the cubicle asking the nurse if he'd been given anything to help him sleep.

Yes, he had been, the trauma team wanted him to rest.

"He'll spend the next few days regaining his strength."

She went back to the cubicle placing her hand over his.

Dan and Regina returned about five asking if they'd talked anymore?

Darlene replied that he hadn't awakened since they left.

Dan suggested they get something to eat and come back. Darlene, not having had lunch was more than ready.

~ D ~

After dinner, they returned finding Ray still asleep. They returned to the hotel finding Dr. Cox waiting for them.

"Mr. Hardy, I have good news. Your brother will be released to me tomorrow. I've already called Duke instructing them to prepare for his arrival. He is sedated and will remain so until we have him in his room at Duke. The excitement of the flight is more than he should be subjected to at this point.

"Have a pleasant evening. I will see you at the hospital in the morning. The transfer is scheduled for nine a.m."

That was a shock but a very pleasant one. Darlene was all smiles now. She was ready to have her husband back in North Carolina. She was ready to be back home too.

She was up, dressed, and packed, when the coffee arrived at six a.m. Dan was too.

"Good morning, Dan. I can't believe that Ray is finally going home. I can only pray that his memory will return soon. I have the rest of my life to wait but I hope it doesn't take that long."

Dan poured her a cup of coffee as he replied,

"Darlene, good morning. I hope that he's back with us soon too. Dr. Cox did tell me that in most cases like Ray's; the brain uses amnesia to protect a person from traumatic experiences and will only allow memory to return when the body is ready.

"We don't really know yet what Ray went through or was subjected to. All we really know is that physically, he's in great shape. His smile is there and the sparkle is in his eyes when he interacts with you. You'll be the one to bring him back. You'll see."

When Regina joined them, they had breakfast at Harry's again, knowing the day ahead of them would be long and strenuous.

~ D ~

The formal transfer took place at nine a.m. and Ray was taken by ambulance to the waiting jet.

When all was secure, Dan told the pilot to take her up.

"We'll refuel in Hilo, Hawaii before continuing our trip. As you recall, it's a nine-hour flight. We'll arrive at in Hilo at ITO around ten p.m. HST. With an hour layover, we'll arrive in RDU at twelve noon on Tuesday."

Although it was a long flight, everyone was upbeat looking forward to having Ray back in North Carolina.

Darlene spent most of her time by Ray's side He didn't know she was there but she did.

When they arrived in Hilo, there were no restaurants open so Dan had a sumptuous meal catered in the Premier Lounge waiting. They still had another nine hours' flight time left and from his vast flying experience, knew a good nourishing meal would certainly help. There was plenty of food on the plane but it couldn't replace getting off the jet for an hour.

The second nine-hour leg of their journey found most of the passengers trying to sleep. Darlene refused to leave Ray's side and slept on a pallet beside his mobile carrier.

~ D ~

When they arrived, Dan insisted that Darlene go home with them. She resisted but knew that jet lag would knock the wind out of her sails soon.

She awakened at seven-thirty Wednesday morning in totally unfamiliar surroundings. She showered and dressed before venturing outside her bedroom.

Smelling coffee, she followed the aroma that led her into a breakfast room. Dan was reading the paper.

"You're up, we thought you would sleep, at least, until noon. Good morning. Welcome to Cary, North Carolina."

Pouring a cup of coffee, she replied,

"Good morning, Dan. I feel rested. Have you heard from Ray?"

"Yes, Dr. Cox says they'll awaken him this morning. She say's he weathered the trip well. All of his vitals are well within normal parameters.

"She asked that we not visit until tomorrow. There are so many tests to run and we would be in the way. I guess we should listen to her. That's what I retained her for."

That wasn't received too well by Darlene but she knew tomorrow would come soon enough.

"Dan, I need to go home and change my wardrobe. Could you, or one of your employees, drive me to the airport in Greenville? I'll pick the car up there and drive to Bath. I'll return in the morning and come directly back here."

"Consider it done, Darlene. After breakfast, we'll drive over the corporate headquarters and one of my pilots will fly you to Greenville on one of the helicopters. It's only a thirty-minute flight. I can fly you directly to Bath and have a car and driver at your disposal it you'd like."

She considered his offer but declined saying it would be better if she had the car.

"I do appreciate all you're doing Dan. I really do."

~ *D* ~

At Prime Properties, she was introduced to the staff before being spirited off to Greenville on one of the copters.

Back at home in Bath, she spent an hour in the Jacuzzi before packing a large suitcase and clothes bag.

Now was the hard part. Everyone had to be called. She knew the redundancy would be grueling but it had to be done.

She called Nellie first saying she had no idea when she'd return.

"Nellie, He still hasn't regained his memory and the trauma team will not speculate. It may be a week, month, or even longer… No, I'm holding up pretty well, considering everything that's happened… I will, as soon as I know something."

She'd been in constant contact with Gail and Arlene. That left her family and Aunt Betty.

"Mama, it's me… No, I'm in Bath but I'm going back to Cary in the morning… No ma'am, not yet. They're allowing him to wake up today but don't want any visitors. I'll see him in the morning… Yes ma'am, he thinks he knows me but nothing positive… Okay, I'll call as soon as I know something… Yes, mama, I called them already. I'm on extended absence leave… I love you too, bye."

"Aunt Betty, Darlene… No ma'am, I'll at the cottage. No, I'm only here to change wardrobes… In Cary, with Dan and Regina… No ma'am, he doesn't recognize anyone yet. Dr. Cox says it may take weeks or months… No ma'am, I'll be up there for as long as it takes. Yes, ma'am, Aunt Betty. I love you too."

~ D ~

That evening Gail came over and they polished off a bottle of wine allowing Darlene to relax for the first time since she'd flown to Australia.

After three glasses, she opened up allowing her pent-up fears to vent.

"Gail, it's been pure hell. Dan and Regina could not have been any more supportive. Every time I tried to thank them they'd reply. *Your family now; we're here for you.* Regina and I have had some time to get to know each other and I really like her. Dan is just Dan, he's like Ray in many ways but much more conservative on his approach to business and I guess to life in general. They are both far more down to earth than I could have ever guessed.

"I don't know how long it's going to take for Ray's memory to return and it makes no difference. I'll be there for him when it does. Yes, it's wreaking havoc with me but that's okay. I can handle it…I hope."

They grilled a steak and Gail left around eleven. Darlene was much more relaxed and sleep came easily.

~ *D* ~

She was up at six with her first cup of coffee. It was chilly out on the main deck but watching another sunrise on Bath Creek tempered the chill in the crisp early morning air.

After a breakfast of scrambled eggs, grits, bacon, and toast, she was ready to return to the traumatic event that had invaded and imprisoned every facet of her very being. When Ray's memory returned, she'd be there waiting for him.

Her Mr. Right, her husband, was almost home. She was, finally, going to get him back.

No God! This Can't Be Happening!"

Ray, I'm here. I love you!

She arrived back at Dan and Regina's just before ten a.m. They were waiting for her.

Dan met her at the door saying he'd just gotten off the phone with Dr. Cox.

"Ray's temperature spiked about two a.m. and he became very restless and nauseas. A red rash has begun to appear on his shoulders, left arm and leg. They've put him back into a coma until they can figure out what's happening. We will not be able to visit him today. I'm sorry, Darlene."

Tears were running down her cheeks when Regina led her into the den. Her nerves were beginning to fray.

"What in the world is going on? Other than not knowing who he was, Ray seemed fine when I left."

Regina didn't know but tried very hard to calm Darlene.

"They're running tests now. It's possible that a spider or something bit him and the effects are just beginning to appear. He's in good hands. We'll just have to have patience. I know that's much easier to say than to do. Let's get your things moved in and then we'll have lunch. I would offer you a sedative but a good stiff drink would probably settle your nerves faster."

After putting all her clothes away, they went out on the sun porch. Dan handed them Jack Black's on ice. Darlene eagerly drank the first one and asked for another. She would never finish it but…just in case, she preferred knowing it was there.

When Darlene calmed, Regina suggested they go out for lunch.

"It will do you good to get out and time will pass much faster that way. What would you like for lunch?"

Much calmer now, Darlene wanted a hamburger and fries

. "Nothing fancy, please."

Dan, let's take her to Big Ed's City Market. They have great hamburgers. Darlene, the food is great. You'll love it."

She knew they were only trying to help so she agreed. There was little to be gained sitting around thinking the worst. Ray was going to get well. She had to believe that he was.

Once they entered the restaurant, Darlene relaxed. It was crowded but not too much to enjoy themselves. She did try the deluxe burger with extra cheese and bacon. She was almost tempted to order the home fries with gravy but chickened out ordering the sweet potato fries instead. For a beverage, Regina suggested the Cheerwine.

"You'll love it."

She did.

Afterwards, they visited several of the galleries in the Moore Square Art District. She had never been exposed to modern art but was fascinated by some of the pieces on display. The more traditional pieces captured most of her interest. She remembered Ray remarking that in modern art. Most viewers interpreted each piece differently. She was absolutely sure that her version would be different from Regina's or Dan's.

Dan fielded a call from Dr. Cox. Ray had apparently been bitten by a mosquito carrying the Barmah Forest virus (BFV).

"It's usually one to two weeks before the symptoms present. Usually, as in Ray's case, nausea and vomiting occur and there's a temperature spike. No, it's not life threatening although it can be very uncomfortable with pain and swelling in the joints. In many cases a red rash appears on the trunk and limbs. Dr. Cox says that in Ray's case, it's probably exacerbated by the trauma Ray's been under."

"It's treatable with…I'm not going to try and repeat all that, NSAIDs. Dr. Cox says it should go away in ten to fourteen days. It may take longer in Ray's case, again, because of the trauma he's been under. They are going to keep him in the coma until the treatment has a chance to work. The stress of a rash and painful, swollen joints, would only antagonize him that much more."

Darlene was visibly uneasy,

"How long Dan?"

Dan, understanding her torment, replied.

"Dr. Cox says three or four days at the most. When the rash dries up, they'll bring him out of the coma. The inflammation in the joints may take several weeks."

Regina, standing beside Darlene, put her hand of her shoulder and suggested,

"There no need to sit around here. We can't see him. Let's go to Duck and see how the project's coming. It's got to be close to completion. Darlene, are you game?"

She knew Regina was only doing it for her. Getting away would probably help since she couldn't see Ray.

"Yes, I'd love to see it."

~ D ~

As they approached, it appeared that the landscaping was complete. Although it wasn't dark, the helipad was bathed in light. Setting down, they saw Ken waiting on the deck. He walked out to greet them as them dis-embarked asking about Ray. Darlene filled him in as they walked towards the house.

He led them up the steps onto the deck and into the house. It appeared to be finished and Regina was jubilant.

"Ken! Are you done?"

"No, I need three more days and we'll do the punch list then. Mostly, it's just utilities. The rep from Wolf and Sub-Zero was here yesterday. Everything checks out and all the refrigeration is operating as specified. Monday, the tech from Pair Electronics checked out the entertainment and communications functions. He made a couple of minor adjustments and said it was ready. Mrs. Hardy, select one of the two hundred recordings you provided on Blue Tooth and let's see how it sounds."

Regina chose one of Yana's and immediately, the whole property was filled with music.

Ken continued,

"Per your specifications, each room, and area, including the deck, and patio, can be controlled from here and the master suite. Each room or area has its own controls but can be overridden by the two master control points.

"This is also the control station for all the lighting and HVAC systems. Each room or area has a dimmer control and thermostat but again, it can all the controlled or overridden from the two control points. This panel controls the elevators and garage doors. There are also controls by the garage stairwell exit and garage elevator doors. As specified, one elevator opens on all floors but is restricted on the master level. It requires a voice code. The other elevator only opens on the first three levels."

"Unless you have further questions, I'll leave you to enjoy your 'almost ready' home. Have a nice evening. Darlene, Arlene and I have you and Ray in our prayers."

He hugged her and was gone.

In moments, Regina had placed a tray of cheese, dip, chips, and nuts on the bar and poured glasses of California Chardonnay. She stood behind the bar while Darlene and Dan took stools.

Darlene, still awed and amazed at the beauty and enormity of the house, remarked,

"Regina, it's all so beautiful. The architect did a beautiful job and it appears to be so functional. It's so you."

Regina, obviously very proud, beamed,

"Darlene, it was two years in the design stage. I went through three architects before Dan introduced me to Jefferson Davis. His firm is in Savannah, South Carolina and he specializes in properties like this. When I left our first meeting, it took place here, I felt he understood what I wanted and unlike the other two, he appeared to be ready to work with me.

"My first two trips to his office were all about what I wanted this house to be. Yes, I wanted it to blend in with the other properties here. No, I did not want to make a statement. I wanted a house we could entertain our friends and of course us and our children. He knew immediately that my kitchen, dining area, and lounge would be the center of almost all our activities. As you can see. He designed exactly what I wanted. I'm so ready to get in here and get started. Can you feel my excitement?"

"Dan, let's take Darlene to the Sandpiper's Trace for dinner before we go back."

Dan called and made reservations at Dune's Retreat for seven p.m. That gave them time for another glass of wine before leaving.

It was only a few hundred yards away so they took the 'road-ready' enclosed golf cart to the resort.

"The Sandpiper's Trace Experience"

Janele's Kitchen

When they were seated, Regina suggested 'Jockey's Ridge' cocktails.

"Darlene, it's honey pecan bourbon, ginger ale and lemon. You'll love it."

She also suggested the local blue she-crab soup along with a bottle of William Hill Bench Blend from Napa Valley for starters.

Darlene found both delicious. She'd never tasted blue crab soup with so much flavor.

Curious, she asked.

"Regina, how much time will you being spending here?"

Regina took a sip before replying,

"I'm not sure. With the children in school, it will only be weekends until summer vacation. I hope to spend most of the summer here unless Dan wants me to accompany him somewhere."

Dan offered,

"We'll spend a lot of time here. It's one of our favorite places plus tidewater Virginia is only minutes away. We really enjoy the Williamsburg area.

"There are some great restaurants there and we enjoy Ford's Colony too."

He laughed before continuing,

"Regina will go anywhere they'll let her in the kitchen."

Regina, wide-eyed, replied,

"Dan…Oh, I guess he's right. I do like to see what's going on in the back of the house."

For salads, Regina suggested the wedge salad.

Darlene took her suggestion but Dan ordered the classic Caesar salad with a side of smoked oysters.

Regina commented that Dan was a sucker for smoked oysters.

"He'd probably put them on ice cream. It wouldn't surprise me a bit."

That brought laughter from everyone.

She knew they were trying to keep her spirits up and had to admit that they were doing a good job. She preferred to be with Ray but knew she'd only be in the way if they would even let her get close to him.

Dan broke her train of thought.

"Darlene, have you ever tried a smoked oyster?"

"No Dan, I've eaten them many ways but never smoked."

He offered her one.

"Here, try one, you'll either love, or hate, it."

She timidly took a small bite and liked it. She would be in the 'love group.'

For her main course, Darlene chose the Bluefin tuna with grilled asparagus and creamy corn.

Regina chose the Prosciutto encrusted Stumpy Point scallops, grilled asparagus, and low-country succotash.

Dan wanted the cast iron seared 14 oz. ribeye, medium rare, with the stuffed sweet potato. He also wanted the grilled asparagus.

While they were waiting, Dan wondered,

"Darlene, are you going back to the hospital? I know you told me that Ray wanted you in school."

"Dan, I'm not sure. If Ray's recovery time is long and drawn out, no, I'll resign immediately. If he still wants me to take those courses, I'll continue doing it. When this is behind us, I'll do whatever he wants. I just want this to end. I'm so afraid he'll go back to Australia to finish his project."

Dan looked at her, smiling,

"Darlene, let me put your mind at ease. The research project ended last Friday. They're packing up and will be back at Duke next week.

"As far as Ray's research is concerned. He had almost completed it. One of his team, Glenda? Took the remaining samples and they'll be waiting for him when he'd ready to wrap it up."

Darlene was all smiles now. She wanted to jump up and scream but managed to contain herself.

"Oh, Dan, that really makes me very happy. Now all I need is for Ray to get well and remember me."

Her whole demeanor changed; she was smiling again.

She commented, favorably, several times on her meal and asked the waiter to thank the chef.

~ *D* ~

They arrived back in Cary a little after midnight and sleep came quickly. It had been a busy day. Darlene knew Regina and Dan had successfully put all her concerns on a back burner. There was no way she deserved them, or Ray, for that matter. Her guardian angel was working overtime.

"The Vigil Continues"

Ray, please come back to me.

Next morning, after breakfast, they went to the hospital for a conference with Dr. Cox

In her report, she was positive in so far as the BFV treatment was concerned. The NSAIDs' was working as expected. The rash would be gone in ten to fourteen days and the swelling in the joints was beginning to diminish.

"We will awaken, Dr. Hardy, Friday morning. He may, or may not, have regained some of his memory. There is no way to tell until he's fully awake and cognizant of his environment."

Looking at Darlene, she continued,

"Mrs. Hardy, I want you to be at his bedside, holding his hand, when we awaken him. Without question, you elicit his strongest desire to regain his memory. I must warn you. He still may not remember you but deep inside, he knows that you are very important in his life."

Darlene was more than ready for him to awaken and was prepared, however long it took, to be there when his memory returned.

"Dr. will I be allowed to stay with him 24/7?"

Dr. Cox, replied, "Mrs. Hardy, lets address that one day at the time."

~ D ~

Afterwards, they lunched at Nosh's near the university. Regina raved about their panini's.

"You have to try them. They're delicious. My favorite is the DeLuca. The Russian dressing sets it apart."

Darlene was sold but Dan wanted to try the Gonzalo. All three wanted the sweet potato fries.

That evening, Regina and Dan attended a dinner at Raleigh Country Club while Darlene spent her evening on her cell and FB.

She called her family first letting them know what was going on.

"Mama, it's probably going to be a long, harrowing, experience but it doesn't matter. Ray's sure he remembers me. I'm sure he does."

Next, she called Arlene. There was little she could share with her twin that she wasn't already aware of.

"Arlie, I'm sorry I missed you when we flew down… I don't know, they're going to awaken him tomorrow… Yes, I'll be by his side… You know I will… I love you too, bye."

Aunt Betty was next,

"No ma'am, I'm not sure. Tomorrow, they'll awaken him. I hope it won't be long after that… I will Aunt Betty… I love you too, bye."

"Hi Gail… I don't know. I'm beginning to wonder if I should resign… Not yet, maybe when they awaken him tomorrow. Hopefully, his memory will be back… No, Dr. Cox holds out little hope. She thinks weeks… You know I'm going to try. He seems to think that I belong in his life… I will, see you soon, bye."

~ *D* ~

Friday morning, they stopped by the Rise, biscuits and donuts, location near the hospital enjoying peach glazed and raspberry filled donuts along with their locally roasted coffee.

Enjoying hers, Darlene commented,

"They should come to Greenville. The line would be five blocks long.

Dan replied,

"Somebody will. Franchises are available.

~ D ~

Darlene was holding Ray's hand when they awakened him. His eyes fluttered for a moment before they focused on her. Smiling, he realized she still had his hand.

"Darlene, please tell me about our wedding, and show me the pictures again."

He listened eagerly to her every word but said something was missing.

She looked at him,

"Missing, what do you mean?"

A radiant smile covered his face.

"Bali Hai, when I proposed."

She almost screamed, he remembered, he was back. Her Mr. Right, her husband, was back!

She smothered his face with kisses as tears dropped from her face onto his. Neither tried to wipe them away. They were tears of joy. The nightmare was over and he was back.

Still holding her hand, he looked at Regina and Dan.

"Hey, it's good to be back. How long have I been gone?"

For the next hour, he listened intently to the accounts of his plane crash and the ensuing weeks that followed. It would take much longer than that to share it all with him but for the moment, it was enough.

All anyone wanted to know now was how long before he'd be discharged?

Dr. Cox furnished the answer about two that afternoon.

"Dr. Hardy's recovery has been remarkable. It is the consensus, of my staff, that he is ready to be discharged. We'll do one final block of blood tests today. In the morning, we'll do a CT-Scan and MRI. Unless something presents itself that we do not foresee, we'll release him at noon."

She looked at Ray saying,

"Dr. Hardy, you are a remarkable man. No one on my staff, including me, would have thought you could have possibly recovered as fast as you have.

"I am quite sure sir, that the relationship you have with your wife played a very significant part in your rapid recovery. Mrs. Hardy, what you did can only be termed as, quite extraordinary. You have your husband back. Good luck."

She turned, nodding to Dan and Regina, then exited the room.

Ray spoke first,

"Dan please take our ladies to dinner."

Darlene started to protest but his smile stopped her. He continued,

"I'm going to need my rest because Darlene and I have some serious mountain climbing to do. She'll destroy me if I don't get some rest."

Dan and Regina were confused but Darlene wasn't.

With a puzzled look, he asked Ray?

"Mountain climbing? Are you serious?"

Ray laughed replying,

"Yes, Dan but our mountain climbing is done in the bedroom."

There was no question about what he meant. Dan looked at Darlene and Regina.

"Ladies, would you kindly follow me?"

Darlene didn't want to go but knew he was right. There was a lot of energy pent up inside her and he probably needed all the rest he could get. She kissed him tenderly saying.

"Get some rest, darling. There's a mountain beside Bath Creek begging to be scaled. I love you."

"Climbing Their Mountain"

Darlene

Ray was released just after noon knowing he was on the way to Bath Creek. Darlene was ready to take her husband home. It had been too long. The cottage missed him, Bath Creek missed him but most of all, she missed him and was ready to give him all the love she had.

Their wedding night was beyond words. Yes, they'd climbed their mountain before but it was different. That night they were truly one. It was heaven but oh so brief. It had sustained her until now. It was all she had but it was all she needed.

No one would, could, ever know the utter despair she'd been through over the past nine months. It was bad enough having her husband on the other side of the world but to exacerbate that, he'd been in a plane crash and was lost for almost a week. Then the memory loss and sickness.

She'd been strong but there were times she wasn't sure she'd be able to hold it together…but, she had and now, she was carrying him home.

They waved goodbye to Dan and Regina as Darlene backed out of their driveway.

The one hundred thirty-one miles melted away as they traveled around the outer beltline onto Hwy 64 and then Hwy 264. Wilson was behind them and they traversed the bypass around Greenville. Washington was next and then Teach's Cove. They were home.

It took only minutes to dispense with their luggage. Unpacking it would come later. The Jacuzzi awaited.

For the next hour they sipped on wine while caressing and kissing. Few words were said. None were needed. It was time to climb their mountain. First, they explored familiar routes and then new ones, totally new and exciting, until they were exhausted.

In robes, with glasses of wine, they spent a few minutes on the upper deck enjoying the warm comfortable May evening. There was just a hint of a breeze coming up Bath Creek as the full moon cast a romantic glow along the shimmering creek. The only sound was of a lonesome Whippoorwill calling its mate.

Darlene had her life's mate, her Mr. Right, her husband. She prayed she'd never have to be without him again.

Epilogue

Three years later:

"Ray, is Danny Owen in there with you? When it's quiet it scares me."

Danny Owen Hardy would be two in January and he was already a handful.

"He's not in here, honey. I'll check the playroom."

The sitter would be arriving any minute and Darlene was trying to make a last minute check on her opening list.

Tonight was the first of two trial runs on her new restaurant. She'd chosen the location on the Washington waterfront beside what had been Haven's Wharf many years before.

From the beginning, she'd planned it to be upscale drawing her clientele from Beaufort, Pitt, Craven, and Martin Counties. Cypress Landing and Pamlico Plantation would produce many clients. She was depending on them but knowing Greenville and Pitt County would be, by far, the largest group to draw from. "Darlene's" would open on Saturday and she was ready. Regina had been a godsend. Darlene never would have attempted it without her.

Tonight, all her family had been invited including Aunt Bessie and Uncle Russell. Gail would be there too with her husband, Rex Tillison. They'd married last June and were living in Greenville. He had a real estate office there and was planning on opening one in Williamston. Gail was working at Vidant Health in Greenville but maternity leave would be soon.

Three years previously, when Ray was released from the hospital, they'd returned to Bath Creek and decided to make it their permanent home.

Going through a maze of federal, state, and county regulations. Ray had finally received a permit to construct a helipad. He'd purchased the cottage adjacent to theirs and was utilizing the space between the two docks. With Ken heading up the project, construction had been completed in less than 60 days affording immediate access to the airport in Greenville, and New Bern and Prime Properties in Cary. It was also their primary transportation when visiting Dan and Regina near Duck.

A year ago, he'd finished his project papers and chose to make Prime Properties, his career.

At least now, when he was out of the country, she'd be with him. Memories of Australia remained fresh in her mind and probably would for years to come.

~ D ~

The trial run went without a hitch, maybe a glitch here and there but they were quickly overcome by the chef and his well-trained crew.

Accolades abounded. Darlene's was going to be a huge success. Reservations continued to pour in from as far away as Cary and Durham. It had been an interesting and very intriguing undertaking but now she could rest on the laurels of accomplishment and turn her full attention to an upcoming event.

Melody Snell Hardy was due to arrive on June eighth and all was in ready.

Life was good. Her Mr. Right did exist and she'd found him.

"Just a Note"

I hope you enjoyed reading Darlene. It's my most thrilling novel yet. As with my previous novels, it's fictitious and all the characters in my story are figments of my imagination.

Some names and locations are from my past but are only there as background for my story.

Thank you again for reading Darlene. If you enjoyed, it; may I ask a favor? Please go to amazon.com and write a favorable review. Like everything else today, it's all about the "clicks."

You may also enjoy one of my other novels listed below.

JD

Gina

She Walked Through His Heart Again Today

III (Three) Islands

I am Janie

You may also enjoy my cookbook.

Bob's Country Recipes and Other Interesting Stuff II

All my books are available online at createspace.com, amazon.com or other online bookstores. Some are available in Kindle and other eBook formats.

Bob Holt

P.S. Look for Randy soon.

His Recurring Dream, a rewrite of my first novel, is in the works also. I've learned a lot since my first attempt at publishing. It's been interesting but also, loads of fun.

41881850R00203

Made in the USA
Middletown, DE
25 March 2017